the TOUCHING

THAT LASTS

stories by

KENT NELSON

CONUN
DRUM
PRESS

AN IMPRINT OF BOWER HOUSE

DENVER

Printed in Canada
Designed by Margaret McCullough
Photography thanks to iStock

First US paperback edition 2020

Library of Congress Cataloging-in-Publication Data
Nelson, Kent, 1943-
        The Touching that lasts / Kent Nelson.
                p.cm.
        ISBN 978-1-942280-58-3
        1. Short stories, American. I. Title.
        PS3564.E467T68   2006
        813',54—dc22
                                            2019957275

10 9 8 7 6 5 4 3 2 1

ACKNOWLEDGMENTS

The author is grateful to the following publications in which these stories originally appeared, sometimes in slightly altered form:

The Chicago Tribune Literary Supplement and *Witness*, "Rituals of Sleep"; *The Georgia Review*, "Tides"; *The Gettysburg Review*, "Starlings" and "What Shall Become of Me?"; *Iron Horse Literary Review*, " Fugitive Colors" and "The Touching That Lasts"; *New Virginia Review*, "The Orange Grove Book of Dreams"; *Prairie Schooner*, "Ringo Bingo"; *Shenandoah*, "Ditch Rider," "Two Minutes of Forgetting," and "Galimatia"; *The Southern Review*, "The Dark Ages"; *The Virginian Quarterly Review*, "Northern Lights" and "The Beautiful Morning of Almost June".

CONTENTS

TIDES

On a late afternoon in May, the sun angles across the Intracoastal Waterway to the island and through the open doorway and high windows of the marina lounge. I should have gone home, but I'd settled a case in Charleston, and Edie and the children weren't expecting me, so I stop in to see Billy and Purvis. My eyes adjust to the separating light and shadow, but in one corner it's all sunlight where Billy Prioleau and Pope Gailliard are playing cribbage and drinking rum and Coke. Purvis looks on, silhouetted against the masts of sailboats beyond the open doorway. Pope and Billy are sixty-something, gray-haired. Purvis is in his late forties now, though he stands old—askew and on one foot, his left hand always in his pocket. I've known them all since I was a kid, from the early days of the island when my father was still alive.

Four crabbers with pitchers of beer eye the two women in shorts drinking margaritas at the bar. One of the women is brunette, thirty, chewing gum a mile a minute. The other's a curly blond with wide eyes, halfway pretty. The way Donna, the bartender, is huddled with them, I assume they're friends.

I sit down a couple of stools away, between the women and the cribbage game.

"All I know is I don't feel safe anywhere," the brunette says.

"They haven't caught the bastard, either," Donna says. She comes over, but doesn't say hello.

"Sam Adams," I say.

"Hey, Scotty," Pope says.

Purvis waves, and I wave back. Billy doesn't look up from his cards.

Donna squints through her cigarette smoke and tilts the enamel handle of the tap. "You hear anything about that shooting?" she asks.

"People are talking about it," I say. "The family was from Illinois. The boy, I guess, was drawing a picture when he died."

"You think it was a colored man did it?" Pope asks.

"You mean, do I think it was racial?"

"'Course it was racial," Donna says. She sets my beer down. "You saying it was an accident?"

"It could have been a stray bullet—someone hunting."

"It isn't hunting season," Donna says.

"Nothing's an accident," Billy says to Pope, "except your mother's having you. It's your goddamn crib."

Pope turns over the crib cards and counts, "Fifteen two, fifteen four, and trips is ten." He moves his peg, and Billy gathers the deck and shuffles.

Light shimmers across the water, and toward the city the sky yellows through sea haze and city smog. Ten years ago, after I finished law school, Edie and I rented a house on the backside marsh. She was from Atlanta, and at first she thought the island was too isolated, but once the children were born—Carla's seven now, and Blair's five—she liked it. She walked them to the playground, and other young mothers were willing to trade babysitting. I was from here, so when my practice took hold as expected, we bought a house on the beach—four bedrooms, a kitchen that looks out to the ocean, and a wraparound deck.

A noise from the front of the lounge draws our attention, where the Rupert brothers, Shem and Marvin, jostle each other coming through the door. Marvin's heavyset, jowly, gray-brown hair in a ponytail. Shem's thinner and taller and has a gold chain around his neck. "Pour us two shots, Donna. Dickel. And give everyone a round, especially the pretty ladies."

The Ruperts stride to the bar as if they own the place.

"Give Scotty two," Marvin says. "Damn right."

"Absolutely," Shem says. "Two for Scott. Without Scotty, we'd have been up shit creek without a paddle."

Billy doesn't look over.

"You saved us a ton of money on taxes," Shem says. He looks at the brunette chewing gum. "Scotty here's the best lawyer in Charleston."

Donna sets up three shot glasses on the bar and pours Dickel.

The Ruperts are old-timers, odd-jobbers and boat painters. My father never liked them much, They were too pushy—but when they came to me for advice, what was I supposed to do?

Donna sets the shots in front of us and fills another pitcher for the crabbers.

"I don't want nothin' from them," Billy calls over.

Shem nudges Marvin. "I told you he seen us."

Marvin nods. "He was awfully slow closing the bridge for us." Then he turns to me. "Hey, Scotty, you see our new Lincoln Town Car? It's out front next to Billy's little bug."

Donna tops off the pitcher and carries it around the bar. "What are y'all going to do with a Lincoln Town Car?" she asks. "You going to be the new Mafia?"

"We're going to travel," Shem says.

"Where?" asks the curly blonde. "Maybe Janine and me'll go with you."

"Miami. The Bahamas. Where do you girls want to go?"

"How're you going to drive to the Bahamas?" Janine asks.

"We'll buy a boat."

"You boys win the lottery or something?" the blonde asks.

"If it was the lottery," Pope says, "Billy wouldn't have a problem with that."

The Ruperts slouch down with the women, one on either side, and Marvin swivels his stool around toward Billy. "Your wife still taking the bus to town, Billy?" he asks. "She still ride with the colored maids and gardeners?"

Pope stops dealing the cards, and Purvis looks over at me, as if to say I should step in. Billy turns slowly toward Marvin, then jumps up. The cards and cribbage board go flying. Chairs clatter. Billy rushes Marvin like a mad dog, though Purvis intercepts him and throws him off-target, so that Billy careens into the two women, who fly sideways and backward onto the floor with Billy on top of them.

Shem and Marvin laugh. Billy untangles himself and gets up swinging his fists. It isn't a fight, really, only that one lunge. Donna comes around the bar with a baseball bat. I get hold of Billy and, because I'm twice as big and half his age, I wrestle him out onto the terrace.

Outside, Billy shakes himself free of my grip. "You can't solve anything by fighting," I say, "especially at your age."

"What's age got to do with it?" Billy glares at me, his eyes sharp blue, his grizzled jaw shaking.

"What'll Arlene say?"

"She don't have to know."

"I could tell her. If I helped the Ruperts, I might do almost anything."

"You wouldn't do that, though," he says.

"Calm down now, Billy. Calm down."

Purvis comes to the door, and Billy turns toward the marina.

"Let's go out in the johnboat," I say. "Let's go up to the fish camp."

The johnboat's a sixteen-foot, snub-nosed piece of tin with dents and scrapes. Billy steps down and maneuvers over the fishing gear and two coolers in the center, one with bait in it, one with beer. He sits in the center, and I push off and hop into the stern. It's my father's old boat, but since I don't have the time to use it, Billy does.

One pull on the Evinrude, and we're underway. I steer around the moored sailboats toward the harbormaster's office, where Purvis is waiting with his hand in his pocket.

Purvis stopped talking when he was fourteen. His father had taken off up to the Piedmont with a woman. Purvis dropped out of school and worked on shrimp trawlers until he was thirty, when, in an accident, he caught his hand in a winch. He still lived with his mother then in a big house down island. A year later she died and I helped him convert the crab shed in back into an apartment he could live in so the main house could be rented for income.

Purvis, in the bow, squints into the sun and holds his good hand up to shade his eyes. I give gas up the waterway. Billy takes a Pabst from the cooler and passes one to me. We ride the choppy water going north.

The steel drawbridge where Billy works comes closer. The evening traffic from Charleston hums across to the island. In the center is a pillbox lookout where the operator sits, and Billy waves to the silhouette of the operator.

We slide underneath and traffic rumbles above us. The sound fades and the paling sky opens out again. No one says anything—Purvis because he won't, and Billy, maybe, because he's ashamed. I don't know what to say because Billy and Purvis are mysteries.

For a half mile we beat against the wind, and then I veer off the waterway into a side creek where a new world takes hold. It's quieter, reeds flower around us, and I have to ease off on the gas. The tin boat glides past mudflats and oysterbanks, and a mudhen croaks. Around a bend, a white egret rises from a pool and throbs low over the marsh.

"You think they were lying in wait," Billy asks, "or did they shoot at a car for no reason?"

"You mean whoever shot that boy? I'm guessing he didn't know a car was there."

"White people live out there, too," Billy said. "Why would anyone shoot a kid?"

I cut the engine to a crawl, entering the end of the creek. The headland in front of us is a scalloped canopy of live oaks muted by the humid air, though we're still a half-mile by way of the serpentine curves. A night-heron on the bank watches us ease by.

Close to the headland, the channel splits into rivulets. I squirm the boat across pluff mud, cut the gas, and tilt the Evinrude up. We coast onto the mudbank.

Billy finishes his beer and opens another. The wind's discernible, keeping the gnats down and rattling the grass. Hermit crabs pop along the bank.

"Is it low tide?" I ask.

"Fifteen, maybe twenty minutes," Billy says.

Purvis looks at Billy again.

"You're right," Billy says. "We could have picked a better time."

Purvis gets out and draws the boat higher onto the flat, then wades through the pluff mud toward the trees. The low sun tints the clouds orange. Billy looks as if he's expended his last bit of energy getting here and now he can't move.

He draws inward to memory, and, though I can't go with him, I'm pretty close. Billy's thinking of camping here with his father every weekend. They sometimes brought along my father, who was Billy's age then, and then later he and my father brought Edgar and me. We fished from the dock, gigged flounder, and caught sheepshead and drum in the snags on the beach on the other side of the island. The remains of the old dock are still visible right here—parallel rotten posts two abreast going back into the reeds.

Billy's father acquired the land in 1926, before the island had a bridge to it, in exchange for hauling a bargeload of polo ponies to Palm Beach. It was sixty acres of shell mounds, palmettos, live oaks, and tick-infested underbrush. At the time, everyone laughed at Billy's father, but now they don't. The Ruperts have sold their abutting thirty-five acres for 2.8 million dollars.

"You want to hike to the Indian mound?" I ask finally.

"I like the view from here," Billy says. "It be easier than walking. Besides, we only have one pair of boots."

I get two beers from the cooler and hand one to him. I open mine and sip.

"You know what I'd buy," Billy asks, "if I had the money the Ruperts got?"

"Is that what you're thinking about?"

"Mixing bowls. Arlene wants mixing bowls. And a new bed. For forty years we've slept on a damned mattress that sags in the middle. I can't escape."

"You never wanted to."

The orange in the clouds shades to pink, and a warbler sings from the moss in the closest live oak. Another egret flies over.

Billy sets his beer on his seat. "You can wear the boots," he says and steps out into the pluff mud in his tennis shoes.

Purvis is in the trees, invisible, as usual, and Billy slogs toward the headland, *slop slop slop.* I take off my wingtips, pull on the rubber boots, and get out of the boat into the mud.

Each step is a pull and a grunt, but toward the high ground the mud lessens. When I get on solid ground, I follow a trail Billy's gone down—not far, maybe fifty yards. I know it's there, but it's still a surprise—a mound of oyster shells, ten feet high and twenty in diameter. This is where we always pitched our tent.

The Indians used the site the same way we did, as a fish camp, and over hundreds of years built that mound of shells. I say I haven't been here for a long time, but that's not true. I come here every day. My father and I camped here the last time we were alone together, and I still hear his voice telling me I should take care of people and not want more than my share. I hear my own voice saying, "What do you mean you're going to die soon?"

"And you have to take care of Billy," he says over and over. "Arlene looks out for him at home, but that's not the same."

"You aren't going to die," I say.

In two months, my father was dead. When I started my law practice, I took care of Billy as much as Edie allowed, and as much as Billy let me. Before I got busy at work, Billy and I took the johnboat to the jetty for bluefish or into the creeks for sea trout. We cast for shrimp in the shallows behind Mount Pleasant and put down crab pots off the dock at Purvis's. Sometimes, with Pope Gailliard, we towed the boat to John's Island where Pope had friends.

Edie understood my excursions with Billy had a meaning she couldn't appreciate, and for a while she accepted them, but after Carla and Blair were born, I couldn't go out with Billy as often. Besides, my law practice assumed a bigger portion of my time. I was absent from the marriage as many hours as before, but with a more permissible reason.

Billy kicks mud from his tennis shoes and walks to the tideline. We're on higher ground and look back beyond the johnboat to the marsh and the Intracoastal Waterway. Car headlights move through dusklight on the causeway, and two TV towers blink red against the darkening sky.

Purvis emerges from the brush, and I give him a sign. We've somehow arranged this moment without conspiring—getting Billy where he is now, by the shell mound and the live oak. I've brought a beer in my pocket for him and open it. He drinks and sets the can gently on the ground. Then he steps forward under the canopy of the oak and kneels at the grave of his son.

On the way back, we're okay with the tide's coming in. Down the waterway, the flashing markers guide me—red, right, returning. All the way, Billy, in the bow, drinks beer.

At the landing, I back the trailer down, and Purvis, standing knee-deep in the water, hooks the cable onto the boat. I winch the johnboat up.

"One thing I like about you, Scotty," Billy says, "is your truck."

We leave off the boat and trailer at Purvis's and drive to the lounge to get Billy's car. The Town Car's gone, but more pickups are in the parking lot. Donna's making drinks for a younger crowd. Her women friends have gone. We get out.

"I can drive," Billy says, but he hands Purvis his car keys. I have to follow to bring Purvis home.

Billy's yellow bungalow is off Coleman Boulevard in Mount Pleasant. Moss grows on one side of the roof. Lights are on inside, so I pull onto the lawn while Purvis drives the beetle into the carport. The street light throws out a purplish glow over the house and the lot next door.

We get the coolers from the back of the pickup, and while Billy puts the bait shrimp into the freezer, I hose the coolers out and turn them over on the lawn.

"We could at least have come home with some fish," Billy says.

Arlene comes to the side door. "There you are," she says.

She's a short, plumpish woman with short hair. Barefoot. Her flowered dress is unbuttoned at the top, and in the carport bug light, her gray hair looks yellow-blue.

Billy closes the freezer and gazes at her. He's a sight—jeans caked with mud, hair sticking straight up from his head. He breaks into a grin and dances over to her singing, *"Five foot two, eyes of blue, has anybody seen my gal?"* He takes her hand, pulls her off the step and into his arms, and twirls her across the cement. *"Could she love? Could she coo? Could she, could she, could she coo? Has anybody seen my gal?"*

Arlene dances a few steps, then shakes him away. "You stop that," she says.

Billy drops his arms and staggers a little.

"It's my fault," I tell her. "We bought some beer and took the boat out."

"I got in a fight," Billy says.

He and Arlene gaze at each other, and then she climbs back onto the step. "It's been a long day," she says. "I'm tired." She glances at me. "Should I call Edie and tell her you're on your way?"

"That's all right. I'm going right home."

"They weren't shooting at him," Billy says. "It was a stray bullet."

Arlene pauses, holding the door open, and looks at me. "What's he talking about?"

"How would you like some mixing bowls?" Billy asks. He dances out of the carport, sidesteps the truck, weaves across the grass. Halfway to the street, he loses a tennis shoe and his muddy sock dangles from his foot. He pirouettes under the street lamp, still singing.

The house is dark, and Carla and Blair are asleep. Edie's in bed, too, though the light's on. I mount the steps to the deck, but instead of going in, I walk around to the ocean. The beach is pale in the starlight, and, farther out, the waves are visible as oblique white lines. Beyond them, barely distinguishable from the sky, is the endless dark water.

I think of the boy riding in that car in the back seat. He's drawing on a lapboard and hears an explosion. He feels what? Pain? Numbness? Blood spurts from his leg, so maybe he screams or cries. He loses blood fast. The parents look around into the back seat...

"Scott?" Edie comes out through the sliding door in her white nightgown.

"Right here."

The breeze lifts her nightgown around her bare legs. "Where were you?"

"I went up-island in the boat with Purvis and Billy."

"Fishing?"

"We didn't fish. How are the children?"

"Fine. Carla had soccer after school. For his birthday, Blair wants a bicycle to ride in the dunes."

"He can't ride anything without a motor in the dunes, and that's not allowed."

"Try telling him that." Edie stares straight out at the sea. "Where were you, really?"

"I've got pluff mud all over me. Call Arlene, if you want a reference."

She says nothing for a long minute. The half-moon drifts out from behind the clouds.

"I'm sorry I was late."

Again a silence.

"Come to bed, Scott. It's cold out here."

I prepare for a trial up in Myrtle Beach—depositions, interviews with witnesses, case research. Is a woman liable for a man's mental illness allegedly caused by her breaking their engagement? Evenings, I drive by Billy's house, then across the causeway and the bridge, and detour past the marina lounge. Billy's car isn't at any of those places.

One evening, I stop at Purvis's. His door's open to the breeze. A television on the counter flicks colors into the air. I say hello through the screen and knock after.

Inside is the smell of tomato and onion and garlic. He's cooking spaghetti and heating up sauce from a can. On the kitchen table is a stack of library books. Purvis turns off the television and motions toward the pot of spaghetti on the stove.

"Edie's expecting me," I tell him. "How's Billy? Have you seen him?"

Purvis shakes his head. He doesn't know any more about Billy than I do, but the moment we're in is more complicated than ignorance. We're used to not speaking, but there's an awkwardness between us, as if we share a loss we refuse to recognize. He knows I'll go home to my family. and I know Purvis will be alone. I scan the titles of his books—*Daniel Boone, Boy Frontiersman,* two of the Hardy Boys series, and a Harry Potter. He envies my time, and I envy his.

The next day, after a deposition, I check on Arlene at Huguley's on King Street. She's in the section that sells greeting cards, wall prints, and Southern cookbooks. She's helping a customer pick out a print of a plantation house with azaleas along the driveway. I sort through cards and messages and remind myself Edie's birthday is a month away.

When the customer leaves, I bring a birthday card to the register. "You look nice," I say. "That dress is pretty."

She's wearing a flowery smock with a gold-plated pin on her lapel. "Thank you." She takes the card and scans the bar code. "How's Billy doing?" I ask.

"He's okay. Quiet, though. He's been working nights at the bridge, so I'm asleep when he comes home, and he's asleep when I leave. Two dollars and eleven cents."

She puts the card in a brown bag, and I give her a five. "I haven't seen his car," I say. "He could call me."

"He's going through something, Scotty. I don't know what it is, but we have to let him. I learned that a long time ago."

"I want him to know— "

"He knows," Arlene says and hands me my change.

My trial's postponed at the plaintiff's request, so I'm out early and stop at the marina lounge on my way home. Pope and Purvis are on the terrace watching a fifty-foot power boat wedging itself into a berth, so I join them. The captain guns the engine, then revs it into reverse, then forward again. Diesel smoke pours into the air.

Donna comes out with a Jack D for me. "They arrested somebody in the shooting of that boy," she says. "It's on the news."

"Who was it?" Pope asks.

"The last person you'd imagine," Donna says. "A twelve-year-old white girl."

We go inside and stand behind the barstools and look up at the television. A reporter's speaking from the courthouse. "It's not clear at this time whether the girl knew the rifle was loaded," she says. "The girl's parents were not home at the time of the shooting."

The girl, apparently, came home from school, found her father's deer rifle, and took it into the woods "to see whether it would shoot." No details are given about whether she loaded the rifle or aimed it at anything.

"Jesus H. Christ," Donna says. "What the hell was she thinking?"

On the screen, a police car drives up to the courthouse. The girl gets out, though someone holds a coat in front of the girl's face. She has on shorts, and her skinny legs are visible.

"How did they catch her?" Pope asks.

"They questioned people," Donna says. "Even your friends only protect you for so long."

The picture switches to where the shooting occurred—a rural road, paved, with a ditch along it. A few feet away is brush and pines. This cuts to a late-model blue compact in a police lot and a close-up of the bullet hole in the rear door.

"Weird shit," Donna says.

"What'll they do to her?" Pope asks.

"They ought to fry the parents," Donna says.

"But we don't know the facts," I say.

Everyone looks at me.

"Like, where she was standing, what she could see? Did she know the rifle was loaded or how far a bullet could travel? Did she see the car? We don't know what really happened."

"A kid's dead," Donna says. "We know that."

Edgar Prioleau died when he was eleven. I was nine. We were at the fish camp on a Sunday. My father was making a picnic lunch, and he and Billy were taking Edgar and me to the other side of the island to cast in the surf. On the trail, I carried a rod and an empty pail, Edgar two rods, and Billy the bait cooler. My father lagged with the rest of the gear.

It was warm and sunny. I don't remember what we saw on the trail or what we said. Edgar walked ahead of me. Everything was familiar—palmettos, vines, the live oaks dappled in sunlight. The only thing unusual to me was how dark the woods were and how bright the light was when we got to the dunes. Edgar had on a red shirt, and when he ran out of the trees and up and over the first dune, his shirt was a kite in the air.

I followed, struggling for footing in the sand. Billy shouted, "Wait up, now." But Edgar was already at the top of the dune and ran down the other side.

Before the crest, I heard the wind in the sea oats, the louder sea, and then, at the crest, the sea itself. I skittered part way down the steep sand

and stopped. Edgar had put down the two rods and was racing toward the horizon.

That's how I remember him—a boy in a red shirt caught against the whole ocean. He leaped into the froth of the waves and waded out into the sunlight.

By the time Billy reached the top of the dunes behind me, Edgar had disappeared.

Monday around eleven, Billy shows up in my office wearing a light blue suit. He's shaved and his hair is plastered down with gel, so he doesn't look like himself. "I have a meeting with Latimer," he says.

"Is that the only suit you have?"

"What's wrong with it?" He brushes a speck from the lapel.

"It's not ironed. It's probably mildewed."

"The Ruperts bought a sailboat," Billy says. He examines my law degree hanging on the wall and, beside it, my admission to the bar. "Did you know Latimer has a permit to dredge for a new marina? The Corps of Engineers caved in, and now he wants to build a second golf course."

"We can't have enough golf courses."

Billy steps along the shelves of law books and gazes out the window at Broad Street. "Should I sell?"

"It isn't my property."

"If I gave it to you, would you sell?"

"That's a hypothetical. Where are you meeting Latimer? You want me to come along?"

Billy gives me a sidelong glance. "Do you know what it's like for Arlene to ride the bus into town every day? Sometimes I meet her at the bus stop when she comes home because she's been on her feet all day. If I sell, Arlene can quit her job."

"You can ride around together in a Town Car."

"Don't be smart."

"Don't wallow in self-pity."

He looks at me and nods. "Come with me, if you want. We're at the Mills Hyatt."

But as I'm getting my suit jacket on, a call comes in from a distraught client. Billy goes ahead. I'm twenty minutes, and at the restaurant, Billy and Latimer are drinking martinis.

Next to Billy, Latimer looks like an altar boy—ruddy cheeks, short hair, wet shiny eyes—though I know from representing the Ruperts he's a sweet-talker who believes God is money. He's dressed in a gray suit, gray tie, and wears a tie pin and gold cuff links.

"Scotty!" He shakes my hand, though I can tell Billy hasn't told him I was coming.

"Hello, Kevin." I sit down without being asked.

Latimer rolls with this. "Have a martini," he says.

A waiter arrives with a menu, and as if by magic, another martini, though it's for Billy. "The soup of the day is New England clam chowder," he says. "Entree specials are grilled salmon in a lobster sauce, and pork medallions with shiitake mushrooms and a browned garlic. Would you care for a beverage?"

"I'm good," I say. "Water."

Latimer raises his glass to Billy's refresher. "Here's to mutual success," he says. He drinks and turns to me. "I was telling Billy the Ruperts sold early. Lots on the interior of the island are going faster than we'd anticipated. In a few months, Billy's land has become more valuable."

The waiter brings my water and takes orders—salmon for Billy and Latimer, seafood salad for me. "And another martini," Billy says. "I'm not paying."

During the meal, Latimer argues his case. His company, Coastal Amenities, owns every parcel on the island except Billy's sixty acres that extends from the beach to the marsh. "The marina goes in first," Latimer says, "but the company's donated five acres for a grade school to encourage age-group diversity."

"Billy can motor his johnboat to the club for lunch," I say.

"And play golf for free," Latimer says.

Billy sips and sets down his martini. "If I sell," he says, "I want four times more money than Ruperts got."

"Acreage," Latimer said. "You have more, so you'll get more."

I have to get back for a meeting, so after lunch I leave Billy and Latimer in the lobby of the hotel. Billy wants to see where the houses will be, the second golf course, and the swimming pool. He promises not to make a decision without consulting me.

Walking down Broad Street, I cross into the sun-shadow of St. Michael's whose white steeple shines above the gray and pastel storefronts. A gust of wind blows a newspaper along. The unfolding scenario of Billy's caving in goes through my mind—the whole future of the island and others like it. Trees are felled, roads cut, and houses built. The middle of the woodland becomes the edge. Trees once protected by others are made vulnerable to storms. Birds requiring space and cover, like sparrows, thrushes, warblers, give way to grackles, mockingbirds, and starlings.

Even if Billy doesn't sell, his land will be diminished. At the shell mound, he'll hear car doors slamming, domestic quarrels, and golf balls teed off. At night, car headlights will shine into palmettos and pines and oaks that have never known other light than the moon and stars.

At my office I tell my secretary, Sylvia, "No calls," and for the rest of the afternoon, I bill my hours at half rate, because all I can think of is Latimer's arrogant assumption Billy is a fool.

At three, Sylvia looks in. "You said no calls, but your wife has an emergency."

I click a button and say hello.

"Billy's here," she says. "He wanted to see the view from our deck."

"What for? He had three martinis at lunch. Is he okay?"

"I gave him a Coke. He's been telling me about his sex life with Arlene."

"I hope you haven't told him about ours."

"What's to tell? Did you know he and Arlene are seventy, and they still make love three times a week?"

"Did he say whether he's going to sell the fish camp?"

"Are you listening to me, Scotty? He says, 'Arlene, you look beautiful,' and she says, 'I think you'd better get to work.'"

"And that's it?"

"Time goes by, Scotty. People change."

"I'm coming home," I say. "I'm leaving right now."

I pack my briefcase, but on my way out, Sylvia asks whether I've finished the reply brief for the Ruisdale case.

"Oh shit, I forgot."

"I assumed that's why you didn't want to be disturbed."

I retreat and take an hour to write the end of the brief. By then, it's already after four. But I text it to Sylvia.

"Arlene Prioleau called," she says. "She sounded upset, but I told her you went home."

"Call Huguley's and see if she's left work."

Sylvia dials, gets the manager, and hands me the phone.

"That woman," the manager says, "walked out the door as if we weren't here. She knows better than that."

"Maybe she won the lottery," I say. "And, you aren't here."

I hang up, and in a few minutes, I'm in traffic north at the apex of the second span on the Cooper River Bridge. White Ibis fly in a vee close above the girders, illuminated from beneath by the sun. The beauty of their precise flight heightens my unease. I don't believe in omens, but I know Arlene's leaving work early has to do with Billy.

At the bottom of the bridge, I veer right to Mount Pleasant and make the right turn on Magnolia Street. But at Billy's, the shades are drawn, and his car isn't there. I stop anyway. No one answers the side door, so I circle the house. The azaleas and roses in the back yard have withered.

I peek in the kitchen window. Inside is evidence of turmoil—a chair overturned, cabinets open, a skillet on the floor, along with boxes of cereal, lettuce, tin cans. A purse I assume is Arlene's sits on the table.

The knob of the back door turns in my hand. "Arlene?" I call out.

No answer.

The purse contains glasses, a hairbrush, a bus pass, no wallet. I step over the debris on the floor into the living room. Cushions from the sofa and cut-up newspapers are strewn around.

"Billy? Arlene?"

I edge into the bedroom in back, but it's empty. The bedspread has been tucked in. The only thing unusual is a newspaper clipping on the floor which I pick up and hold to the window light. It's of a child's primitive drawing of a beach with the wide blue sea and the sun going down into the waves. The caption says, "Brett's Vision of Edisto Beach State Park where the Herzberger family camped the night before Brett was shot." The colors are blue, yellow, tan. The sun has no reflection on the water. A bird is sketched in brown at the tideline.

Are these the boy's last thoughts before he was shot? Who can know?

I backtrack to the kitchen, pick up the phone, and call Edie.

Carla answers. "Hi, Daddy. I thought you were coming home early. What's wrong?"

"Is your mother there?"

Edie comes on. "What's going on, Scott? Where are you?"

"Is Billy there?"

"No, he left an hour ago. He was going to work."

"Tell Carla I'm sorry I was short with her. You and I—we'll talk later."

I take McCants to the causeway and merge with the line of cars going toward the beach, No one's moving, though. Horns honk. A few cars squeeze in and turn left, but on the main road to the island, people crane from their car windows for a view ahead. No cars are coming the other way, because the bridge is open.

I wheel around the cars in front of me, and instead of turning left, go straight ahead into the empty oncoming lane. Ahead a mile, the highway's tilted into the air, and police lights swirl across the tops of the waiting cars.

Either side of the causeway is salt marsh. A few cars turn around and come toward me, but I veer to the berm and scrape the oleanders to get by. Up ahead, I see Arlene striding along the pedestrian path. She has on a print dress, straw hat with a wide brim, and sturdy black shoes. She disappears behind a dump truck and reappears behind a Mercedes. I stop opposite her and lean across the seat. "Arlene!"

She turns and sees me and comes through the line of cars. She snaps the passenger door open and gets in. "He's in the pillbox," she says. "He opened the bridge but won't close it. And he won't come down."

"How do you know?"

"His supervisor phoned. I called you, but your secretary said you'd gone home. I've walked here from the bus stop."

Sailboats are stacked up, too, on either side of the bridge—dozens of masts stuck up in the air. The bridge is open enough to block the cars, but not enough to let boats go through.

"Did you see the boy's drawing in the paper?" Arlene asks. "This is his response."

"I saw it at your house. He sure tore up the place."

A policeman ducks among the cars ahead of us and holds up his hand. I stop and he comes to Arlene's window. "What do you think you're doing?" he asks.

"I'm Billy's wife," Arlene says. "Billy's up there in the bunker."

The cop looks at me. Two navy helicopters roar in over the marsh, and egrets and herons fly up from the reeds.

"Scott Atherton," I say. "I'm his lawyer."

"We think he has a rifle," the officer says.

"Billy doesn't own a rifle," Arlene says.

"But it isn't hard to get one," the officer says.

"Can we talk to him?" Arlene asks. "We can solve this."

The cop gets on his walkie-talkie. "I've got a wife here," he says, "and a lawyer."

We get the go-ahead, but we're still a half-mile from the bunker. The closer we get, the fewer cars come the other way, and we pass a half-dozen dump trucks and suburban assault vehicles waiting in line to cross.

The highway is broken by the open bridge, a stretch of ungainly metal against the blue sky. Sailboats are waiting in the inland waterway, too—sloops, yawls, ketches, and a trimaran. Two helicopters hover above the pillbox.

Billy's Volkswagen is parked in the turnout before the bridge, along with four police cruisers with their red lights whirling and two television vans. Several marksmen crouch behind the fenders of the cop cars with high-powered rifles at the ready. I pull up beside the nearest cruiser, where the sergeant is leaning against the hood. In the pillbox above, the Venetian blinds are pulled down against the sun.

Arlene gets out and holds the brim of her hat against the breeze. "What's this about a rifle?" she asks. She shouts above the noise of the helicopters.

"Stay down," the sergeant shouts back.

"I'm his wife," Arlene says.

"He's as likely to shoot you as anyone else," the officer says, "maybe more likely."

"Has he said what he wants?" I ask.

A helicopter drops to the window level of the pillbox, a man poised with a rifle in the passenger seat.

Arlene throws her hat into the truck cab, skirts the highway barricade, and aims for the steel catwalk at the side of the bridge.

"Ma'am?" the officer calls. "Ma'am, stop. Please."

Arlene doesn't stop, so I go after her. I follow her along the grating of the catwalk.

"If he's going to get himself shot," she says, "I want to say goodbye."

"He's not going to get shot."

"That boy did," she says.

The waterway beneath us is choppy, and swallows dart around the bridge girders. To the north, past the sailboats, the waterway recedes in a wide blue triangle, the border of which is marsh grass and, farther away, billowing trees. At the end of the catwalk a metal ladder leads up to an anteroom beneath the pillbox. Arlene holds a rung in her hand and steps up. "Billy?" she calls up. "Billy Prioleau, you listen to me!"

The helicopters are so noisy, Billy can't possibly hear a word.

"You go up there, Scotty," she says. "Talk to him. What do you say when you're fishing?"

I look up at the pillbox. "They should back off the helicopters. Let him breathe."

"I'll tell them." Arlene takes my two hands in hers and squeezes. "He loves you, Scotty. You bring him down."

She walks back along the catwalk, while I climb the ladder.

The helicopters are still loud, though muffled, and I wait to see whether they move off. Beside the trapdoor is a keypad, but I don't know the code, so I call up, "Billy, it's me, Scotty. You in there?"

A few seconds go by. Outside the reinforced window, the sailboats loll on their anchors, hatches open, crews hidden belowdecks. Another sloop motors toward the bridge with its sails furled. In the cockpit the captain holds what I imagine is a gin and tonic.

He's already dead is what I think. He opened the bridge and keeled over from a heart attack. In their siege mentality, the police have invented the scenario of a lunatic holed up with a rifle.

"Come on, Billy, open up. It's me."

The roar of the helicopters diminishes, and an occasional car horn sounds in the distance.

I hear scraping above me. "Who?" Billy says.

"Let's talk about Edgar."

There's another long pause. It's a risk to say this, but I've drawn the same connections Billy has, though not in the same way. He cut out the boy's drawing from the newspaper; he wanted to see the view from my house, which is roughly what Billy saw that day when Edgar disappeared—at the top of the dunes he saw the ocean and the beach spread out before him, but he didn't see Edgar. He saw me.

The trap door hums open slowly, and the inside of the pillbox appears—space rather than detail—and a wedge of Billy's forehead, his blue eyes, gray hair. I can't tell whether he's drunk or angry or deranged.

"I'm alone," I tell him. "Arlene— "

The door opens wider, and I climb up into the pillbox. The room's spartan. Except for the blinds on the west side, the windows are open and a breeze flows through. On one side is the control panel for the bridge hydraulics, a chair nearby, and a table with binoculars on it. Billy's splayed out on the floor with a six-pack of Pabst—one left—and he's holding a rifle.

"A pellet gun," he says. "I want them to think I'm serious."

I slide down next to him. I take the last beer. "Serious about what?"

"You know as well as I do."

I crane my neck and look over the sill. Light's fading from the blue triangle of the waterway. The motor sailer's closer. East, beyond the island, the blue ocean is wide and flat to the horizon. South, where the helicopters have retreated, the city skyline patterns the horizon in jagged shapes. Gulls fly leisurely above the houses on the island.

I pick up the binoculars and focus on a tern hovering over a tide pool, then swing the glasses to the marina lounge. "There's Purvis," I say. "And Donna and Pope and some other people watching us from the terrace."

"They haven't seen anything yet," Billy says.

I scan the cars and trucks backed up along the causeway and in both directions on Center Street. The dump trucks on the island are empty. I follow the marsh up-island to the live oak tree, but I can't see the oyster mound.

"Latimer's started filling in the ponds," Billy says. "That's what gave me the idea. All these dump trucks are Latimer's."

I lower the binoculars. "So you stopped him by opening the bridge?"

"One of those boats down there is the Ruperts'."

"Which one?"

"I don't remember," Billy says. "How many are there now?"

"Dozens. And a Coast Guard cutter is bringing in reinforcements."

I focus on the cutter entering the waterway from the harbor. The sun whitens the sky above the trees and clouds drift across the blue, though a sunset threatens.

"We need more beer," Billy says. He shakes his empty can and pulls the phone toward him. He dials a number. "We'll get room service."

"Maybe we should eat something."

"Donna, it's Billy. Yeah, we're up in the bridge. Listen, Scotty and I need a case of beer. Sam Adams is good. A case. And a half dozen corndogs. What else have you got there? Some beef jerky and onion chips. Put it on Scotty's tab." He listens a moment. "Purvis can deliver it. He can take the johnboat across the waterway." Another pause. "Now, yes, right now. We're thirsty."

He clicks off and hands me the phone. "You're my lawyer," he says. "Call the newspaper and have them tell the police to let Purvis up here."

The number's on his phone—he's already called once—and they switch me to their mobile unit. "It's Scott Atherton. I'm with Billy Prioleau in the pillbox. Put on the police."

I stand up, hold back the Venetian blinds, and see a man get out of a media van and run across to one of the cruisers. In another few seconds, the sergeant comes on.

"It's Billy's lawyer," I say. "Billy wants the dump trucks off the causeway."

"He wants what?"

"He doesn't like the dump trucks. And we've ordered some food from the marina. A friend of ours, Purvis Neal, will be bringing it up here. Billy also wants to talk to his wife."

"No, I don't," Billy says.

"She's right here," the sergeant says.

I hand the phone to Billy.

"Hello," he says.

I'm close enough to hear Arlene. "Are you all right?" she asks. "What are you and Scotty doing up there?"

"Nothing much so far."

"I want you to come home."

"Maybe in a while."

"You have to get to work, Billy."

"I will," he says. "You're beautiful."

She says something I can't hear, and Billy hands me the phone again.

"Are you making any progress?" the sergeant asks.

"Billy hasn't offered to surrender his weapon yet," I say, "but we're talking."

"We want to defuse the situation," the sergeant says. "We want to get the traffic moving."

"Get rid of the dump trucks," I tell him. "Give me your phone number so I can be in touch when we have other demands."

He gives me the number.

"Don't do anything rash," I say, and I click off.

The police on both sides of the bridge talk to the dump truck drivers, and in a few minutes the trucks are turning around on the causeway. On the island, they disappear behind the Episcopal church on Center Street. It takes fifteen minutes or so, and by then Purvis is in the johnboat coming up the waterway. He maneuvers through the maze of sailboats and ties up near the bridge pilings. A police officer helps him offload the case of beer.

"You still think it was an accident about that boy?" Billy asks.

"I don't know for sure."

"What's an accident?" Billy says. "When you think about it, everything's an accident. Life is an accident."

"You mean Edgar's drowning."

"Up here I watch the seasons change," he says. "I watch the tides flow in and out of the creeks."

"Is that what you think about?"

"It's not thinking," Billy says. "It's feeling."

We hear a noise below, and Billy opens the trapdoor. Purvis is in the anteroom, and Billy opens the door wider. The beer's on the catwalk, but Purvis has looped a rope around it and tied the rope to his belt. With his good hand, he tosses up the food. I help him up after into the pillbox, take hold of the rope, and hoist up the beer.

Billy opens the case and passes me one. "Help yourself, Purvis," he says. "You're an accomplice now."

Purvis doesn't drink much, but for this occasion, he takes a Sam Adams and sits down crosslegged beside Billy. Billy doles out the corndogs.

I pull the Venetian blinds up a little. The helicopters are poised off the end of the island. The line of cars extends back on Main Street on the island and all the way to Mount Pleasant in the west. Fifty or so boats are in limbo on the waterway. The sun's in the trees now, and rays of pink shoot out into the clouds. Sky colors—all we can see—brighten everything around us.

I join Billy and Purvis on the floor. For a while we don't say anything. Billy and I finish our beers and open two more. Purvis munches on his corndog.

The beer loosens me up, and I like the new ground it takes me to. Billy will want immunity from prosecution, or at least a reduced charge, if he agrees to counseling. He'll need an assurance the highway department won't fire him. A transfer, maybe—they can't be expected to let him back up here. These items are negotiable, but the other demands won't be so easily met—to stop the dredging and filling, to end the cutting of trees and the building of roads, to purify the air, cleanse the water, keep the rich from getting richer. He'll want Edgar's grave undisturbed.

The pink clouds fade to gray and the pillbox darkens. I rock forward and look out again. The causeway's silent and many of the cars have turned around, but the police and the media are still there. The marsh is dark and the creeks and tide pools are silver-gray, tinged with red. Across the harbor, Charleston glimmers in the dusk.

"They aren't going away," I say. "I should call Edie to let her know where I am."

"She knows where you are," Billy says. "You're with me and Purvis."

Billy opens his beer and chews a piece of beef jerky. "You know the oyster mound?" Billy says. "Guess what Latimer says that's going to be." He waits a moment. "The fifth tee."

Billy laughs. Purvis grins and drinks his beer. Then we're quiet again. The sun makes a last burst from the trees, dances into the clouds—its deep orange and red lighting up the pillbox, even as the darkness comes down over us.

NORTHERN LIGHTS

We were east of Hot Springs, South Dakota, on the gravel toward my uncle's farm. I was riding in the backseat of the Chevy between my aunt and my mother, but leaning up between the front seats to hear what the men were saying. My uncle was driving. He had on a gold-colored jacket and a green John Deere cap. It was September tenth, and we'd been to town to celebrate his birthday. The women had had hard feelings because my father and my uncle sat in the lounge for a long time while the rest of us looked at the menu in the restaurant. Finally my mother had gone to get them. My uncle was cheerful, though, even when he sat down and my aunt gave him a look. He'd ordered another bourbon and coke from the waitress and said, "You only turn fifty once."

Then we'd eaten. Nothing more was said about the drinking until we got out to the car. My aunt didn't want my uncle to drive, but it was his car, he said, and he'd damn well drive if he wanted to. So he did.

It was getting dark, then, and big gray sledrunner clouds curled up at the ends slid over the Black Hills, which were blue-black against the sky. The gravel road jogged east and north, east and north along the section boundaries. It was rolling hills mostly, climbing to the mesas which then dropped down to my uncle's place ten miles away. My uncle sprayed stones on the turns and weaved a little across the road, and now and then my aunt said, "Easy does it, Luther," under her breath.

My father liked to come back to the Lakota. He and my uncle had grown up there, over by Oelrichs, and I think he felt the going home.

My uncle and aunt had two older boys—one in college and one working for General Mills in St. Louis—and my father held them up to me as what to strive to be like. They'd worked on the farm and had done well in school, and now they were making names for themselves. My father thought the farm instilled values. "You learn from the land," he said.

But the farm to me was just someplace different from Denver where my father was a veterinarian. He knew about animals, and my uncle knew about farming. When they got together they talked about cows and sheep, alfalfa and corn and wheat, and the weather. And machines. My uncle could take apart any machine—tractors, pickups, windrowers—and when we visited, he and my father were always tinkering in the shop.

Driving along, they were talking about the Case tractor and the broken three-point on the ditcher—nothing I understood—but it was better than listening to my aunt and my mother discussing books. "We can weld the three-point," my uncle said. "No two ways about it. I'll do her in the morning."

"But the tractor still has that bearing about to go," my father said.

"We'll get through ditching the borders and put water on them for spring. I can replace the bearing this winter when hell freezes over."

My uncle slowed and turned at a section, but took the corner too fast, and my aunt tipped toward me. I felt the words she didn't say tighten in her body. We made the corner and ran straight north toward the mesa.

For a moment quiet ruled in the car. I heard the engine and the rocks cracking up under the Chevy. Then my father said, "Maybe we should let Les drive."

My uncle stared ahead. He kept both hands on the wheel.

"Not with so many people in the car," my mother said. "Not at night."

"Couldn't do worse than Luther," my father said.

"We're still on the road, aren't we?" my uncle asked.

"You want to drive, son?"

"Not really," I said.

We kept on north for another mile. I'd been driving some on the farm—the half-ton Ford mostly—back and forth from the fields to take lunch or to deliver gas for the tractor or to practice with the gears and get used to the feel of the engine. But I hadn't driven on the county road.

My uncle pulled on the headlights, and the land was closed away, all but the tan stripe of gravel, the weeds and dead sunflowers in the ditches, and the fences on both sides of the road. A few arc lights blazed in the distance.

"When's the irrigation district cut back the water?" my father asked.

"Two weeks," my uncle said.

"If it snows, you'll be all right."

"If it snows, we'll be cold," my uncle said. "Can't plan crops on snow." He slowed a little, then took one hand off the wheel and pointed ahead through the windshield. "Look there."

I ducked down between the seats to see what he saw. Wisps of white and yellow and pink drifted up vertically into the sky, diminished, then burst again like curtains of colored rain.

"Northern lights," my father said. "I'll be damned."

"Haven't seen them in years," my uncle said.

My aunt and my mother leaned forward. "They're from sunspots," my mother said. "I read about them. The sun throws out bunches of atoms."

The lights diminished. My aunt sat back. She asked about how much schoolwork I'd have to make up coming to visit on a long weekend.

"Not that much," I said. I looked back out the windshield.

"We thought it important to see Luther," my mother said. "And Les likes the farm."

My uncle slowed down. "You want to drive?"

"It's all right," I said.

"Go ahead," my father said. "You have to practice night driving sometime."

"He's fourteen," my mother said. "He has plenty of time."

My aunt leaned up. "Luther, it's late. Why don't we get home now?"

My uncle pulled over to the side of the road and stopped. He put on the hand brake. "It's pretty flat from here," he said. "And I don't want to sit in the back."

He opened the door and got out and walked a little ways away from the car to urinate.

"Sometimes I don't understand that man," my aunt said.

My father opened the door on his side, too, and the cool air with the smell of sage and cut hay rushed through the car. "Come on, son," my father said.

I climbed up between the seats and got behind the wheel. My uncle came back and got into the passenger side up front. "You can drive a stick," my uncle said. "This gear's in a little different place. All you have to do is follow the road."

My mother slid to the middle of the backseat, and my father got in behind me, though he didn't lean back.

I was tall for my age and looked right out over the wheel. I shifted a couple times to get the feel, then left it in first and gave some gas. The car jerked forward. I accelerated and shifted again.

"Don't shake out my teeth," my aunt said.

We got up speed and I shifted again. "Look at the northern lights," I said.

They'd come back in a different place, or maybe the road had turned slightly, but a band of shifting colors drifted way up in the sky.

"Watch the road," my mother said.

The road dipped and rose and then ran straight for two or three miles. It was dark, but I knew where we were. The bright light off to the left was Fosters' farm, and farther on, TePaskes'. I wasn't going fast, maybe thirty-five, but no one spoke. It was as if they were waiting for an accident.

I passed Fosters' and TePaskes' and turned east. The sky was darker ahead of us, a few stars, but no moon. The road was straight. We were still a mile or two from my uncle's farm, and I felt the softness return to the car. My aunt and mother resumed talking.

I picked up speed to forty, maybe a little more. We came up on some brush on the right and two cottonwoods loomed bright yellow at the edge of the headlights. Then an animal bounded out from the brush and into the road.

"Coyote," my father said.

I was surprised by his voice so close behind me. I slowed. I thought the coyote would cross the road—it had plenty of space—but it swerved and loped along in our same direction a few yards in front of the car, as if it were racing with us. It was a big one, gray and reddish-brown, broad-shouldered. Its bushy tail flopped down as it ran. Any second I expected it to veer off into the weeds.

I took my foot off the gas again, but suddenly the coyote darted left in front of us. We heard a terrible crumpling noise, then nothing. The car passed. The engine kept on. The gravel slid under us.

"You did the right thing," my father said. "You kept the car steady."

"I didn't think it would cut in front," I said.

"Blinded, maybe," my father said. "Animals get lost in that kind of light."

"It might have dented the car," I said. I looked over at my uncle. He was staring ahead at the road, but maybe seeing something else. He didn't say anything, and I looked back at the road.

"Turn in there," my uncle said.

"Where?"

"There, at the lane. Turn the car around."

I slowed and turned into the lane and stopped.

"What are we doing?" my aunt asked.

"Reverse is in and up," my uncle said.

I got it into reverse and backed out into the main road, shifted down to first. I drove back.

The coyote was lying in the road. At first I was sure it was dead. How could it not be dead? But as we got closer, it rolled up and lifted its head.

"Get the lights on it," my uncle said.

I aimed the headlights at the coyote and pulled closer. It had weird eyes—black, but flecked with yellow—and a thin nose. Its ears were raised alertly, and it was panting. Blood frothed in its mouth.

We stopped.

"Okay," my uncle said, "that's enough."

We were in the middle of the road. I backed up a ways and turned and went forward and backed up again. I was shaking. No one said anything.

The last couple of miles to the farm took forever. At the lip of the mesa the arc light on the barn appeared, but it was stationary as a star. But it wasn't a star, and we got there. When I pulled in under the light, I was relieved.

"That was some birthday," my aunt said.

My father patted my shoulder. "Good driving, son," he said.

Everyone got out except my uncle. I went around to the grille to inspect the damage, but there wasn't a mark on the car.

My uncle rolled down his window. "Go fetch the .22," he said. "We have to go back."

My aunt had already gone inside and had turned on the light in the kitchen. A rectangle of gold spread out into the yard. My mother paused at the door. "Luther, he's tired," she said.

"I'm tired," my uncle said. "I've been up since five-thirty, and I've worked all day."

I thought my father might make a case for me, but he didn't. "I'll come along," he said.

"No, I want the boy." My uncle looked at my father and then at me.

There was a pause. Then my father said, "Get the .22, son."

I started to cry. I don't know why. I felt the tears beginning in my body. I knew I shouldn't cry, and I didn't make a sound. No one else knew, but I knew. The tears came, and I couldn't stop them, and to get away, I went into the house and took the .22 from the glass cabinet in the living room. He had a 30-30 and two shotguns, too. The key was in the lock.

I stood for a moment facing the glass. The crying passed. I touched each eye to each shoulder to soak the tears. Then I got a box of shells from the drawer.

"Are you all right, Les?" my mother asked.

"I'm all right."

"You don't have to go."

"I want to go," I said.

I turned around. My mother wanted to hug me, but I was holding the gun sideways in front of me.

"What's that man asking now?" my aunt said.

I broke away from my mother, passed my aunt in the doorway, and went on through the kitchen. I let the screen bang behind me.

When I came out, my uncle was in the driver's seat talking to my father. The car was running, and the passenger door was open. My father backed away from the open door, and I got in with the .22 between my knees, barrel up. My father closed the door.

My uncle turned around in the yard and headed back down the driveway. He didn't say anything for a while. We bounced along, and the headlights jumped across the dark fields of alfalfa. At the mailbox, we got onto the smoother gravel of the county road and climbed the long hill to the top of the mesa.

We turned south, and my uncle glanced in the rearview. "Those lights are still playing their games," he said.

I looked around. The northern lights had flared up again, an eerie wash rising and disappearing. "I thought northern lights were in Alaska," I said.

"They're everywhere," my uncle said. He glanced into the rearview again and back to the road. "I've seen them a few times, but never like that."

He was quiet again. I could feel the lights like some odd force translated into my body, flaring and fading, and flaring again.

"I've lived out here thirty-five years," my uncle said. "By the time I was your age, I knew everything I know now. Maybe I'm a little better at fixing a tractor or a windrower, but I'm worse at others."

"What are you worse at?"

"I can't run a tractor straight down a row anymore," my uncle said. "Takes concentration. My mind wanders. And I'm worse at talking."

"You talk all right," I said.

"I keep things to myself," my uncle said. "Sometimes I walk into that house and wonder what's there. All those hours up and down the fields—disk, plant, spray, harvest. That's what I know. We talk about the crops and weather and the work, but I'm out there in the darkness." He pointed to the side of the road where the headlights didn't reach.

I thought it was booze talking. My uncle was quiet again for a while. We turned west onto the straight stretch where I'd hit the coyote, and he slowed down.

"So what about the coyote?" I asked.

"He's a trickster," my uncle said. "That's what the Indians say. He shows you one face and means another. That's the legend."

"I don't know any legends," I said.

"Two faces and one name," my uncle said. He slowed down to maybe fifteen.

I thought he was looking for the coyote. "He's farther on," I said.

My uncle seemed not to hear. "My sons hate me," he said.

I didn't say anything.

"They hate me. You understand? They didn't call me today, did they? My birthday? Fifty years old. They didn't call."

"Maybe they called while we were in town."

My uncle shook his head.

"Why would they hate you?"

He speeded up a little. We passed the farm lane where I'd turned around the first time. My uncle leaned closer to the windshield. "I made them work," he said. "I told them what to do, how to do it. Do you see? I made them windrow and drive the tractors and combine because it was work that had to be done." He paused. "I never let them want to do it."

The coyote appeared in the road ahead of us. I made out its shape beyond the headlights. I'd hoped it wouldn't be there, that it would have healed itself and run off, but the way my uncle was talking, I was glad to see it. Maybe it was dead already. That's what I hoped.

We came up on it slowly, and right away I saw it wasn't dead. It was lying down, but had its head up and ears raised. It panted blood and looked directly into the headlights.

My uncle stopped and put the Chevy in neutral and pulled on the brake. He left the engine running and the lights on. We got out. I held the .22 at my shoulder, barrel pointed at the sky. The clouds had dissipated a little, and a half moon wove its way through them. "What do you want me to do?" I asked.

My uncle didn't answer. He stepped in front of the headlights and stared at the coyote for a minute. Then he took a couple of steps forward and crouched down. He was maybe fifteen feet away.

The coyote stared back.

"Turn off the engine," my uncle said.

I leaned into the driver's window and turned off the ignition. It was suddenly quiet. The headlights dimmed a little.

My uncle got down on his hands and knees and crept forward a few feet. I didn't know what he was doing. I put a shell into the chamber and pulled the bolt. I didn't know much about coyotes, but I thought any wild animal would protect itself.

A few crickets were buzzing, and in the near distance other coyotes yipped and barked.

"Turn off the headlights," my uncle said.

I opened the car door and turned the knob for the headlights.

It was dark. The moon had gone under the clouds, and only a rim of silver outlined where it had been. The wisps of the northern lights were gone, too. The road faded into the distance and ended at the horizon of stars.

The coyote was a dark shape in the middle of the road. My uncle was a dark shape crawling toward it. As he got closer, he started talking softly, in a voice I hadn't heard him use before, a sweet voice, almost singing. I'd never heard him sing before. A lullaby, maybe, is what it sounded like. I couldn't make out the words. The crickets and the coyotes in the distance and my uncle's voice were all mixed together.

I don't know how long this went on—minutes. The coyote didn't move, but it started to sing, too, louder than my uncle, as if the pain in its body were its voice. It whined and howled and cried. I wanted to sing, too. I don't know why, but I did. I wanted to get down on my hands and knees right there on the gravel with my uncle.

Then a car appeared, coming from the other direction, far away so it was only a pale glow of headlights moving across the darkness. I didn't think my uncle saw it. He kept on singing. The car lights turned north toward us, still a ways off, but close enough to cast my uncle and the coyote in silhouette. I was certain my uncle would get up then, but he didn't. He stopped singing and crawled forward.

He was two or three feet from the coyote when the coyote lurched up from the gravel. My uncle rushed forward—lunged, but the coyote eluded him. I was surprised how quickly it moved with only its forelegs. It dragged itself into the weeds and kept moving. The weeds swirled in a jagged line. I raised the .22, but it was dark, and I couldn't see well enough to aim, and I lowered the rifle again.

The car came on, still a quarter mile away. My uncle lay face down on the gravel, a big man in his pale jacket. The headlights closed in and then turned off at the section marker toward TePaskes'.

I unloaded the .22, set the rifle on the backseat, and helped my uncle up from the ground. He'd had too much to drink. I got him into passenger seat, and I got behind the wheel.

I turned around at the section road and headed back east. We passed the place where the coyote had been, and I slowed, but I didn't see him. My uncle didn't look. He was slumped against the passenger door with his eyes closed. The northern lights over the mesa were not so bright anymore, just faint streaks shimmering, like nerves firing in the night sky, like the pain all through my body.

THE BEAUTIFUL MORNING

OF ALMOST JUNE

I live alone forty miles from Tucson and work at home translating movie scripts from German into English. Before this, for ten years, I worked at Farrar, Straus and Giroux in New York, handling German novels and film rights, which I parlayed into freelance. Agents send me scripts from Zürich, Berlin, and Los Angeles. A translator could have any name, but let me call myself Ruth.

Señora Astacio, the weaver, lives across the street. We're neighbors by proximity in what is not a neighborhood but, rather, two adobe houses built years ago on a dirt lane that deadends north into the arroyo. It's a bleak landscape. To the east are the rocky ridges of the Galiuro Mountains and the dry bajada fanning down from the canyon; to the west is pale blue distance. Sporadic birds and mammals, along with snakes and lizards, survive on next to nothing in the saguaros, mesquite, and palo verde.

This noon in April, the mountains are hot, and wind shakes the ocotillo in my yard. Señora Astacio, across the road, sits by her window where the sun illuminates her gray hair and weathered face. The mailman's told me she's a weaver, that her cloth bags are in museums, but I've never been in her house, nor seen anyone carrying anything away. Maybe she weaves at night, a secret sharer, a counterfeiter, Rumpelstiltskin weaving straw into gold.

When I first moved in last fall, I tried to befriend her. I offered peaches and plums from the slight trees in my backyard, firewood a friend gave me, cookies I baked. Once I took over an article I'd cut from the newspaper about rabies in raccoons and foxes I thought she might not have seen, but each time, though my Spanish is sufficient, I was met with silence.

Movie scripts are not books. Each word bears intolerable weight because there are so few of them. Take this slugline from the Jakob Becker script:

EXT. HAUS – MITTAG

Ein Viertel der Arbeiterklasse. Eine Frau, etwa 25, gräbt ihren Rasen auf.

EXT. HOUSE – NOON

A working-class area. A woman, 25, digs in her lawn.

What appears on the screen? A cloudy day in autumn, revealed by the yellow in the nearby poplars. A busy street runs in front of the clapboard duplex. On one side is a ratty porch, and on the other, a metal chair beside a refrigerator. Children are coming home from school carrying their book bags and knapsacks. A rusty red Fiat is parked in the drive. A blond woman, pretty in a frowsy way, and dressed in a white blouse and frayed jeans, is digging ferociously with a shovel in her lawn.
All of that you'd see, and more, in a split second.

Darkness focuses close work. The outer landscape is cut off, and pages and words are more visible, more comprehensible, more luminous in the gooseneck lamp that bends over my desk. I've been working at night for several months, from after supper until three in the morning, and in a burst of speed, I've finished one project and started on the Becker script. Then, in the midst of it, about a month ago, I was wakened at 8 a.m. from a sound sleep by bulldozers. In a single day they carved a road across the bajada above Señora Astacio's house. A day later, at the end of the road, a backhoe dug a big hole. Each succeeding day, someone new appeared—a cement truck poured basement walls and footings, an architect inspected the site, a landscaper came out and took measurements.

When I lived in New York, people complained about the end of daylight savings time, of not having a view, of the cold, but for me it was the noise—car horns, screeching subways, jackhammers, airplanes, *voices*. People yelled for taxis, scalped tickets, preached the gospel. Even at night, an elevator hummed, a car passed in the street, or a siren blazed.

Silence is Señora Astacio's native language. I asked the mailman whether she ever spoke, and he said yes, but she'd never been a talker. She wasn't deaf, though. She was shy and ornery. She used to live where I do now, in my house. Her parents built it when she and her husband got married, and when her parents died, Señora Astácio moved to the bigger house, thinking the son would want the smaller one. The son, though, moved to San Diego to build boats.

As a girl, my mother lived in Arizona outside of Willcox. She said the desert made her feel clean, and I remember when she talked about it, her voice got dreamlike, as if she were tasting the air or smelling the cactus blooms. Her memory spawned my wistfulness for distance. I bought my house the modern way, over the internet. I saw a photo of a low-slung adobe with two fruit trees the seller promised to water. The interior was a living room and a rough kitchen, with a wood stove in the corner. The house was forty miles from Tucson; the yard was desert. I had the vague idea of reliving what my mother had experienced, but the expanse around the house was unexpected. It never occurred to me to ask how far away a grocery store was, whether fire and police protection existed, or who one called in an emergency.

Every day Señora Astacio and I watch the new house take shape. The carpenters arrive in the early morning—two pickups with four or five Anglos, and a pickup and a van with a half-dozen Hispanics. They swarm through the shell of the house, hauling, lifting, POP POP POPPING their nail guns. A generator hammers most of the day so the saws can whine like car engines. The house has risen by degrees—the ground floor, the second, the third—see-through studs shaping the sky at angles. It's not a house, it's a palace. I've seen manors on the Hudson, glitzy ranchhouses in the hills above L.A., the gem castles of France and Germany, and this house is a synonym. I've asked the mailman who's building it, who will live there, and he says he's heard it's a dentist from Oregon, or a high-tech baron from Boston, maybe a movie star.

Since I can't sleep in the daytime, I work. I don't know whether my translations suffer from their being done in that ubiquitous light, but they're different—long-winded (I can cut later), florid, tentative. I want to be precise the first time, to trust my intuition, but working in the daylight opens up the world. I've taken to getting up at 4 a.m. to utilize the few hours of darkness and quiet, but I'm aware of dawn's coming. This is new to me: the emergent shapes of the hills, the gathering pinks and yellows, the songs of wrens and towhees and the calls of doves.

Because of her son, I think more about Señora Astacio than I might otherwise. He appeared one afternoon a few days before the construction started. I happened to be awake after a night's work, and I was out getting the mail when I saw dust rising from the road a long way off. I heard a motorcycle coming, and finally a rider materialized through the heat waves and pulled up at Señora Astacio's broken down wall. I assumed it was her son, a man about thirty-five, with long black hair in a ponytail. We're so far out from other houses, I didn't remember I was still in my nightgown, a white one with lace at the collar and sleeves. The man stared at me directly and without subterfuge, the same way I was regarding him. He was well-built and wore, not biker's leather, but a white shirt and tie.

He stayed two hours in his mother's house, and, when he came out, I was working on my rock garden. My mother had grown cactus in a solarium in her house in Connecticut where I grew up—barrel cactus, agave, prickly pear, cholla. Until she died and I moved out here, I had never considered them more than oddities, but now, living where they are native, I admire their efficiency at storing up what water comes to them and protecting their resources with spines. I liked arranging and rearranging the stones so it looks as if I've created a design. The man put something into his saddlebag and then came across the road to where I was.

In a movie, what happens must not only be possible or plausible, but inevitable. Events lead one to the next, not by coincidence (though coincidence may start a sequence), but by what must be perceived as logical extension. If a good-looking man were to fall for a beautiful woman, that's to be expected, but if he falls for one not so pretty, he needs a convincing reason—she's rich, she's smart, she's principled and courageous. If he were unusual, he'd understand more than the representation of a woman by her physical appearance.

My yard has no fence, no separation from the gravel road, so Señora Astacio's son walked right up to me. He was less beautiful and more serious. His eyes were dark, his nose a little squashed, his chin stubbled with black. "I see you changed your clothes," he said.

"I'm a late worker and a late sleeper," I said.

"I wonder if I could ask you a favor." His voice was serene.

"Why don't you tell me first who you are?"

"Benito," he said. "I grew up in your house. I'd ask someone else, but…" He scanned the empty road and the dry arroyo beside the house.

"I know," I said. "No one else is here."

"Keep an eye on my mother. See that she's up and around every day, that she gets her mail. No more than that. She's old, and her health isn't good. If you notice anything unusual, call me. Would that be too much of a burden?"

"Call you where?"

"I'm in San Diego. I'll give you the number."

Neither of us had a pen or paper, though he might have written the number in the dirt with a stick. Instead, I led him around to the back terrace where the door was open to the kitchen. The house was cool inside, shadowy from window light and absolutely still. No birds or insects sang at midday, no breeze, no airplanes. Benito waited in the doorway, but his presence followed me to the desk by the telephone. That's how it felt. The feeling was so unexpected I was overwhelmed. I forgot what I was doing. I stood at the desk and stared at the telephone, at a ruler, a piece of blank paper.

After a few moments, Benito came up behind me. "Are you all right?" he asked.

He was genuinely concerned. I heard that in his voice. I thought I'd simply ask him what I was looking for, but when I turned, there was only the light from behind him, the cool air, no other language but his. He held me; I held him.

Translating is an attempt to render meaning similar to the original, to straddle two cultures and mediate between what the author intended and what the reader will understand—to take a little here, give a little there, as priests are wont to do when they're interpreting symbols for the laity. But as soon as words are attached to ideas, havoc breaks loose. Ideas change, relationships among things, even objects. If I were to transcribe "Jahre" as "year," we'd have to agree a year is the duration of the earth's rotation around the sun, or the number of days in the Gregorian calendar, dismissing the days lost in conversion from the Julian Calendar. We say winter's cold and summer's hot, but in other hemispheres, January is summer and July winter. Does a year feel the same to a Chilean as to us? Or the same to a six-year-old girl as to a man in prison or to a woman in a bad marriage? You see the difficulty. Multiply that by every noun and verb, every adverb and adjective. "Slow" is relative. "Clouds" are thick or thin or threatening. What about words like "admiration" or "love" or "waiting"?

I lived with a German for three years after college and before I took the job in New York. I met him when I was studying in Santander. I should have known living in his hometown of Würzburg wouldn't be the same as when he was in Spain on vacation. I found work in a *Verlag* that was bringing out German editions of American novels.

We had a tiny apartment. He cooked the meals, showed me off to his friends, brought me presents. He called me *roseschätzele*, but he refused to see a flower can be killed as readily by watering it too much as too little.

The construction workers are putting on the roof, one crew steering sheets of plywood up three floors with block-and-tackle, while another saws the sheets to size, and a third hammers them into place. The various planes of the roof are so steeply pitched the men have to rope themselves to the other side of the house to be free to use their nail guns.

At noon they eat in groups, the Hispanics on the steps leading to the entry, and the Anglos in the shade on the north side of the house. This separation is a daily ritual born of history and language, but, though their behavior is not determined, each day they choose the same configuration.

To my knowledge I haven't seen the owner of the house, man or woman, or owners. They're nameless, faceless, but rich. I know that much. Maybe they've been at the site when I haven't noticed; maybe someone sends them photographs, though I've not witnessed anyone taking pictures. Maybe they fly over the house in a small plane. I see these from time to time and pay no attention.

It's evening, almost dark. The construction workers are gone, but it's not quiet. Nighthawks buzz in the air, and coyotes sing back and forth across the arroyo. These noises are different from those I knew before. They're not noises, but sounds. The light is on in Señora Astacio's house—gold divided into squares that shine across the road so perfectly I can't look. I sit on the terrace in the impending night and wait for her to come out. She's been stirring every evening, sometimes walking out to the steep hillside behind her house or up the empty road gathering twigs and dry husks of ocotillo and saguaro, which she puts in the woven bag she carries over her shoulder.

This evening I go out into the road and call to her, "¿Puedo ayudarle?"

She doesn't hear, or pretends not to, and for a few minutes I walk alongside her gathering the small twigs as she does. "I met your son," I tell her. "Su hijo."

"No me lo diga Usted."

"Me gustaría verlo otra vez."

"El no está viniendo," she says, with finality.

I stop and consider why her son won't come back again. San Diego is only a short day's drive. It's been more than a month since his last visit to her and his first visit to me. In New York I rarely went out with men, and when I did, I was reserved, unwilling to be hurt. I took to heart my mother's admonition: men can be forgotten. Neither Benito nor I has called the other, but that's our choice. To make love as we did so suddenly was a revelation, a moment that needs no discussion or analysis. It happened for a hundred reasons, and no reason at all. Possible, plausible, inevitable.

Señora Astacio rests and looks up at the house above her. Stars have come out, but their pattern is not the same now, with the sky broken by the silhouette of the dark house.

"Who would live in such a house?" I ask.

Señora Astacio doesn't answer. The nighthawks have stopped chirring, and the coyotes are silent.

Over the next weeks, my work slows down. I'm troubled by nuances in the Becker script—a void, an absence, a space between what the words say and what I feel from them. Someone in Hollywood has bought the rights to the script for $100,000, but meaning isn't a function of money. I see the printed page, the individual words and phrases in German. I conjure the woman digging in her lawn, follow her on buses and trains and through the death of her husband, searching for something that isn't buried, isn't in the air, or in the sea. I'm paid to decipher words, but what if words are not enough? Or the mind is insufficient to understand them? I'm at fault and not Becker.

In the midst of this labor, on a morning clouds swirl down over the mountains, Benito visits his mother again. I don't hear his motorcycle for the generator at the construction site, but when I go out to get the mail the bike is there, leaning against the wall.

The mail has catalogs and a postcard from a girlfriend in France. So little comes to me now except over the internet. I retreat to my office and wait. Will Benito remember me? Has he any idea how difficult the last time was, how joyful, how perfect? It took no courage at the moment; I was too stunned to think. My body acted, and afterward, inevitable or not, it took all my strength to embrace what I'd done.

A mist falls outside, the first precipitation I've seen here, what the cactus desire. I open wide the windows. The ocotillo in the yard slowly unfurls its leaves. The distance west is shortened by clouds. What I notice most are the smells wetness engenders—moist blossoms, sage, earth.

Benito finds me where I am. He knows what distance is, and unlike the workers, knows rituals must be broken. He kisses me long and hard, unbuttons my blouse, lets the moment speak. Cool air flows over my skin.

Later, returning to the strangeness words require, I ask him about this place—where the adobe came from, whether the well ever ran dry, how much rain fell in the spring. "What was it like when you were a boy?" I ask.

"In those days, it was really far out from anywhere," he says. "We rode on horseback down the arroyo to the intersection of roads. A wax camp was there and a couple of trailers and a mercado where the Kwik Mart is now."

"Who planted the fruit trees?"

"My mother. But all of us watered them—six children. We carried buckets from the well. It was a pain in the ass, but I remember it differently now. We loved the fruit."

"Where are your brothers and sisters?"

"Gone," he said. "Somewhere. I don't know…away."

"I offered your mother some peaches and pears last fall, but she refused to take them."

"She couldn't. She had to know you first."

"How can she know me if she doesn't talk?"

"She watches what you do. That's her way of knowing." Benito smiles. He gets up and pulls on his jeans, wrangles his white shirt over his chest, and turns to me. "Have you been up to that new house?"

"No. Why would I want to?"

"My mother has."

"She climbed that hill?"

"That's what she says." He goes to the window in bare feet. "Look there."

I rise from the bed, cover myself with the sheet, and look out. The sun's broken beneath the mist and clouds, and across the desert is a curtain of pink and yellow rain. Benito pulls the sheet away and puts his arms around me. In his embrace I am released from myself.

After that day, Señora Astacio's different toward me. Benito must have said something, or she's seen he was at my house. When I work in the early morning darkness, her light is on, too. I imagine she's weaving, braiding the intricate strands of wool into a rug or a shoulder bag. The yarns fill my imagination with rusts, blues, blacks—the colors I saw before. One morning a coyote appears in the early light, lopes down the bajada and along the road, and stops between our houses. I open my door to watch him, and Señora Astacio opens hers. We nod at one another. The coyote moves on.

That afternoon she comes out of her house and stands in the street beside her broken-down wall and stares at me on my knees in my rock garden. Her expression is fierce, as if she's about to yell, but for a long time she says nothing. Then she says, "Me ayudaría." It's not a question. You will help me.

"How can I?"

"No dice nada."

"¿Es eso todo?"

"Si, es todo."

Later, I risk a call to Benito. "She told me not to say anything," I tell him.

"That should be easy."

"But about what? Say nothing about what?"

"You share the same place," he says. "She likes you. Otherwise she wouldn't bother."

"That's no answer."

"Keep an eye an her," he says. "Thank you for calling. Next time it's my turn."

Our watching each other like this goes on for a week, two weeks. Now that the walls are up and the roof is on, the palace is quieter. Workmen are more scarce. Then comes the beautiful morning of almost June when I'm wakened by an Elf Owl calling in the arroyo. It's four o'clock, my work hour, and I go outside in a thin nightgown. The half moon bathes the terrain in a pale glow, bright enough to see shapes and shadows. The owl is in a thicket of palo verde on the far hillside—I make out the direction, but the bird is hidden. It chirps and chatters, but what is the meaning of its call? To summon, to protest, to celebrate?

Is it by accident the owl wakens me?

I listen until the bird flies deeper into the arroyo. Light sifts gently from the east, and the moon loses its power. Señora Astacio's windows fill with the pale blue of dawn, but her doorway is in shadow, the house is dark. Westward, the stars still shine. I imagine the sorrow I'll feel for Señora Astacio's death, the changes her passing will require—a new neighbor, the hours to be filled learning in the ways I realize I have been for months, not in the measuring of words, but in their absence.

I walk along the road watching for snakes, but keeping my eyes open. I am looking for her in her absence, and I know she is there. I smell her, feel her without seeing, sense in our days together our conspiracy. Then on the hill above, I catch a furtive movement. At first I think it's a coyote; it has that way, but no, of course not. It's a shape leaning on a stick. Señora Astacio descends haltingly along an animal trail. How did she get up there in the dark? I run along the road for a quarter mile, then veer off through the brush and up the hill, heedless of scratches and cactus spines and snakes. I connect to the animal trail lower than where she is. "Wait for me," I call to her. "Espéreme ahí!"

She pauses, bracing herself on her stick, her woven bag over her shoulder. Behind her at the top of the hill, dark smoke ascends into the blue dawn. I climb again, faster, and by the time I reach her, flames are tearing through the monstrous house, brightening and brightening above us. She takes my arm and leans into me, and, saying nothing, together we go down.

RITUALS OF SLEEP

At night, no matter the season or whether we had made love, we had a ritual for sleep. We lay under a quilt, naked and silent, our arms wrapped around each other. Hannah's body fit into mine and mine into hers in perfect alignment of skin and live bone. Her breasts pressed against my chest, my leg was thrown over hers in the precise curve above her hip so neither was discomforted, our heads on the same pillow so we breathed the same air. It was the moment I wished for the whole day, the peace of it, the comfort, the death-wish. I imagined her thoughts and mine the same, her peace and mine the same, her blood and mine equal. I desired to die at such a moment, having knowledge I'd missed nothing in the world.

After minutes, Hannah's breathing slowed, her heart steadied, and she slept. I knew in that quiet we were growing together, the stems of our bodies entwining, the leaves overlapping above, the roots below absorbing the moisture and nutrients from the same earth. I wanted more than anything to remain still in this way and let her sleep, but my arm under her tingled. I moved my leg, flexed my shoulder. Disturbed in this way, she slid her arm from around me, gave up our unspoken alliance, and turned over.

It was early fall in the mountains of Vermont, and a warm afternoon had cooled to evening. The door of my studio was open to circulate the air. Outside the wind stirred the leaves in the nearby apple trees. I'd washed the dishes and settled Catherine into bed with some songs on my guitar; Hannah had been on the telephone with a student from the academy so I'd slipped away to the workroom I'd built for myself—a place where once apples had been pressed and made into cider. I sat under a gooseneck lamp, contemplating blocks of cherrywood of different sizes. I was going to carve a bird—perhaps an Upland Sandpiper, resident of farmlands from New England to Idaho, or a Dipper, the only North American species of the family Cinclidae, a stocky shorebird of high mountain lakes and streams in the West. It was as much a problem to choose the wood as the bird to carve from it.

My usual habit was to carve three birds in succession, then to paint all three so I could feel a distance from each and yet achieve a rhythm in the work. But lately I had felt a curious need to carve one thing and to finish it. I had no upcoming exhibit or crafts fair, no client who'd commissioned me, no *rush*, but I'd found myself waking early and staying up late at night in odd turmoil or fear. Perhaps it was the darkness coming earlier, or the clearer air of autumn, or the way the water in the creek outside the studio had quieted now that the summer melt was over and new snow was about to fall.

I chose a piece of wood 12" x 18" x 18", perfect for the Dipper. I made drawings of the bird on a pad—different angles in flight and perched on stones—to get the feel of it, to absorb it into my fingers the short neck and legs, the wingspread, the gentleness of the bird's demeanor. I liked the dipper's nickname—water ouzel. As I sketched, I hummed the tune of Catherine's favorite song of the moment and thought the words to myself.

The waltzing fool's got lights in his fingers
The waltzing fool he don't ever say
The waltzing fool keeps his hands in his pockets
And waltzes the evening away.

In the midst of drawing a Dipper in flight, I realized Hannah was outside. I felt her there like a shadow, though my back was turned to the door and she was not blocking any light. She was silent. The wind had ebbed, though the apple leaves still rattled on the branches. I wanted Hannah to speak, but why would she? I knew already what she wanted. My pencil constructed wing feathers—primaries, scapulars, tertials. I imagined an alpine valley with a fast-moving stream. Hannah waited.

Finally I turned, thinking I had invented her presence. But no, she was in the yard not far beyond the door where the light from the room diminished and the darkness began. Her face was hidden by the shadows of branches. She had on a long paisley dress and an open beige windbreaker. "I need your help," she said. Her voice was soft, but her inflection gave her words the urgent meaning she wanted them to have.

I rose from the chair as if commanded and went outside. She embraced me, pulled me down with her onto the lawn—I gave way beneath her—and we made love on the ground in the apple leaves, she above me, my bare skin cold against the yellow grass.

Hannah had grown up in Dublin, Georgia with three older brothers who persecuted her because she was ungainly and didn't care about dances or sports or boys. Her parents had been as confused by her as her brothers—why did she read books? Why did she like to be alone? Why, when they belabored the correct paragraphs of society's handbook, was she not of the order of Southern women who minded their hairdos and their chances for marriage?

She went to Davidson, graduated with honors in English, and was doing graduate work at Princeton when her father got sick. It had been a difficult time for her—she'd dropped out of school and took a job in Atlanta to be near her father. We met shortly after he died. It happened that two of my sculptures had been in an exhibition at a gallery in Atlanta, and she had been drawn to a delicate hummingbird in the window. That I was there, the maker, was to her a sign.

We visited back and forth between Vermont and Atlanta—I was freer than she to travel. She was quiet. That's what I liked about her.

Her manner was quiet. She liked stillness. Her movements were easy, comfortable and appropriate to herself, and whatever awkwardness she had endured as a child had dissipated. She was tall and solidly built, connected to the place she was. We often walked in the park near her apartment, without speaking, sometimes holding hands, but often not, and I was aware how the actual touching made no difference.

We were married the next year, and Hannah took the job teaching literature at the academy in the town in Vermont where I lived. Our life in the ensuing years went smoothly. Catherine was born and flourished. My work improved, and for a time was sought after. When its popularity diminished, I supplemented Hannah's income with random commissions. We evolved a way of taking care of Catherine that suited all three of us: Hannah tended her mornings while I carved my birds, and I watched her afternoons while Hannah taught her classes. Catherine prospered, and I knew she felt our love.

There was a joke in Hannah's family that Catherine was Hannah at the same age. The resemblance between them was so strong her brothers suggested virgin birth, and though I laughed at the idea (Catherine had longer second toes and my slightly protruding sternum), I had seen the pictures in Hannah's childhood photo albums. The shape of Catherine's head was identical to Hannah's; Catherine's nose was the same; her eyes were set deep. Hannah's mother said even their voices were alike, and sometimes I thought I might understand Hannah by studying Catherine.

At four, Catherine was a whimsical child who knew what she wanted. She liked to wear her hair in barrettes, mimicking the child in the movie *Digging to China,* but when she saw *Snow White*, she cut her bangs with sewing scissors. She liked radishes and beets, salmon not steak, real maple syrup, Little Lulu and Wily Coyote, the Beast and not the Beauty. With other children she was demanding, earnest and generous, bossy, yet well-meaning. One morning, for instance, after chiseling the general shape of the Dipper, I came in to get coffee. The house was cool; I turned on the heat. I heard Catherine's voice from the playroom talking to a friend. "You have to eat fiber, so your bowels will function smoothly," she said. "Oat Bran is all right. So is shredded wheat. And you must floss your teeth. Daddy says so. And don't ever throw Tampax in the toilet."

There was no reply, and I turned the corner to see which friend she was lecturing, but there was no one else there. Catherine had made a bed for her doll Grace out of a cardboard box and her own comfort blanket.

"When do I tell you to floss your teeth?" I asked.

"Hello, daddy," she said.

I sat down on the floor beside her. "What's going on here?"

"I'm practicing for the new baby."

"What new baby?"

"His name is August, after grandfather, but mommy says we'll call him Augie."

"She's named him, then?"

Catherine gazed at me directly. "Didn't you know?"

"No," I said. I tucked the blanket around the doll. "Where is your mother?"

"Asleep."

I got up, paused at the door. "If it's a boy," I said, "he won't use Tampax."

Catherine looked at me. "It's still a good thing to know."

In the next weeks, Hannah moved through the house serenely, as if all within her was harmony. As usual she was silent, absorbed in thought. One particular day she wore a long skirt, lilac-colored, a white blouse, and Birkenstocks, and she bent forward slightly with purpose to her stride, apparently intent on some good she had yet to accomplish. Catherine and I were finishing our lunches sitting in the bay window in the kitchen, and as Hannah passed, Catherine put down her jelly sandwich and the plastic sorrel horse she was making leap over her plate. She didn't say anything, and Hannah slid open the door and walked outside into the sunlight, into the orchard with its shriveled apples and sweet scents.

The fallen leaves exploded lightly around her feet. She passed through the orchard onto a path we couldn't see in the high grass. In the distance were the playing fields—a vast green space—and beyond them the hills and the trees beginning to turn red and the white buildings of the academy.

I measured Catherine's expression of puzzlement and concern. "It's all right," I said. "She's going to school."

"She didn't go yesterday."

"Yesterday was Sunday. Every day isn't the same."

"Will she come back?"

"Of course, she'll come back. She always has."

"Do you think she notices the wind?" Catherine asked.

"I don't know."

"I notice the wind." Catherine gave a sigh deep with worry.

"You notice everything," I said.

Mornings during October, Hannah did not come down to breakfast. She was awake: I heard the shower upstairs go on and off. The floor creaked. A door opened and closed. I sent Catherine up to check on her, and Catherine came down alone.

"Where is she?" I asked.

"In the sewing room."

"What did she say?"

"She's not hungry."

I went up myself and found Hannah sitting, staring out the window. The trees on the hillside had turned red and yellow. The light came in from the east. "Are you all right?" I asked. "You don't want breakfast?"

"The faculty wants me to give a meditation." She spoke without turning from the window.

"That's the series in the chapel?"

Hannah nodded. "I wouldn't know what to say."

I understood her dilemma: she was private. But the school had its interest in her. She had taught there five years and was revered by students and faculty for her calm and self-assurance. Each term her courses were oversubscribed. I'd seen the lucky ones so properly deferential in her classroom because they had been admitted to her sanctum sanctorum. They sat as if in a library around a heavy wooden oval table, listening in rapt attention to Hannah's hushed voice as she spoke of Whitman or Durrell or Joyce. I'd heard her lecture once on the idea that Stephen Daedalus discovered he did not have to live every other person's life, only his own.

The faculty was equally devoted. In meetings she listened carefully and well, gave deference to others' ideas of what should happen when, cared enough to believe what other people said was true. She volunteered for committees, arranged for visiting writers, took the classes of those out sick. To be asked to do a meditation was an honor—people wanted to know her—and to decline might be interpreted as distance or arrogance. In her solitude, she didn't want to displease anyone.

"You'll think of something to say," I said. "When is it?"

"Not till December."

"Then you have time for breakfast."

She looked up at me and smiled vaguely, but she shook her head no.

When she was pregnant with Catherine, Hannah at odd moments had put my hand on her stomach so I could sense from the outside what she felt within. She embraced me so that I felt between us the shifting foot or the moving hand of the child that would be ours forever. I remember once coming into the bedroom and finding her sitting on a low stool brushing her hair. I knelt behind her and spread my fingers over the rise in her belly, and she gazed at me in the mirror, deep in the pleasure of our history. Her hair was in sunlight, and her hand moved leisurely, as if she were brushing the light.

But carrying August, she was different. Because of her discomfort, she stayed up late grading papers or preparing her classes or doing committee reports, and when she came to bed, she lay on her back with her hands at her sides. I knew her eyes were open, and knew, even in the dark while she was beside me, she was thinking something I couldn't imagine. I wished she'd turn and assume the position I loved, welcome me, but she didn't, and her breathing was all sighs.

One rainy Saturday when she was four months pregnant, Hannah came downstairs mid-morning in a loose blue dress. I'd made French toast for Catherine and had saved some in the oven, but Hannah went straight to the closet and got her overcoat. "Do you want anything at the store?" she asked.

"Can I go?" Catherine asked. She was watching the rain from the alcove window.

"I don't think so, sweetheart."

"There's a list of what I need by the telephone," I said. "Why can't Catherine go?"

Catherine turned from the window. Her face was gray with the outdoor light, and I saw she wanted us not to argue. "Will you buy me a Milky Way?" she asked.

Hannah put on her overcoat, while I got the list from the bulletin board. "I shopped Thursday," I said. "We don't need much—laundry detergent, milk, and coffee. I could use some stamps."

"You don't mind being with Catherine this morning?" she asked. "I'll take this afternoon."

"Catherine and I will go for a walk," I said.

"It's raining," Catherine said.

"Not that hard. I might carry you."

"Goody."

"Part of the way."

"I won't be long," Hannah said. "No more than an hour."

I added stamps and a Milky Way to the list and gave it to Hannah.

Hannah left, and Catherine and I put on warm clothes with slickers over, and rubber boots, and we walked out through the orchard. The branches were bare, and the low gray sky hovered close by. I was not used to being outside in the morning, but I liked the change from habit. The rain had slacked to a drizzle and was soft on our faces. The world was alive with a misty breeze, the air visible beneath the wavering wings of crows flying east toward the academy, in the webs of tent caterpillars in the birch trees, in the space between us and the dark hills.

We descended the slope to the creek by an animal path. The water was low, and I held Catherine's hand and lifted her from one boulder to another across the slow current. We worked our way upstream, stopping to look at the leaves floating in an eddy, or at the clear gray and amber stones on the bottom, or at the swirling reflection of trees and clouds. I imagined Catherine was fascinated by the mutable surface, the riffles and the placid pools we could not see the bottoms of. Each moment the stream looked the same, but in fact different molecules surged in different light. I liked watching her when she was so attuned to things not herself, when everything around her mattered. Once she bent and touched the water in such a gentle way I could not help but think she believed it magical. Yet I knew she would forget the moment she was in, that whatever caused her then to dip her hand, whatever she loved at that moment, would become something else, and no promise could arrest it.

We kept on along the creek bottom. My idea was to intersect the road and get a ride with Hannah when she came back from the store. There was no trail. Catherine labored over the slippery stones, so I held her hand or sometimes I carried her. The rain fell harder. Catherine was cold, and we ducked into a thick dry pine grove where we huddled on a bed of needles. The wind hushed above us, and the creek and the rain made music. Our eyes accustomed themselves to the pale light.

Catherine saw the owl first. It was well-camouflaged in the dark boughs—a tiny Saw-whet, only seven or so inches tall, brown-and-white mottled on the back and wings, and reddish streaks on the breast. It stared at us, as astonished as we were.

"Is it a baby?" Catherine asked.

"No, it's a grown-up. Small owls can be very tame."

"It's wild, isn't it?"

"Yes, very wild."

She stood up and held out her hand, as if to let the bird have her scent.

"Not too close," I said.

She took several steps toward it. The owl fluffed its feathers but didn't fly, and they stared at one another for a long time.

As soon as the blue Volvo pulled into the driveway, Catherine ran out the back door. "Mommy, guess what!"

I followed Catherine outside. The rain had stopped, but low clouds still banked in against the ridge. It was three o'clock, and Hannah had been gone four hours.

"We saw an owl," Catherine said. "It was in some pine trees by the creek."

"What kind of owl?" Hannah asked.

Hannah opened the back of the Volvo, took out two sacks of groceries, and handed them to me. "Where have you been?" I asked.

"It was tiny," Catherine said, "but not a baby. I almost touched it."

"Really?" Hannah slammed down the back door of the Volvo.

"I could show it to you."

I took the groceries into the kitchen and set them on the counter. Hannah brought in the jug of milk and put it in the refrigerator, while I stowed packages of pasta in the cupboard.

"Did you get me the Milky Way?" Catherine asked. She climbed onto a chair and looked into one of the sacks.

Hannah paused at the refrigerator door. "I didn't think of it."

"What about the stamps?" I asked.

"I forgot."

I closed the cupboard door and looked at her.

"I forgot," she said again. "I'm sorry."

"She forgot, daddy," Catherine said. "Sometimes we forget. I forget, too."

Just after Thanksgiving, it snowed three days in a row. The orchard filled with white, and except for the yellow tufts of grass poking up, the meadow beyond was indistinguishable from the manicured playing fields. Classes were cancelled at the academy, and Hannah stayed home. In the long white mornings, she slept. This seemed right to me: she was weary of her classes and obligations at the school; her body was changing. Catherine and I played Concentration, Go Fish, Battle; we watched a nature video in the den with the door closed to mute the sound. Several times I took her to my shop so she could draw and I could work.

The Dipper was taking longer than I wanted to spend. It wasn't a particularly complex project— simpler in line than a heron or an avocet, less delicate than a warbler—but I struggled. Perhaps Augie's coming had unnerved me, or the weather got into my hands; certainly I'd spent more time than usual with Catherine.

The third morning of snow Catherine sat near the wood-burning stove drawing on my sketch pad. She wore one of Hannah's shirts—it looked like a smock on Catherine—and Hannah's shoes several sizes too large. But she concentrated on her work at least as well as I did on mine.

"Have you ever seen that bird you're making?" she asked finally.

"Yes. In Colorado."

She looked at me in a way that encompassed more than the room, more than what she and I were doing. "Do you think the owl is still there?" she asked.

"We could go look."

"I don't want to."

"Why not?"

"If it isn't, I'd be sad. Where is Colorado?"

"A state in the West," I said. "I saw this bird along a stream high in the mountains."

"What is it?"

"A Dipper, also called a water ouzel. It flew upstream and landed on a rock and bobbed a few times—that's why it's called a Dipper—and then it waded into the rushing water and disappeared."

"Where did it go?"

"I don't know. It can walk on the bottom of the stream. It can swim. I didn't see it come out."

"Were you ever at that place with mommy?"

"No."

"Why not?"

"I had another life before her."

Catherine considered this a moment and studied the drawing on her sketch pad. "What is another life?"

"I mean, I was lonely without your mother."

Catherine turned her drawing to me. It was of a recognizable family— a woman, a man, and a baby. "It's mommy and you and Augie," she said.

"Very nice," I said. "And where are you?"

"Silly," she said, "I'm drawing the picture."

When Hannah wasn't sleeping, she was reading novels. She gravitated to the farthest part of the house—upstairs in the back bedroom if Catherine and I were in the kitchen, in the study if I was upstairs putting Catherine to bed, and so on. She read Doris Lessing, Henry James, Colette, Nabokov. She didn't hide the books—she brought them to the kitchen sometimes—but she didn't talk with me about them in the ways she had in our first years together. In earlier times, she often read aloud affecting passages, or brought up ideas that struck her as brilliant or troublesome. "Do you think crime is a condition of existence?" she asked once, or "Do you think we owe it to our own mental health to protest injustice?" That was then, and now was now.

I suppose if I cared to know what Hannah knew, I'd have read the books myself. Or to follow the tracks where her mind had been, I'd have asked her to mark the passages she found intriguing. But I couldn't bring myself to this simple directness. If she didn't want to tell, I didn't want to ask. In some way, I didn't wish to comprehend why she was distancing herself from me. I wanted her to come back. Yet it was borne on me like suffering that silence required two voices that remained at rest, two hearts that did not speak.

One still night in December, not long before her meditation, Hannah was at the academy for a meeting, and I sang Catherine to sleep. Her favorite song then was "Hush-a-bye, My Baby," which I had sung twice:

> Hush-a-bye, my baby,
> Hush-a-bye, my darling child,
> You can tell, you know darn well,
> Daddy wouldn't lie to you.

Catherine sat up in the dark room, her frail body and face illuminated only by a wedge of light from the hallway. "Is that true?" she asked.

"Not exactly," I said. "I can't catch you a star, as the song says."

"I know that, but did you lie to me about the water ouzel?"

"No, why would I?"

"It's such a funny name."

She lay down again and closed her eyes. I sang her "All La Glory" and "Bridge Over Troubled Waters" and "Waltzing Fool," and she was asleep before I finished.

I went downstairs and found Hannah in the kitchen putting on water for tea. She'd come in from a walk and still had her gloves on and was wearing her long black wool coat. She turned the burner knob, and the blue flame burst under the kettle.

"I didn't hear you come in," I said.

"I was in the chapel thinking about what to say."

"Did you come up with something?"

"Maybe." She paused and looked away. "It's not a good idea to sing her to sleep every night."

"She likes it. And I feel useful."

"She'll get accustomed to it, though, and won't sleep on her own." Hannah found the tea she wanted in the cupboard and got down a mug. She looked at me calmly. "I've signed her up for child care next term. I want to teach mornings and have afternoons free."

"Without asking me?"

"Your schedule won't change."

"But Catherine's will. What do you need to do in the afternoons?"

The water boiled, and Hannah poured it into her cup and swirled the tea bag. She didn't look at me, and I saw, beyond her serenity, a darkness I hadn't noticed before, as if she were a cave and I were leaning toward her at the threshold, hoping for a glimpse inside.

"I want peace," she said. "That's all I ask. I want these next months before August is born to be peaceful."

Her meditation was a Thursday night before exams. Hannah had gone to the chapel early to compose herself, and it was dark when Catherine and I started over. The tangled branches of the apple trees were black against the stars. I held Catherine's hand, and we followed Hannah's worn path in the snow. I pointed out Cassiopeia's Chair, the Dipper and the way north.

"The Dipper is the bird you're making," Catherine said.

"Same name, different picture. And those three bright stars are Orion's belt. Orion is a hunter, and, if he's in the sky, we know it's winter."

"We already know it's winter," she said.

We crossed the playing fields toward the quadrangle. Pairs of lamplights along the stone walk shone on the piled-up snow. On the far side, the chapel blocked the way, its doors thrown open to the cold and a pale yellow light flowing out. The silhouettes of students and faculty going inside threw shadows at us.

We sat three rows from the back so as not to make Hannah nervous, and because I wanted to give Catherine some remove. Candles burned on the altar. A violin concerto, composed and performed by a student, drifted into the nave and diminished in the air. We waited until the chapel filled and every seat was taken. Students stood two deep along the outer aisles.

The music stopped, and Hannah rose from the front pew and stood at a lectern at the head of the center aisle. She had on a long black dress with a white collar, and her hair was down over one shoulder. She let the place settle, and the students and faculty which had been quiet before grew quieter still, intolerably quiet.

"My father was ill before he died," she said in a hushed voice. "I had been at Princeton studying and went home to Georgia to be with him. He'd had a stroke, one small blood vessel blocked, one tiny blood vessel the diameter of a pin. Blood had poured through that minute opening all his life—sixty heartbeats a minute, thirty-six hundred an hour, thirty-one million a year for seventy-two years, and then in one moment…" She paused and took a breath.

"My mother was with him when it happened. The two of them were walking across their lawn under the magnolia tree in our front yard, and suddenly my father sat down on the ground. His eyes rolled back in his head, and my mother thought he was dying. Her husband, my father.

"But he didn't die. He recovered. He had therapy. He sat up. He walked. I took a job in a bookstore in Atlanta to be closer by, but it was my mother who cared for him and coaxed him to do rehab. She emptied his bedpan. Wednesday afternoons and weekends, I spelled her. His improvement was incremental. Each day we did what we could and were grateful he lived.

"One day, as random as the first, he had another stroke. I was shelving books at the store, and my mother telephoned. She said, 'He's going to die.' I went home. What I was most conscious of was my mother's self-abnegation. She'd never have spoken of her own pain. She had, her whole life, kept up the house, waited for my father to come home from work, listened to his stories of what he'd done that day. She accepted his jokes, his smoking, and his excessive superstitions—we had to place the salt on the table before someone else could pick it up—and now she had to watch him die. She sat by his bed for hours…"

Hannah didn't speak of her own sadness, of her withdrawal from Princeton, of the hours she'd driven back and forth to her parents' house to sit by her father's bed and watch him sleep. She spoke only of her mother in her soft voice, the voice from the cave that everyone bent to hear. It was true her mother had grieved, that Hannah was herself grieving. But I imagined what her father felt. He'd been blind his whole life to a woman who endured him and was helpless in such a moment to make his life comprehensible or to speak the truth or make his longing known. In listening to Hannah—how she kept us all looking into the darkness!—I wanted to stand and ask her whether she loved me.

But of course in the chapel, with Catherine there, I couldn't interrupt or make a scene. I sat and trembled and held tightly to my daughter's hand.

That January I finished carving the Dipper. I painted the white undercoating and the pale gray breast and the darker gray head, the gray feathers of the wings and back. In February, I began two new carvings— a Canvasback on a much-needed commission and a Kirtland's Warbler, whose small population in upper Michigan was dwindling, for a museum in Boston. In the spring, August was born. The academy gave Hannah the term off, and the pattern of our days was new. Every morning while I worked, Catherine went to child care, and in the lengthening afternoons the baby had to be looked after. Sometimes Catherine and I took Augie for walks in his stroller or a backpack. The creek was high from the snowmelt and too dangerous to cross, so we often hiked across the playing fields to the woodland beyond. Catherine was solicitous of Augie—she made him keep his hat on, pointed out to him pictures in the clouds, and warned him about getting cavities, if he ever got teeth.

At night, Hannah wanted Augie to sleep close to her so she wouldn't have to get up to feed him, and, after some weeks of sleeplessness, I gave him my place in the bed. I took the spare cot in Catherine's room, but I didn't sleep well there. I lay on my side, listening to the wind race under the eaves, or if there was no wind, to the house creak or to Catherine's light breathing.

One night Catherine woke crying in the dark and called out for me and sat up in bed. I came quickly across the room. "Did you have a dream?" I asked.

"Yes. What are you doing here?"

"You called me."

"I mean *here*."

I didn't know what she meant, whether *so soon*, or *here, in this house*, or whether I were a part of her dream in which I had disappeared or had died. She didn't explain, and all I could do was settle her back into bed with Grace and pull the covers up. I sat on her bed for a few minutes and rubbed her back and sang "Waltzing Fool" until she was asleep, as I wanted to and wished I could, every night of her life.

THE DARK AGES

That September my mother took sick in Kansas City. I was twenty-nine and living in Utah in the foothills of the Wasatch Mountains with Tom Dunbar whom I'd met skiing the winter before. Tom thought I should go back to see her, but I had a landscaping business—four projects underway and bids out on three others. I had to order fertilizer and railroad ties, oversee two or three workers at each site, and present ideas to new clients who might tide me through the winter. Besides, I was afraid to fly and didn't want to drive across Colorado and Kansas alone. My brother Larry and his wife lived in Shawnee, so it wasn't as if my mother weren't looked after.

Her illness was undiagnosed—shortness of breath, dizziness, nausea, general weakness. She was in the hospital for tests and observation, and when I telephoned her, she sounded far away, but spirited. Larry checked on her every day, and she wasn't feeling neglected. She asked me more questions than I asked her—how was the weather in the mountains? Was business going well? How was Tom? In two days, she was out of the hospital. After a week with a nurse at home, she resumed her normal routine—she shopped, went to lunch, played bridge with her friends. According to Larry, she was as fit as before.

But her illness lingered in me. Sometimes, during workdays, stuck in traffic, I called her on my cell phone. I interrupted her cooking, her reading, or a conversation she was having with a friend on the terrace.

I was intrusive but couldn't help it. If I didn't call, I thought of her. Digging in the earth or sketching a project, I might feel a darkness surround me like clouds suddenly blocking the sun. Once in the middle of the night, Tom woke me. I was sweat-soaked and my heart was pounding. "You were dreaming," he said.

I couldn't remember the dream, but I was certain, in the way one knows the depth of the unknowable, it was about my mother.

The next morning I began to write things down. I was not a writer. The telephone, fast and reliable, was my medium. Sometimes when Tom and I went rock climbing in Colorado or to Canyonlands or Zion, I wrote postcards, and at Christmas, I wrote thank-you notes, but I had never written to write anything.

That first time, this was what I wrote:

> When she was a girl she had brown hair and wore it long and straight and parted in the middle. Her nose had a rise in it. Her ears were never visible. Her eyes were black. Her skin was smooth as pewter. Her body was round. Later her hair turned early gray. She still parted it right in the center of her forehead, as though her head were divided in that way—left and right. The ridge of her nose became more prominent. Her ears were invisible, always. Her eyes were black. Her skin was rougher and sandy-colored. Her body was solid and strong. In her old age she's gained weight, but she still stands up straight. Her skin is loose, splotched. Her hair is salt-and-pepper, cut at the beauty parlor in a way that covers her ears. Her eyes are paler, softer.

I made mistakes when I wrote, errors of grammar and punctuation which I've corrected. The writing was simple and self-conscious, and I took too long to write each sentence. Compared to writing, landscaping was easy. The terrain was there before I started—the slopes, the shade, the angles of light. The soils could be tested for what might grow in it. Drainage was a mathematical calculation. I made drawings, figured where shade was needed, where sunshine. I didn't have to lie.

The descriptions I had written of my mother contained only a passing reference to her posture or her voice. Her eyes were not black, really, but brown. She must have worn her hair in other ways.

One day we went to an orchard to pick apples. My mother drove the old Packard—a robin-egg's blue sedan—with my brother and me in the backseat. We picked apples, though I was too young to climb the ladders into the trees. I had to cull good apples from the wormy ones on the ground.

On the way home, my mother sat erectly, her two hands on the top of the steering wheel. A dark spot blotched one of her hands, the right one, and smudges of dirt were on the nape of her neck where she had scratched a mosquito bite. She wore a blue kerchief over her black hair. The basket of apples on the front seat exuded a sweet smell. While she was driving, I filched her wallet from her purse and took out all the bills.

Lies. It was true we went to pick apples, and I remember mother drove the Packard, but it wasn't particularly old. And the words *culled* and *nape* and *exuded* were words I'd learned much later. *Filched*. To write such words changed the meaning. The spot on her hand, for instance, was a birthmark she usually covered with a glove. And was her kerchief blue? What shade? I was eight at the time. The apples could have been Romes or MacIntoshes. Had my mother sat erectly or had she pulled herself forward on the steering wheel?

And the omissions: how old was my brother? He was twelve. What had he said? I don't remember. What were we wearing? I don't know. I left out the darkness. The orchard had been some distance from our house, and it was late when we were driving home. Larry had leaned forward over the backseat to sing songs with my mother. I was on the far side of the backseat. The darkness let me steal her wallet.

Every morning at 7 a.m., Tom ran eight miles. I used that hour to scratch out my ideas on a pad of yellow paper. Most of what I wrote was mundane—memories from my childhood, what shoes or cars or boyfriends I'd acquired over the years, how landscaping intrigued me for its obvious requirements. One morning, by accident, I wrote about my father. He'd left us the winter I was seven, and his absence was a fact like air. I'd thought nothing of it; I barely remembered him. I had very little to say.

But Tom came home from his run and found me weeping.

"What's the matter?" he asked. "What happened?"

I shook my head, unable to speak.

"What did I do?"

I turned my pad over and stopped crying because his presence changed the room. I made coffee and waffles, and we talked about the winter's skiing.

Till then I hadn't thought much about my arrangement with Tom. I don't mean I hadn't thought about *him*: I was aware of him all the time. He was a carpenter. He had a degree in history, but he liked seasonal work so he could rock-climb and ski. He was younger than me by two years, but he knew things I didn't—how to tie knots, directions to places, how to make others feel at ease. I owned the house, but we split utilities and food. Tom did repairs. He wired the garage, replaced tiles in the shower, hung new gutters. He was honest. He had a past which he wasn't ashamed to reveal. He told me about a Mexican woman he'd slept with in Oaxaca, about an episode with a woman climber dangling a thousand feet over nothing.

Usually I didn't think of the past, but that night, when he wanted to make love, I eased away from him. He rubbed my back instead.

"Are you all right?" he asked.

"I was thinking about your making love with that woman in the hammock on the Spire."

"That was a while ago. I'm with you now."

"I know, but what you learned with her, you bring to me."

"If I hadn't loved her, I wouldn't know how to love you."

"Still, I wish…"

"I love your hair, your eyes, your lips."

He held me tightly. I knew he was with me. I felt it. But I didn't know whether I could endure the pain of knowing about the past.

One evening at supper Tom was telling me about a chimney route on Powder Mountain. The chimney had petered out into an overhang near the top, and he'd spidered out in a free climb. He paused with his fork in his hand. "Are you listening to me?" he asked.

"You had to free climb."

"It was getting cold, and…"

I gazed at him, imagined his clear, physical responses to the world, how his arms and legs reacted to problems on rock, how his body coiled and lifted in powder when he skied, and how at night he was composed in a sleep I could never reach, even after love.

He took another bite of his pork chop. "You're not here," he said.

"I want you to build me a room," I said.

"A room?"

"A room to write in."

"I was about to fall three hundred feet from this overhang."

"You're here," I said. "So you didn't fall."

He sighed. "In case you've forgotten, you have an office downtown."

"I'll pay for the materials."

"What's wrong with the breakfast nook?"

"Too public."

Tom smiled. "No one lives here but us."

"I know," I said.

He built the room off the kitchen—a lean-to with a desk in it and a window looking west toward the lake and the Bear River Wildlife Refuge. I kept up with my landscaping projects, but the hours I'd spent before looking for new work I now spent in the lean-to. I wrote about the grasses turning yellow, the shadows moving toward the south, about the cloud patterns over the lake. I wrote about the bluebirds and hawks and the ancient people pushed elsewhere because the fields where they had hunted were under a sea of houses.

But always I came back to my family. I revised the reminiscence of the afternoon in the apple orchard and was surprised to remember Larry's plaid shirt (and how bright his red hair was), the darkness falling across a cemetery nearby, my mother's laughter which, after my father left, never came back to her.

The singing was closer to me—"Parsley, Sage, Rosemary, and Thyme" was one of the songs— but something was not right about it.

One day I wrote this:

Spring, already dark. My father took us owling, all of us, except my mother. It was a school night, and she'd argued with him. We took back roads toward the river, and I sat by an open window and felt the humid air flow into the car. "The male owl stakes out a territory and calls," my father said. He made a low eerie whistle. "That's a screech. This is a barred owl. *Who-cooks-for you?*" We all laughed. "The female decides which male is strongest, or maybe the sweetest."

We parked in a grove of trees at the river, and my father turned off the engine and the headlights. We got out and sat on the warm hood of the car. It was so dark we couldn't see one another, and Larry flashed the light into the trees. "Turn off the light," my father said, "and let's hear what there is to hear."

Whip-poor-wills called, and crickets and katydids. Once a heron splashed in the water nearby. Stars were everywhere through the blackleaves of the trees around us.

We heard a screech owl across the river, and my father called to it. It moved closer. "We're in its territory," he said.

We were quiet again, listening. Then my father thought he heard another owl off in the distance, and he took one of the flashlights to go look. Larry was scared and went with him. But I stayed with the other flashlight and waited for the screech owl. It called again right nearby. I heard it above me in the trees.

"Listen!"

In my lean-to room, I stopped writing. I said the word aloud, "Listen." That's what I'd written on my yellow pad. *Listen.* The voice that spoke that word was not my voice, but my sister's. *Listen.* Why had I not been able to remember until now, until, on my page, I was ready to shine the flashlight into the dark canopy of trees.

Over the next few weeks I was quieter. I was not so eager with Tom in bed. When the first snows came, he oiled the ski bindings, waxed his skis, and dug out his gloves and sweaters. When it really snowed hard, he was ready for Alta. "Deep powder's what you need," he said. "We'll ski and sit in the hot tub."

"I'm not going," I said.

He paused. "Is there someone else?"

"Yes," I said.

Tom was silent.

I was sad for his pained expression. "I love you, Tom," I said. "There's no one else."

"Then I want you back," he said.

He went alone. I spent my days in the lean-to. I watched the snowy mist fall across my window, deaden the distance to gray, blend the roofs of the houses with the air. I was absorbed in something I couldn't put a name to, but knew what lay in the darkness ahead of me was both beautiful and terrible. I was afraid to know one for the other, and I willed myself to put down words.

We are born without choice to words and language, and
language to me is like dreaming.
    Where did my father go? He went beyond the prairie and
into the air. What have I done all these years except hold onto
what is not in my grasp and to wonder at what I cannot know?
    That night coming home from the apple orchard they
were singing, *Are you going to Scarborough fair? Parsley,*

sage, rosemary, and thyme. We stopped for gas. That was how
my mother discovered her wallet was missing.

My sister had stolen it, but I was the one who got punished.

On Monday my brother called. My mother was sick again with the same
illness—shortness of breath, dizziness, nausea. She was at home with a nurse.

"What can I do?" I asked.

"Nothing really. Call her. She's all right."

But when we hung up, *I* was not all right. That night I dreamed of my
mother—terrible, realistic dreams of her pain—and, in the morning, I
left a note for Tom and flew back to Kansas City.

It was dusk when an Uber delivered me to my mother's house. It was
the same red-brick house I grew up in—white shutters and two columns by
the front door. A stone wall bordered the yellow lawn and paved driveway.
With the leaves gone from the trees and the grass yellow, the place seemed
stark and joyless. Larry's BMW was parked in the driveway.

I was surprised how cold it was for October. The wind came from
a far distance across the plains. I carried my bag to the side door, went
into the kitchen, and set my suitcase on the floor. I knew the sound of the
clock, the configuration of the counters, the way light entered from the
south and fell on the print of "Flaming June" on the wall in the sitting
room. To open the cupboard for a glass, I had to swing the body away
from the stove. I got down a glass just to hold it in my hand.

"Jane?" Larry came in through the swinging door.

He'd put on weight, especially in the face, and he had done something to his hair—a new short style, or maybe he'd touched it up. He gave
me a cursory hug. "You didn't have to come," he said.

"I wanted to."

"Mother's asleep. Would you like a drink?" He looked at the glass in
my hand and got out the Wild Turkey from the closet. "I'll join you."

"That's where the liquor has always been," I said.

Larry got another glass and ice from the freezer and held the bottle
out to me.

"No, thank you," I said.

He poured his own pretty full.

"Tell me what happened this time," I said.

"One of her bridge friends called me. She hadn't shown up for their luncheon, and when they phoned the house they got no answer."

"She was here?"

"She'd decided she didn't want to play bridge but hadn't bothered to tell anyone else. She wanted them to miss her."

We went through the swinging door into the dining room. The rosewood table had a bowl of flowers on it, and the crystal in the cabinet glimmered. The mullioned windows let in a pale light. "Is the nurse here?" I asked.

"I let her go until after dinner. Mom doesn't need a nurse."

We continued into the living room, neatly arranged with flowered sofas, wing-backed chairs, and a Kazak rug. Larry opened the drapes. "I wouldn't have called you if I'd thought you'd come."

"What a terrible thing to say."

"Why did you?"

My mother interrupted us. She hobbled down the stairs, clutching the railing, and paused midway on the landing. She looked old—that wasn't a surprise—but her hair was disheveled and her dress sagged from her shoulders. "I thought I heard voices," she said.

"Jane decided she could spare the time," Larry said. "How long has it been?"

"Four years," I said.

My mother descended the stairs. She was medium height and her posture was skewed, but no more so than when I had last seen her. Her hair was cut short, above her ears. She was the person I knew, but not the one I had written about.

I embraced her gently. "How are you feeling?" I asked.

"I'm tired. If Larry wouldn't hover, I'd get better."

Larry helped her sit down on the sofa. "How did you sleep?" he asked.

"I don't sleep," my mother said. "That's the problem."

"Why not?" I asked.

She looked at me and said, "How is Tom?"

"Tom's fine. He's skiing in Alta."

"Doesn't he work?" Larry asked.

"Not in a bank."

"Larry disapproves of your living with a man," my mother said. "He's a neo-con."

"I don't want her taken advantage of," Larry said.

"Why do you think I am?" I asked.

"I want you to be happy."

"And what if I don't want to be happy?"

My mother focused on me. "Why wouldn't you want to?"

"I'd rather be honest."

"Is that why you've come to see me?" my mother asked.

"I want to know about Shelley," I said.

"Who's Shelley?" Larry asked.

"I heard her voice," I said. "I remember her."

My mother stared ahead. "Her voice?"

"She sang with us that time we picked apples."

"What's the use in remembering what happened twenty years ago?" Larry asked. "That's history."

"I remember she said *Listen* when we looked for owls."

My mother sat straight on the sofa and gazed at me. "What did you do to your hair?" she asked. "It's brown."

"It's always been brown," I said. "Shelley's was red like yours and Larry's."

That night I felt the currents of air through the hallways, the rhythms of the rooms, the way night came to every corner. I couldn't sleep, so I went across the hall to my mother's room. Her light was on, and she was sitting up in bed doing a Sudoku puzzle.

"Did you take your sleeping pill?" I asked.

"I never do," she said.

"Don't you want the pain to stop?"

"Not any more than you want to be happy."

I took the pillow from behind her head, shook it, and put it back again. "Why were you so hard on her?" I asked.

My mother put her puzzle on the nightstand, closed her eyes, and leaned her head back on the pillow. "Shelley was an unruly child. She could be cruel."

"Larry..."

"She shut everyone out. Even at school she wouldn't speak. She was in the dark ages."

"Maybe you didn't listen."

"Your father wasn't here. I had so much to tend to."

"Daddy loved her, and she followed him, didn't she? That's what she wanted to do."

"I don't know, sweetheart. No one does."

That night I woke from a dream that was true. I turned on the light and found my pad and pencil. All the way down the first page I wrote:

Listen.

Listen.

Listen.

Listen.

I woke because the room was cold. A quilt had fallen off me. I was trying to find it, when I realized the window was open. Shelley was standing on a chair in front of the moving curtains, her white nightgown billowing around her. "What are you doing?" I asked.

"I'm looking for him."

I found the quilt and pulled it around me. The light of the street lamp outside gave her red hair a halo of silver.

"Goodbye, sweetheart," she said.

She climbed to the window sill and jumped. I heard her body fall through the trees and land heavily on the driveway.

I put down my pencil and wept.

In the morning I took an early flight to Salt Lake. My mother was relieved I was leaving, and I understood her illness—she couldn't get over the past. I didn't say goodbye to Larry.

In the air, over the plains, it was clear, but clouds along the Front Range of the Rockies banked in so that, passing over, I couldn't see the mountains. We descended into the gray above Salt Lake City. It had to be snowing in Alta. Tom would be happy to be stuck there because, when the storm passed, ski conditions would be perfect.

That suited me. I'd have the house to myself, and through the window of my lean-to I'd watch the snow fall and fall. I'd write about my sister, gone to find our father, and, in writing, I'd make them both alive.

RINGO BINGO

Joanette wanted to join Costco because you could buy frozen shrimp for $4.98 a pound, cheap paper towels that weren't flimsy, and all sorts of computer and technical gadgetry. She was tired of hearing Adrienne and Joy talk about the bargains they got. But Lenny had no interest in belonging. If she'd asked, "Can we join Costco," he'd have said, "What's Costco?" or, "You should try shopping a little less, sweetheart. It's not good for your heart."

Lenny was no more of a skinflint than anyone else, but he hated shopping. He'd never been with her in a grocery store since the first year of their marriage—his second, her third—four years ago. As long as he had his Ford Bronco, his TV, and missionary sex every week, he was happy. Not Joanette, though. She wanted more.

Joanette occupied the middle ground between doing what Lenny wanted and what she liked. They had no confrontations about this, no arguments, but they had an unspoken agreement they lived in separate universes.

It was a Tuesday evening in July in Colorado Springs. Next door, Bill Gordon was edging his lawn, and down the street a car with a bad muffler revved and faded. The mountains were the horizon to the west, and clouds scudded across the blue sky. Joanette had marinated the chicken, and Lenny was cleaning the grill in the backyard. Joanette watched him from the kitchen scrubbing off charred salmon with a wire brush. His face was handsome; with his mustache, he looked like a character actor on TV. He was forty-two, but looked older, and he'd been upset recently when someone asked him if he was in AARP. He was paunchy, but not heavy, and kept in shape yelling at sports events on TV. It was baseball season, so he had plenty to scream about with the Colorado team.

What Joanette liked about Lenny was his kindness. Her other two husbands had been hotheads—one had died in a road rage motorcycle accident and the other of a heart attack—and, compared to them, Lenny was sweetness and light. He was nicer to her mother than she was and listened to the stories she repeated ad nauseam. He was good with Shannon, too, the neighbor's daughter, from whom last week he'd bought six boxes of Girl Scout cookies.

He put the grill back into place and lit a match, but nothing happened. He lit another match, and another, and then swore a blue streak of words she couldn't hear from behind the window. He unscrewed the grill canister and came inside.

"Out of gas?" she asked.

"Propane," Lenny said.

"You want me to go to the hardware?"

"I can go, Joanette. You don't have to go."

"We could go to Costco," she said. "It's cheap. We could buy one of those Cadillac grills with the big tanks so you wouldn't run out of gas so often."

"I didn't run out of gas. I ran out of *propane*."

"Over time we'd save a lot of money."

"Over time? How much time do you think we have, Joanette?"

"Thirty more years," Joanette said. "At least."

"So where's this Costco?" Lenny asked. "You sure they sell propane?"

In the Bronco, on the way over, they talked about movies. Joanette liked thriller romances—her favorite was *Rear Window*—and Lenny liked space movies. Joanette wouldn't have guessed that about him, but he'd seen dozens of them—*Alien, Space Cowboys, Star Trek, Destination Moon*. His favorite was *2001: Space Odyssey*. They'd watched *Shakespeare in Love* on video, but Lenny called it boring.

"It wasn't boring," Joanette said. "You liked *Tootsie*."

Lenny stopped at a stoplight behind a long line of cars. "You have to tell me where I'm going."

"Turn right up ahead there," Joanette said.

They waited through three red lights, Lenny humming a nasty tune the whole time, and then he made a right turn into an immense parking lot filled with a sea of cars.

"Dinner looks far away," Lenny said.

They found someone backing out of a diagonal space a good quarter of a mile from the entrance, and Lenny slotted the Bronco into it. "I'm not going in there, Joanette," he said.

"What do you mean?" she asked. "It's just a store."

"It's a madhouse."

"What about the gas?" she asked.

Lenny didn't say anything. Neither did Joanette, but she was shaking and tears welled up in her eyes.

Lenny snapped open the door, jumped out, and stalked off toward the crowd at the entrance. Joanette dried her eyes, powdered her face, and hurried after him at a pace faster than a walk. People surged toward the doors and scattered back into the parking lot—families, singles, people pushing huge cartfuls of dog food, boxed fans, broom handles and vacuum cleaners sticking out.

She didn't spot Lenny anywhere in the swirling mob. What color shirt did he have on—blue, was it? She went in to look for him.

The check-out lines snaked back into the aisles. People pushed against the customer service desk. Boxes were stacked high on the shelves. Would Lenny have ventured into this maze? Doubtful. Besides, you had to be a member to get in.

Joanette waited at the exit. No Lenny. SUVs and station wagons were lined up at the entrance, and people loaded their goods into the backs of their cars. After a few minutes, Joanette walked back toward where they'd left the Bronco, measuring the distance and the angle from the entrance. She couldn't remember if they'd parked a row over, but she was sure the car was somewhere in the vicinity. She turned full circle, scanned the cars, and then it struck her: Lenny had ditched her.

She was angry and hurt. She'd never been stood up in her life, not by either of her exes or by any boyfriend in high school. What could have possessed him? It was seven-thirty. Maybe he'd probably gone to get a beer, but that didn't make sense when he was going to grill the chicken. Or maybe he'd gone to Ace Hardware. They had gas.

She walked back to the entrance and paced. Lenny might come back. And she thought of calling Adrienne or Joy and asking one of them to come get her, but either of them would think she was hysterical or overdramatizing. She couldn't tell them Lenny had deserted her.

A half an hour went by. Lenny wasn't going to sneak up behind her and yell, "Surprise!" the way he did at the bus stop that one time. God, she'd nearly jumped into traffic. Whether he'd gone for a beer or to Ace Hardware didn't matter: he'd abandoned her, pure and simple.

At the end, she did the only thing she thought reasonable. She went inside and bought a thousand-dollar grill and all the food she thought could fit into a taxi.

The garage door was closed when she got home. She assumed Lenny had come home, but he hadn't. The garage was empty. She busied herself with dinner—made rice in the ricemaker, cut tomatoes, avocado, and red onion for a salad, and uncrated the new grill. She didn't know how to put it together, though, and anyway, she hadn't bought gas. So she heated the oven.

Then she called Lenny's office. She didn't expect him to answer, but she was surprised by the message, especially his tone of voice. He was so cheerful: "Hey, this is Lenny, your favorite insurance peddler. I'm out of the office, but I haven't gone to Mexico yet. Leave a number where I can get back to you."

That was definitely odd. For years Lenny's message had been somber, his voice played at three-quarter speed to inspire fear and guilt. What made insurance companies wealthy, Lenny said, was the idea that something bad was going to happen. Tornadoes, floods, earthquakes, fire, cancer, old age, burglars, accidents—take your pick. You had to protect yourself and your family. Lenny even kept a list of freak occurrences—a woman hanging up clothes who was struck by lightning, a motorist in rural Arkansas whose windshield was shattered by a golf ball and ran head-on into a cow, the couple who'd left their three children to get dinner at McDonald's and returned to find their house leveled by an explosion.

"Lenny, it's Joanette," she said. "I apologize for whatever I said. I didn't mean to hurt your feelings or threaten you. So, listen, come home, okay?" She paused. "What's with this message on your machine? Of course you're not in Mexico."

Lenny hadn't come back when the rice was done, so she called Jed Sanborn and Arnie Blaisdell, Lenny's closest friends. Jed said he hadn't heard from Lenny in weeks, and Arnie, according to his wife, Sherry, was at the Rockies' game. Lenny hadn't been by.

"Is anything wrong?" Sherry asked.

"Not yet," Joanette said.

She called Chuck Wier in Dutch Elm Village. Martin had the ad agency adjacent to Lenny's office, and sometimes on slow afternoons he and Lenny hacked at golf. She asked straight out whether he knew where Lenny was.

"That rascal," Martin said. "We were supposed to play the Target course last Friday, but he didn't show. You know Lenny."

"I thought I did," Joanette said, "but he's not home, and he should be."

"Tell him I made a hole-in-one," Martin said. "That'll get him."

"I will," Joanette said.

Ten minutes later, as Joanette figured, Adrienne Frost called. "Martin called me," she said. "What's going on? Are you all right?"

"Nothing is going on."

"Martin said Lenny's disappeared."

"Maybe he has a mistress," Joanette said.

"No man is perfect," Adrienne said. "That's why God made women. If Gerry had a mistress, I'd be glad. He wouldn't want sex every day with me. So consider yourself lucky."

"I'm worried," Joanette said.

"Did he pack a suitcase? Men don't leave their wives without packing a suitcase and taking their fishing equipment."

"Lenny doesn't fish," Joanette said.

"See? He has one good quality."

"He's got a new message on his machine at work that says he hasn't gone to Mexico yet. Goddamn it, I didn't do anything."

"Don't go berserk, Joanette. Now listen, if I'm going to sympathize, you'll have to tell me what happened. Otherwise, I have to do the dishes."

"We were going shopping at Costco—"

"—Oh, Jesus. You're nuts, Joanette. You took Lenny to Costco? You can't do that to a man. That's bananas. I'll talk to you tomorrow."

Adrienne hung up, and Joanette pondered why a crazy person was called a nut and not a banana.

All the while she was eating roast chicken, Joanette wondered whether she was crazy for caring about romantic thrillers and a good grill and all there was at Costco. Afterward, in the shower under hot and then cold, she pondered the same question, and after that in bed in her nightgown with the light on, and then again with the light off. She examined from every side what had happened, even from Lenny's. What monster would drive away without telling his wife where he was going?

She'd married Lenny because he was responsible, witty on occasion, but not so often as to be obnoxious. He was predictable, too. She liked that. He had a morning ritual and an evening ritual. He was pretty normal. He liked to eat but wasn't a gourmet by any means. They had movies in common, even if they didn't like the same ones. He was sanitary. He shaved every day and used deodorant. (One of her husbands hadn't.) He went to bed at 10:30 and didn't snore or drool. As far as she could tell, he barely dreamed. His lovemaking—she had comparisons to make—was adequate but not great, no worse than her previous husbands. Sex with Lenny wasn't knock-'em-dead, but he didn't use chains or rubber items, either.

It was past midnight when she heard the car pull into the driveway. The garage door didn't open, but she heard the engine of the Bronco shut off, the front door open and close. "Lenny, is that you?" she called.

Who else would it be but Lenny?

He didn't answer, though. His footsteps crossed the living room and went into the kitchen, but the light didn't come on. She'd have seen it through the bedroom door. She got out of bed and put on a robe and walked out into the living room in her bare feet. She paused there and listened. The sprinklers had come on outside. The faucet in the kitchen ran and then went off. She stepped around the La-Z-Boy. Gray light from the street played across the vinyl tile and the clean counters, a sheen like moonlight over water. Lenny was sitting in a straightbacked chair by the bay window, looking outside.

"Lenny?"

"I think so," Lenny said.

"What do you mean, you think so?"

"Don't turn on the light."

Joanette came into the kitchen, aware of her shadow behind her. She wondered whether he'd been in a fight and didn't want her to see the damage. "What happened?" she asked. "Are you drunk?"

"No, I'm not drunk."

The light gave what she could see of his face a weird, silvery appearance. "I don't think what you did was right," she said.

"What I did?"

"Are you denying it, Lenny? You left me at Costco."

"That's the way you see it."

"What other way is there?"

Lenny turned. "You had to have been there."

"I *was* there," Joanette said. "I got you a new grill."

"I mean where *I* was."

Lenny looked back out the window. At that time of night, what could he see?—the neighbor's fence and the house protruding above it, not even a color, and maybe the blank sky, almost white from the city lights. Joanette inched closer. She smelled the lingering aroma of chicken and salad dressing, but no alcohol or marijuana. "Where were you then?" she asked.

"I was agitated," he said. "I thought I'd go to a bar and wait things out, let myself calm down. I even *went* to a bar—Circle Drive I was on—but it was too crowded. It's what night tonight, Tuesday? Wednesday? I didn't want to be around people so I drove out farther, past some buildings, lots of churches. Do you realize how many churches there are in this town?"

"People go to church," Joanette said. "Some people believe in God."

"Maybe they're afraid of dying," Lenny said.

"I wouldn't mind if we went to church once in a while."

"If I were dying, a church would be the last place I'd go."

She looked at Lenny closely. His lips were pursed into a smile, or in what was almost a smile. "Where did you go?" Joanette asked. "Really."

"I drove a while," Lenny said. "I don't know how far. I thought I'd get somewhere—you know, to a place I wanted to be. I passed bars and clubs. I thought I'd know when I got there, but nothing was familiar. You know where I ended up?"

"Where?"

"In an arcade."

"You mean pinball, video games, and peep shows? You went to an arcade instead of coming back and getting me?"

"It was huge—like a warehouse, sort of. Other worldly. The games were so big you could get inside them. The virtual golf had trees and real sand traps and grass in the fairways. I felt as if I were striking a real golf ball."

"Martin said he made a hole-in-one."

Lenny seemed not to hear. "The most amazing game was Ringo Bingo."

"Ringo Bingo?"

"It was off in a corner, and no one was around it, no one within fifty feet. It was as if it were off limits or something. It was a big box, big as a house. You walked inside it, and... I don't know what happened... you were converted. That's the best word for it, *changed*. It was sort of like being in a hall of mirrors, except you didn't see yourself in funny shapes, but in real shapes."

"You aren't making any sense, Lenny."

"I know. I can't explain it. What happened was—this sounds crazy—I felt new things, not from my side, the way we say, but from the *other* side, as if I were myself and everyone else at the same time."

"You're making this up."

"It doesn't sound possible, does it? But it *felt* true. I felt hatred, not the way I might—when you come down to it, what do I have to hate, right?—but the way George might."

"Who's George? Are you all right, Lenny?"

"You know, George, Jorgé, the Hispanic guy down the street."

"The one with the too-loud Mercury?"

"He has a Tercel with a bad muffler," Lenny said. "He might hate us."

"What are you talking about, Lenny? Why would he hate us? If he lives on our block, he's doing all right."

"I'm giving you an example, Joanette. He's got to be superhuman. Think about it. Imagine how hard it is to be extraordinary? That's what I'm saying. I do okay. I'm ordinary. But Jorgé, he's got to be so much better."

"You make a good living, Lenny. Only a few people can be right at the top."

Lenny looked at her, as if she were far off, as if maybe he didn't know who she was. He had that look.

"You protect people from harm," Joanette said.

Lenny shook his head. "Harm happens no matter what I do. People's houses burn down, they have accidents, they get sick. I don't protect them from anything."

"You make it easier on them."

"Someone dies, the company pays. The disaster still happens. Money only makes the loss easier. Do you see what I mean? Maybe it's come to that."

"Come to what?" Joanette asked.

Lenny was quiet for a moment. Then he said, "I felt love, too. Real love. The whole history of love, like all the way through time."

"If you were feeling all this love, why didn't you come back for me at Costco?"

"It wasn't that easy, Joanette. Believe me. It wasn't that easy. We can't go on this way. We have to know what's what."

"What are you saying? You want a divorce?"

"I want love that transcends time."

Lenny was silent again, drifting. He looked confused, dazed, as if he were an accident victim in shock who wasn't sure what had happened to him.

"Maybe you should take me there," Joanette said.

"Where?"

"To this place, wherever it was—Ringo Bingo—where you felt all these things."

Lenny turned from the window and stirred from his chair. "You sure?"

"Yes."

"All right, I'll take you." Lenny stood up.

"I don't mean right now," Joanette said. "It's almost one o'clock. It's the middle of the night."

"So what?" Lenny said. "Time doesn't matter. Bedtime, daytime, lunchtime. What difference does it make?"

"If it doesn't make any difference, let's do it tomorrow. Noon lunch."

"Lunch," Lenny said. "All right, lunch." He took his day planner from his jacket pocket and wrote it down. "Noon, Thursday."

In the morning, nothing was said. Lenny rose and showered and shaved and brushed his mustache. She heard all of his regular activities. She hadn't slept well. Last night Lenny had made no effort to appease her or to lessen her anguish. She'd turned off the light, got into bed, and pulled the covers back on Lenny's side. Then she'd waited, hoping Lenny would come in right away. Events whirled through her head: running out of gas—propane!—being abandoned, the phone calls, then everything Lenny had said. It was as if her life had veered off course, like a star that for light-years had kept to one path and then was struck by a meteor. She'd heard Lenny shuffle to the bathroom and turn on the water. He washed his face, his hands, brushed his teeth. Ringo Bingo—what was that? She pictured Lenny strapped into a seat like an electric chair, with wires attached to his head. He was being subjected to hatred, love, and worst of all, curiosity. How terrible it must have been for him to want to know everything in the world. She'd heard the tap go off, felt more than saw the light disappear from the doorway. Then Lenny padded away into the living room.

Now where was he going?

She waited. Finally he'd appeared in the doorway with something in his hand. "I thought you'd like some hot milk," he said. "I put a little Ovaltine in it."

She sat up, overwhelmed by gratitude.

"It's hot," he said.

The cup passed between them, the vapors of steam, the fragrant smell of malt. Lenny circled the bed and slipped under the covers.

She'd expected, then, after a few sips of Ovaltine, a caress, an embrace that would ameliorate the pain she felt. They'd miscommunicated, but she still felt close to him. He was a plodder, but a good provider, a partner. She cared for him. But he didn't touch her. He lay beside her on his back, staring at the ceiling. She waited for him to turn toward her. After a while, she heard his breathing even out and realized he was asleep.

Now it was morning. He turned off the tap in the bathroom and came back into the bedroom. Instead of opening the closet, though, he pulled out a bureau drawer, and she opened her eyes. Lenny was putting on jeans and sneakers.

"Aren't you going to work?"

"Of course I am."

He pulled on a pale yellow short-sleeved shirt.

"Are you playing golf?"

"Not that I know of."

"What are you doing then?"

"I'm being me," he said. "Don't forget lunch."

He kissed her on the cheek, and then he was gone. She drifted back to the night before. He hadn't touched her, but she hadn't touched him, either.

Her morning was jagged fits and starts of doing nothing. She couldn't concentrate on the how-to-shop-on-the-internet booklet. A delivery man brought the steaks she'd ordered from Kansas City. There was a UPS package from Sears. She sat outside for a few minutes, but the phone rang: she'd forgotten her appointment at the beauty salon. She scheduled a makeup on the next Monday.

Finally she put on slacks and a thin blouse and sandals. That gave her the option of restaurants, though Lenny rarely ate at fancy places, and he wasn't dressed for one when he left. That didn't mean she had to look as if she were going hiking.

Back outside, she was surprised how gray the air was, not cloudy, but hazy and smoggy, as if there were a distant fire. The sun was discernible in the background, present but not present, like an unseen eye.

She drove the main stop-and-go streets to Lenny's office, glad she wasn't a commuter. His building was low-slung, with a gray stucco exterior, six offices in a row like motel rooms. Lenny's was closed, the shutters drawn over the windows. His Bronco wasn't in the lot.

She went next door. Chuck Wier was doing hand-weight reps in the receptionist's area. "Have you seen Lenny?" Joanette asked.

"About a month ago," Chuck said. "Lenny... He's the guy with the limp?"

"Don't be smart," Joanette said. "He was supposed to meet me for lunch at noon."

"It isn't noon yet." Chuck lifted the weights over his head, then did wideouts. "He'll be here. You know Lenny."

Joanette went back outside and sat on the steps. At 12:20 Lenny's Bronco turned the corner and pulled up to the curb. Joanette stood and bent down to the open window. "Where were you?" she asked.

"A client called."

"You could have let me know, written a note or something."

Lenny leaned across the seat and snapped open the door for her. "Are you getting in or not?" he said.

Joanette got in and Lenny drove ahead. He stopped at a sign and turned right. She checked his face: normal. "Was the client all right?" Joanette asked.

"He totaled his Lexus," Lenny said. "Listen, Joanette, I'm quitting."

"What do you mean, quitting?"

"The business. I'm getting out, saying uncle, no más. You know what quitting means."

"What would you do?"

"Why do I have to do anything? What law says that?" He stopped at a light on Tejon Street, then kept on straight, away from the city center.

"I thought we were going to lunch."

"We are, but I thought first we should..."

"This accident, is that why you're upset?"

"Jorgé in his Tercel would have been killed, but this guy walks away unscathed because he can afford a Lexus."

"You can't quit," Joanette said. "We have to eat."

"I don't suppose *you* could work," Lenny said. "Maybe get a job in a restaurant or a clothing store. You're not powerless."

They drove out Vermijo to Circle Drive. Traffic was heavy, and carbon monoxide floated in the air. Gray buildings eased by. Joanette had never noticed the rigid blocky buildings, garish curves, colors that clashed. And the churches! Spires and parking lots—a church occupied every corner.

"Costco is on the right up ahead," said Joanette.

They passed Costco and kept driving. A mile, two miles. Malls and crowded intersections, gas stations, convenience stores—the first cancers. They stopped at a half dozen traffic lights and waited in silence. It was hot, and Joanette turned on the air-conditioner.

"That wastes gas," Lenny said.

They drove on, the air-conditioner whirring and cooling.

"So where is this place, Lenny?"

"Out a ways."

They passed under the interstate and aimed toward the mountains, hazy and blue ahead of them. Circle Drive ended; they turned south. Housing developments grew over the foothills like noxious weeds, poised to spread their seeds far and wide. Beyond the city limits, the country became piñon and juniper and red sandstone. Another church rose up.

"We are a godless people to need so many churches," Lenny said.

"This isn't zoned for business out here," Joanette said. "Where are we going?"

"You don't believe me?"

"I want to believe you, Lenny. There has to be a reason for what you did."

"You mean besides cruelty."

"Yes."

"I'm looking," Lenny said. "All I remember is I drove for a while."

They crested a hill and leveled out on a mesa. The air had

cleared—no more haze or smoke or smog. A half mile ahead, a small adobe house appeared in among the junipers and piñons and Lenny pulled over to the side of the road.

"This is it?" Joanette asked.

"This is where I came."

"I thought you said it was a warehouse."

"In back," Lenny said. "In the trees back there." He pointed into scrub oaks. "See?"

Hidden among the scraggly oaks was a white tin building with rust on the edges of the roof.

"This is where you came last night?"

Beyond the building was a sandstone cliff, odd rock formations, and more trees. Lenny drove around the house and up a rutted driveway and parked.

"This isn't what I imagined," Joanette said.

"Nevertheless," Lenny said. He turned off the engine and got out of the car.

"There isn't even a sign," Joanette said.

"What do you want to do?" Lenny asked. "You want to go in?"

"I don't know."

Lenny got out and walked toward an unmarked door at the side of the building. It had a silver handle, stainless steel, Joanette thought. She had a weird feeling—she wasn't sure what it was or how to describe it, but it was more than nervousness. She couldn't *do* anything. Lenny was going in there and she was helpless to stop him.

Lenny turned the knob and opened the darkness inside. He stood for a moment silhouetted, his hair defined clearly, his pale yellow shirt framed in black. He waved for her to come with him, but his expression was unclear, almost a smirk.

She didn't move.

He waited.

She waited.

Then Lenny shrugged and stepped into the darkness, and the door swung closed.

He'd left the keys in the ignition—why had he done that?—and Joanette climbed over the gear shift between the seats and settled herself behind the steering wheel. She started the engine and the air-conditioner came on, blasting cold air. She shifted to reverse and spun the tires, stopped, and put it in first, afraid of what she was doing, afraid, afraid, afraid, as she drove down the rutted driveway to the main highway.

STARLINGS

1.

The townhouse Guy Williams rented at Woodgate after his wife died was modern sterile, as he called it, carpeted completely in speckled green. He hadn't got much furniture yet—a dining room table and two chairs, a half sofa, and from his daughter, Peg, a mattress he put on the bedroom floor. For most of the month of April, since he'd moved from the farm, he'd read history and listened to the radio, read more and slept.

That noon he made a pickle-and-tuna sandwich and was carrying it and *The History of the Cold War* into the dining room when he heard through the screen door an eerie noise like a train wheel scraping on metal. He wasn't used to the natural sounds in Wichita, but this sound was not natural. He set the plate and the book on the floor and went out onto the patio. Several children were yelling on the playground at the end of the walk, but Guy saw no workmen whose saws or scrapers might have made such a noise. The vista was pale—the other brownish-gray townhouses like his, the clipped juniper hedges, and the manicured lawns. The sound came from beyond the attached garages, an erratic screeching and whistling high up in a row of dying elms. Guy stepped to the edge of the patio and, over the roof, caught a glimpse of several dozen dark birds zooming away.

By the time Peg called that afternoon, he had forgotten the birds.

"I'm sorry I couldn't come and make you lunch," Peg said. "We had to run three emergency blood tests at the lab. Now I've got to pick up Troy at school. What did you do today?"

"I've breathed," Guy said, "and I've read two hundred pages. You don't have to make me lunch."

"Dr. Lytle wants you to exercise," Peg said. "Why don't you do calisthenics? Or you could swim. You have a pool right there."

"The pool doesn't open till this weekend," Guy said. "I didn't decide to live here. I'm renting."

"You could play golf. Edward had some clubs, didn't he?"

Guy looked out the window and saw a black cocker spaniel sniffing along the hedge around his patio. "You do that, buster, and you're history."

"What?" Peg said.

"A dog," Guy said. "He's going to shit on my grass."

The dog squatted down, and a blond woman about thirty, holding its leash, said, "Good boy, Chipper," in a high-pitched voice.

"Maybe you should take up music again," Peg said. "You liked to sing."

"He did it," Guy said. "God damn."

The woman was slender, though Guy couldn't see much of her through the hedge. She had on a pink blouse, and her hair was short, puffed over her ears. She guided the spaniel two gates up and let it in.

"I have PTA tonight," Peg said. "Do you want me to bring you dinner beforehand?"

"You don't have to make me meals," Guy said. "I'll go to Furr's. I'm fine."

"You're not fine. You need to take it easy."

"I thought I was supposed to exercise."

They hung up, and for a minute Guy looked out at the discordant collection of dead trees and live ones leafing out. The horizon was crisscrossed with jetstreams and crows undulating past, fighting the wind. The blond woman appeared by his hedge with a pooper-scooper.

For most of his life, Guy Williams had grown wheat on four hundred acres near Hays, Kansas. He and his wife Martha had been married thirty-three years and had lived in the same house. She was a substantial woman, tall and large-boned, generous to a fault, and, until Edward had disappeared, believed in the Lord Jesus Christ. That had been six years ago, six years of torment during which he'd sold most of his land to pay for Martha's search-and-rescue efforts.

He'd not begrudged Martha her grief. Edward was their only son. He'd been a freshman at Kansas State, and one Friday night in October—he'd been in Manhattan only a month—he hadn't come back to his dorm. His roommates assumed he'd met a girl and was spending the weekend with her, but on Monday, when he was absent from his history class, they called Martha and Guy, who called the police. They found no evidence a crime had been committed, but Edward's bank account with eighteen hundred dollars in it had been closed. The police put out a bulletin on Edward's truck, an '89 Toyota, and filed a missing-person report.

Guy and Martha considered every possibility: Edward had been murdered; he'd been kidnaped by a cult; he was gay and ashamed to tell them; for his own reasons he had decided to drop out of school and explore the world. Every theory was plausible. Except for the truck and the money, nothing was missing.

They hoped for a phone call from him, a letter, some clue delivered by a stranger. Guy kept on farming as he always had, because doing something was better than doing nothing. The land needed him. Gradually, he gave in to the notion that Edward had made a choice and would call if he wanted to.

But Martha refused to let Edward go. She visited every person he had known at college and all his friends from high school, even teachers who'd moved away and 4-H acquaintances from state fairs years before. She telephoned police commissioners in all the towns she thought Edward might go to. She got crazier. She imagined Edward was in Spokane, Washington, and went there to look for him. She dreamt once he was in Bradenton, Florida, and she searched the beaches. She remembered Edward had talked about visiting the Grand Canyon, so she flew there and stayed two weeks talking to people on the South Rim and in Flagstaff where he might have got work.

Guy couldn't talk her out of these visions; he loved her. At home she prayed and waited, blasphemed God, wept at her own failures. Her only escape was sex. It was as if only her flesh could release the pain in her mind, and she needed it, craved it. Sometimes when Guy came home from the fields she met him at the door half-undressed, begging him. "Please, Guy. Love me. Do it for me. I can't help it."

Guy sat under a Cinzano umbrella reading the sports page, and now and then looking at the swimming pool whose surface danced in the sunlight. It was Saturday, opening day, and half the residents of Woodgate were there. Children, couples, and retired people were a blur of noise and color around them. "Well, grandpa, what kind of birds were they?" Troy asked.

Troy was nine, pale, skinny as Peg and Edward had been, though Peg was not skinny anymore. Troy was afraid to go into the water.

"I don't know what kind," Guy said. "Birds are birds. What kinds are there?"

"Hummingbirds. Eagles. Warblers."

"None of those."

"Pigeons and ducks."

"Ducks wouldn't be in trees."

"Wood Ducks roost in trees. So do whistling-ducks."

Guy turned to Peg lying face down on a chaise. "How does he know these things?"

"He reads nature books."

"They weren't ducks," Guy said. "I know ducks." He turned to Peg again. "What kind of birds were in the Hitchcock movie? Gulls, I think. They weren't gulls, either."

"You don't have to get mad," Troy said.

Guy looked back to the sports page. "I'm not mad. The baseball season's barely started, and already the Rockies are 0 and 4. Do you know who the Rockies are?"

"Colorado," Troy said.

Guy folded the paper and dropped it beside his chair. Then the blond woman whose dog was named Chipper came through the pool gate. She had on a pink one-piece suit, very frilly above her breasts, and she carried a pink towel. She made her way past the vending machines to the line of chaises on the other side. She had an odd hitch to her step, not a limp exactly, but an awkwardness. Her knee turned outward and her foot splayed slightly, and Guy was touched by this imperfection.

He got up abruptly and walked to the curved edge of the pool.

"Are you going swimming?" Troy asked.

"I'm thinking about it," Guy said.

Children and parents splashed in the shallow end, and teenagers and young boys lined up for cannonballs off the diving board. He had never much liked swimming pools, jacuzzis, or hot tubs. Water wrinkled the skin and turned the brain to mush, but the doctor in Hays said his circulation was slow, and exercise, particularly swimming, would be good for him.

The sun flashed brightly in the swells, and a few mirrored clouds were fractured on the surface of the water. Then, suddenly, a dark whirl of birds appeared in murky reflection, and Guy looked up. "There they are," he said to Troy. "What kind of birds are those?"

The birds were dark and fast, not large, flying toward the city, fifty, a hundred of them. "Starlings," Troy said. "They're common everywhere."

Guy watched them swoop down beyond the trees. He felt Troy's hand press into his back and give a push. Guy teetered, fixed his gaze on Troy's gleeful grin. "You little bastard," he said. He saw the blond woman step down into the shallow end and push away from the edge, and he toppled into the water.

Guy stopped his grocery cart in the vegetable aisle. Vegetables in stores were vile and worthless, but he had run out of Martha's canned tomatoes and beets and the peas and beans she'd frozen, and now he was required to buy broccoli crowns and bib lettuce, the best of bad choices, bathed in mist.

"You're the new neighbor," said a woman's voice nearby.

He looked around at the blond woman and was surprised by her Southern accent. "That depends on what you mean by new," he said.

She put out her hand. "I'm Janet Keltner," she said. "How are you liking Woodgate? Isn't it convenient?"

Guy did not see what there was to like. "I won't mind not mowing the lawn and cleaning the gutters. It'll give me more time to read."

"Was that your daughter and grandson at the pool? I saw you swimming."

"Not voluntarily."

"Where's your wife?"

"She died," Guy said.

"I guess I should have known that," the woman said. "Otherwise, you wouldn't be shopping by yourself."

"Men can shop," Guy said.

"We moved here three years ago from Mississippi," the woman said. "My husband works for Cessna." She picked out several broccoli crowns and tore a plastic bag from the roll. She tried to figure which end to open.

"They make these things that way on purpose," Guy said.

"So what do you read?"

"Whatever the library has." He took the bag from her and opened it. "I've discovered in my old age you can still learn new things."

"My husband is a fabulous cook," she said. "You'll have to come over for dinner sometime."

"I have to eat," Guy said. "Thank you."

The next three days Guy woke to the raucous noise of starlings. They weren't secretive, not at all. According to the bird books he looked in, they had been introduced from England into Central Park in New York City and in less than a century had spread across the continent like a plague. *Sturnus vulgaris.* A pair was nesting under the eaves of his townhouse, and another pair above the drainpipe by the garage. "They're already feeding their young," he told Peg that afternoon. She and Troy were driving him down Fifteenth Street to look at furniture.

"I thought birds were supposed to feed their young."

"Not in April. No other birds are nesting yet."

"What are you going to do about them?" Troy asked from the back seat.

"Do? What can I do?"

"I'm glad you have a hobby," Peg said. "Tell me about the dinner invitation."

"What's there to tell about something that hasn't happened yet. You know the joke. We'll have lunch, the check's in the mail, and…"

"Stop," Peg said. "Remember who's here."

She turned right into the parking lot at Weberg's and stopped the car. "Now, Dad, please don't make this difficult."

"It's already difficult," Guy said. "I own a houseful of furniture in Hays."

"You need a TV," Troy said, "and a bed."

"You think it's a health code violation to have a mattress on the floor?"

Peg opened her door and got out. "You might never sell the house," she said. "And then what?"

"I'm not buying a TV," Guy said. "At my age I don't want to acquire, I want to divest." He opened his door reluctantly. "What I really want is binoculars."

Guy knew more about birds than he'd thought. Loons, albatrosses, terns, puffins, owls, hawks, jays, hummingbirds, thrushes, finches, warblers were all names he'd heard before. But he was surprised, reading journals in the library, how many species there were. He'd never paid much attention to birds on the farm, except for blackbirds and meadowlarks and maybe a blue heron or a hawk. Martha had had Blue Jays at her feeder, but there were also, somewhere, Gray Jays, Green Jays, Brown Jays, Scrub Jays, Pinyon Jays, and Steller's Jays. Of course, what you could see depended on geography and habitat. He didn't know what was around Wichita.

Even with the new binoculars, he was slow to learn. He couldn't tell a Song Sparrow from a Field Sparrow, or Northern Flicker from Red-bellied Woodpecker. But he got better. He had good eyes, and looking for birds got him outside. He walked the fields and the river park and found Rufous-sided Towhee, Brown Thrasher, Black-capped Chickadee, Belted Kingfisher, and an early Barn Swallow. Above the meadow he saw Red-tailed Hawk and Northern Harrier. His list got longer.

One Saturday, Janet invited him to dinner. "Tonight," she said, "if you're not busy."

"I'm never busy," he said.

It was a warm evening, and the narrow sky pulsed with city lights. When Guy arrived, Warren was sifting mesquite charcoal into the grill on the patio. He was boyish, early thirties, and hefty— someone, Guy thought, who really needed exercise.

"I hope you like swordfish," Warren said.

"We don't get much swordfish in Hays," Guy said.

"Can I get you something to drink? Janet's still at the store."

"A beer, if it isn't light."

"We have juice, Pepsi and Sprite, and milk."

"That's all right," Guy said. "I'll drink water." He looked around the patio which was identical to his own. "Janet said you work for Cessna."

"Good pay, good bennies," Warren said. "I can retire early." He lit the mesquite and stepped back. "I'm what's called a coroner. You know, ninety-nine percent of the time when a plane goes down it's pilot error, but the manufacturer gets blamed. I do the post-mortem on materials to see whether we could have made the plane better."

The automatic garage door whirred, and inside the condo Chipper barked. A minute later Janet appeared at the sliding glass door holding a grocery sack with a loaf of French bread sticking out. "Sorry I'm late. The traffic was terrible."

"Can I help?" Guy asked.

She peered into the sack and took out a bottle of white wine. "You could open this."

The swordfish was good. The asparagus and hollandaise were good. The brown rice was too crunchy for Guy's taste, but he doused it with sauce. Janet asked Guy questions about the Cold War, but Warren dominated the conversation. The Russians and the Chinese had been the least of the problem. Outlaw nations like North Korea, Libya, and Iran were keeping the civilized nations on their toes. They had to police the proliferation of nukes but also to continue their own weapons research.

"What do you mean by 'civilized nations'?" Guy asked.

"What about dessert?" Janet said.

Dessert was peach meringue, very sweet.

After dinner Warren went out to walk Chipper, so Guy cleared the table and Janet scraped the plates and put them into the dishwasher. "I'm sorry about Warren," she said. "He likes to talk."

"You were right. He's a good cook."

"He's gained sixty pounds since we were married."

"How long has that been?"

"Almost five years." She rinsed the rice dish. "But tell me about your children."

"Well, Margaret's in Wichita. She's a lab technician. And there's Edward. Martha named them after British royalty."

"Where's Edward?"

"He disappeared quite a while ago—six years. That's what killed Martha, really. She died of grief."

"You have no idea where he is?"

"He was in college and emptied his bank account, which may or may not mean he's alive. The police never found his truck."

"The world is full of mysteries," Janet said. "I'm sorry."

"What about you," Guy said. "Do you work?"

She stopped and turned off the water. "Not anymore."

"But you did once? What did you do?"

"Guess." She said it as if she were a child. "Come on, guess."

Guy poured the last of the wine. He looked at her make-up and her hair, her pale pink dress. He didn't want to guess. "A waitress, but in a fancy place."

"No, I had to go to college," she said.

"Lawyer? A stockbroker?"

She laughed. She liked stockbroker.

"A teacher?"

The garage door whirred beneath them. "Warren's here," she said. "I'll let you ponder it. It's another mystery."

On a Sunday in early May, Guy took Peg and Troy to the river park for a picnic. The sky was clear, bluish-white, certain to deepen as the sun climbed. A mist lingered above the water and blurred into the leafy canopy of trees. Peg sat at the picnic table and did a crossword, while Guy and Troy walked up the river along the worn path.

Guy recognized a thrush's clear scale, and Troy pointed out a warbler— a Black-throated Green, they decided—singing from an open branch.

"Do you ever wonder what we're not seeing?" Troy asked.

"You mean like owls?"

"I wasn't thinking of birds necessarily."

"Sometimes people aren't interested in being seen," Guy said, "like Edward."

"I didn't mean people, either."

Guy saw movement high in a tree across the river, and he trained his binoculars, but couldn't find the bird. "Give me some hint, Troy. I'm not a mind reader."

"I mean the future," Troy said, "the things we're not seeing because they haven't happened yet."

"That's a given. We can't know the future."

"But we make predictions," Troy said. "We do that all the time."

Guy saw a vermilion streak flash through the burnished sun. "Tanager," Guy said. He trained his glasses on it. "Summer Tanager. All red, yellow bill." He gave the glasses to Troy and paged through the bird guide.

Troy didn't look through the binoculars. "What will happen to the ozone layer? The rain forests? The oceans? That's what I mean."

The picnic was pleasant. Peg spread a checkered tablecloth and set the places with silverware and plastic dishes. Guy had made lemonade and had bought chicken and ham-and-cheese sandwiches and potato salad at the Safeway deli. The sun was warm, and the river curled through the trees and past them as if it were unmoving.

"How was the dinner party?" Peg asked. "What'd you have?"

"Swordfish. The wife rescued me with a bottle of wine."

"You shouldn't drink, Grandpa," Troy said.

"That's what you say. You're only nine." Guy looked at Troy, then back at Peg. "Afterward, the husband walked the dog, and when he came back, we watched a movie. Why rent a movie when you have a guest for dinner?"

"You're not easy to talk to," Peg said.

"What movie?" Troy asked.

"Something violent," Guy said. "I left in the middle."

"Dad, they won't invite you back."

"I won't go back," Guy said. "Besides, in every movie, you know the hero or heroine isn't going to die, so what's the point?"

"The point is to be polite," Peg said.

"I'm too old to be polite," Guy said. "And poor Janet Keltner was chewing her knuckles as if the movie were real."

Guy swam laps. The first day he'd done four, two days later six, then eight. He thought he could work up to twenty. Once, to see, he swam as long as he could and did fifteen, but when he got out of the pool, he was out of breath and his legs shook. When he staggered up the steps at the shallow end of the pool, Janet Keltner was waiting for him with a towel.

"Overexertion is as bad as no exercise," she said. "You could have a heart attack."

Guy rubbed his arms and chest with the towel. "Me? What about Warren?"

"Warren doesn't overexert. Do you want a soda?"

Guy flopped down into a chair. "I want a gin-and-tonic."

It was a weekday morning, and the pool veranda was nearly empty—an older couple and two fat men asleep side by side on chaises. The pool was calm, reflecting the silver-blue of sky in its curved basin. Janet lay down on a towel, face into the sun.

"So you won't tell me what you used to do?" he said.

"I might tell you sometime."

"I could ask Warren."

Janet propped herself on an elbow. "Do you think what you do is who you are?"

"I still think of myself as a farmer."

"But now you're a reader."

"I suppose so."

"Then I'm nothing," she said.

Guy looked at her. She'd lain back and closed her eyes to the sun.

2.

July. More starlings. Guy knew of twelve nesting pairs. Some had raised two broods, and the pair in the heating duct had raised three. He couldn't tell how many birds had fledged, but he guessed four or five from each brood—something like 120 birds altogether. They flew overhead when he did laps at the pool. They foraged on the lawn as he rode his stationary bike on the patio. He watched them in the evenings join other flocks and descend on the dead elms on the far side of the playground.

One hot afternoon he was listening to Beethoven and puffing away in his underwear on his Exer-Bike in his air-conditioned living room when the telephone rang. He didn't want to stop, but Peg worried if no one answered. He didn't want her to come looking for him. He got off the bike, turned the radio down, and answered the phone on the third ring. It was Renee Brockman, the real estate broker in Hays.

"We have an offer on your house," Renee said. "$175,000 from a woman taking over Dr. Lytle's clinic."

"If she's a doctor, counter at one-ninety," Guy said, "and $20,000 earnest money."

"What do you mean, if?" Renee said. "One-ninety is pretty stiff. Don't you want to sell?"

Janet appeared at the sliding door on the patio and put her hand up to the glass to shade her eyes. Guy waved her in, and she slid open the door. "I thought you might want to go to the pool," she said.

He signaled with a finger for her to wait, and she pulled her robe around her. Guy turned off the air conditioner, and the room went quiet.

"When does Madame Doctor want it?" Guy said into the phone.

"As soon as possible," Renee said.

"Stick with one-ninety," Guy said. "I can move my stuff next weekend."

He hung up and looked at Janet, still waiting by the door. "You're rich," she said. "You sold your house."

"If it goes through, I'll be less poor."

Janet glanced around the room. "I like your new furniture."

"It's not that new. Peg picked it out."

"Should I meet you at the pool?" she asked. But she didn't turn away.

Then he realized he was in his underwear—a pair of blue briefs. They were the same as swimming trunks, really—his legs and chest were bare—but they weren't swimming trunks, and they weren't at the pool. "I was on the bicycle," he said.

Then, the last thing he expected: he got an erection.

Janet stared for a moment, turned, and went out. A flash of pure light burst from the sliding glass door.

Guy took a deep breath. He hadn't had an erection since Martha had died. He touched his cock, as if to make certain, and felt the pleasure of his hand.

Another burst of light came from the doorway, and Janet entered again, came across the room, and kissed him.

She came over the next afternoon, and the next, and the following Monday morning he waited for her naked in his bed. It was raining outside. A storm was passing though. He heard the drops striking the window pane with a dull ache. A pale gray light flowed through the Venetian blinds.

He had no urgency, but waiting created desire. The memory of the first afternoon was still vivid—the kiss, the embrace, Janet's saying, "Let me do that." She'd touched him and opened her robe and kissed him again.

Now the front door opened. He heard the swish of her clothing being taken off and dropped on the hall floor. She stood in the doorway to the bedroom in pink panties and a thin undershirt. Her nipples poked out against the fabric.

"Do you like me this way?" she asked.

"Come here."

She walked with her hitch-step to the bed and stopped a foot away.

He put his hand on her bare leg and pulled her closer still. "You are beautiful," he said. He skimmed his hand behind her knee, up the back of her thigh, and over the smooth fabric of her underwear. He leaned forward and smelled her, pushed his hand under her shirt and grazed her nipples. She lifted her shirt over her head, sighed at his touch. He moved his hand down again and under the cloth between her legs. Then she bent to kiss him, as if she knew his desire was light and he too wanted to be free of the darkness.

3.

He arranged for the Mayflower van to arrive August first in Hays, and, early on the Friday before, he and Peg picked up a mid-sized U-Haul and got on the interstate north. Guy steered with one hand, and chatted with Troy about his Little League team and summer camp—Troy was a third baseman—and about the roadside birds. He pointed out the enormous sky, how the wheat was progressing in the fields, the light in the clouds.

"You're in high spirits," Peg said. "What's wrong with you?"

"How do you want me to be?" he asked. "Should I be moaning and groaning?"

"I thought you might be nostalgic."

"I'm relieved the house is sold." He pointed to a hawk dipping and gliding over the prairie. "Northern Harrier. See, Troy?"

"I just want you to be happy," Peg said. "I'll drive if you want to look at birds."

They arrived in Hays before noon, bought groceries, and drove out of town past hot, breathless corn and wheat. For a mile and a half they raised dust on the county road, then slowed into a hollow and turned at the drive. The house was a two-story woodframe, white, with two gables upstairs in the rooms where Margaret and Edward had slept. A wide porch wrapped around the curve of the living room. The lawn had been mowed and the shades on the windows were open as if Guy still lived there.

That afternoon, Peg packed the china from the dining room and kitchen and went through the attic full of old books, National Geographics, costumes, toys, and the paraphernalia of Guy's and Martha's parents. Guy boxed or threw away the relics of his and Martha's room—the potpourri in bowls, the lacy curtains, the photos Martha had kept in albums. In her closet were clothes he'd never looked at after she died, and he heaved these and what was in her bureaus—sweaters, overalls, house dresses—and carried them downstairs and out to the growing pile of giveaways on the lawn.

Troy explored the garage and brought curious things to Guy—a 78-rpm Victrola, an iron without a cord, an age-old Gibson with a very loose E-string.

"My father gave me that guitar," Guy said. "I gave it to Edward, but he never played it." He took the guitar, tightened the E, and played a chord sequence. "You can have it, if you want."

"Why didn't Edward play?"

"I guess he didn't want music in his life."

That night Troy slept in Peg's old room because Martha forbade anyone ever to sleep in Edward's. Guy tuned the guitar and sang "All My Trials" and "Blowin' in the Wind" and "Standing in the Need of Prayer," all of which he'd sung to Peg and Edward when they were little. Troy went to sleep in the middle of "Where Have All the Flowers Gone?"

At dawn, Peg was asleep in the hide-a-bed in the sewing room, and Guy and Troy went looking for birds. It was warm for so early in the morning, and a haze obscured the distance. The dirt road they walked on faded into a faraway hill.

"You remember what we talked about that morning at the river?" Guy asked. "About what there won't be when you grow up?" Guy pointed to a silo at Pederson's farm. "I thought this place—the fields, the rolling hills, the shape of the sky—would always be the same. But it won't be. It can't." Guy paused and listened. "Hear that?"

"A meadowlark," Troy said.

"When I lived here, I barely noticed the birds' singing."

Troy and Guy listened together. Another song came from farther away. "What's that?" Troy asked.

Guy listened to the thin whistle and trill from the east where the sun was coming up. "I don't know everything yet," he said.

Guy sorted through his office and threw away files, receipts, and cancelled checks from thirty-three years of paying bills and taxes. He boxed up the tools in the shed—chisels and saws, routers, planes—nothing he had use for anymore. Danny Pederson loaded the pile of clothes into his truck and hauled them to the Goodwill.

Peg emptied the den downstairs and rolled the rug. "I'm putting everything in here we don't know what to do with," she said, "and everything we need to talk over."

"Like what?"

"Some of mother's things and Edward's stuff."

By afternoon, Danny had made three runs to the landfill and four to the Goodwill. The kitchen was clean enough. Except for Edward's room, they'd closed the upstairs. The boxes and beds and mattresses and furniture the Mayflower people were going to store in Wichita were ready to go, and they'd loaded the U-Haul to near-capacity with the bureaus and tables and rugs and small appliances Guy wanted.

"I think you should supervise Edward's room, Peg," he said. "I don't want his ice skates or tennis racquet with broken strings or his posters of sunsets."

"What about the standing lamp he made in shop?"

"No."

"Can I have anything I want?" Troy asked. "I want the golf clubs."

"Take them," Guy said. He sat on the porch steps and looked out into the deepening haze. Clouds had built up in the west, huge, dark-hearted cumulus clouds, but where they were the sun was still shining. Guy had no idea how many hours he had sat on those steps. The horizon of low hills was a landscape familiar as his hand, but he'd have to live without it now. This was his old world, and Woodgate, in Wichita, was the new one.

Troy carried Edward's things he wanted to the U-Haul—a wireless radio, the lamp, a debate trophy, the guitar—and brought out Edward's golf clubs and drew out an iron.

"Did Edward play golf?" he asked.

"Edward wanted to do a lot of things but didn't do them."

"You mean he didn't practice?" Troy swung the iron back and forth a few times as though he were hitting a ball.

"He liked having the equipment."

Peg came out onto on the porch carrying Martha's sewing machine. "We're about ready," she said.

Troy put the iron back and took the sock off a wood. "What is this?" He tugged a bit and pulled a shotgun from the golf bag.

"Hold on there," Guy said. "Let me see that." Guy came down the steps and took the shotgun out of Troy's hands.

"Is that the gun you told Edward to get rid of?" Peg asked.

It was a sixteen-gauge with a wooden stock that had on it a notch above the trigger guard. "I think so," Guy said. He broke open the barrels, both empty, and snapped them to.

"There are some shells in the golf ball pocket," Troy said.

Guy took those, too. "You can't have this, Troy."

"What did Edward do with it?" Troy asked.

"He didn't do anything with it."

Guy slipped the shotgun into the center of a rolled rug in the U-Haul and pulled down the door. "Are we ready, then?"

The clouds that had promised rain dissipated by evening. Troy was asleep with his head in Peg's lap, and she stared out the side window at the fields passing by. The sharp orange light of the last sun illuminated the edges of the trees and fence posts and jellyroll bales from the second cutting and cast a vivid light and shadow across the hills.

"Did you know Edward kept the shotgun?"

Peg turned from the window. "No."

"He lied to me about it. He said he'd given it away."

"I was at college," Peg said. "How did he get the shotgun in the first place? You never liked guns."

"He brought it home from school. Mr. Whitten had given it to him. I don't think you knew Whitten. He was a history teacher from Kansas City."

"Why'd he give it to Ed?"

"For some reason that year Edward wanted to shoot a pheasant for Thanksgiving. He told us at the dinner table one night. Your mother had said the blessing, and Edward announced he had this shotgun. He said Whitten had inherited it from his father, and he wasn't a hunter. I said we'd buy a turkey, same as always, and your mother gave me a look. 'What you like and Edward likes don't have to be the same,' she said. 'Why don't you take the boy hunting instead of criticizing?' 'I wasn't criticizing,' I said. 'Since when?' Edward said. He said it in a tone I'll never forget."

"And then what?" Peg asked.

"Edward got up from the table and ran out."

"Did you take him hunting?"

Guy nodded. "I had to. We went out early one morning in October. It was overcast and windless, but cold. We could see our breaths in the air. We were down in the west field over by the Pedersons'. The plan was for Edward to walk around the field and wait on the far side under that cottonwood by the irrigation ditch. I was going to crisscross the stubble south to north and push the pheasants in front of me. Once the birds ran out of cover, they'd fly, and Edward would have a good shot. So I waited a few minutes to give him time to get into position. I hoped Edward would shoot a pheasant and figure out death wasn't so pretty."

"You wanted it to be a lesson," Peg said.

"Everything is a lesson. He'd see the bloodied feathers and be sick to his stomach."

A semitrailer truck passed, and the wind gust shook the U-Haul. Guy slowed to forty. The sun had slid beyond the horizon, and the land was pale greens and browns.

"We'd had hail damage that year, and the west field was silage. The stalks were head-high, but nothing on them, and real brittle. Once I got into the middle of it, I couldn't see anything, and I navigated by the irrigation troughs, back and forth, scraping between the rows, moving slowly so the birds wouldn't fly. I don't know how long I walked. I saw one cock pheasant sneaking along the ground, head low, the tail down. Then a breeze came up... "

Guy paused a moment and pulled on the headlights.

"It was a terrible noise—all those dry leaves—and I knew then Edward was going to kill me."

"Kill you?"

Guy stared ahead at the road. "I panicked. I thrashed through the field, not caring how much noise I made. I beat through the cornstalks and yelled and pheasants flew up with a clatter and whir of wings. The funny thing was I was running *toward* him. Edward was waiting at that cottonwood tree, and I aimed for it. Then suddenly the shotgun roared, and I fell down weeping."

"Did he shoot at you?"

"No. I don't think so. No."

They were quiet a moment. The motor of the U-Haul hummed. Darkness fell around them, and arc lights of the farms they passed shimmered across the fields.

"I made him get rid of the gun," Guy said. "But he didn't. He got rid of himself."

Guy unloaded the rental truck Monday morning out in the apron by his garage—chairs for the patio, blender, toaster-oven and coffee maker, the round oak dining table, and several rugs, including the Oriental in which he had sheathed the shotgun. It was 9 a.m. Warren must have already gone to work, but he didn't see Janet. Two doors up, their garage was closed.

When he finished unloading, he drove the U-Haul to Peg's and dropped off the sewing machine, the half-sofa, the boxes of keepsakes and photographs. Then he returned the rental truck and took an Uber home.

Janet hadn't left a message, so he went to the pool. She wasn't there, either. A mother and her baby were in the shallow end, but otherwise the pool was quiet. Guy did ten laps and took a break. He felt awkward looking for her. She'd never seemed to care who saw them together, but now that they'd made love, he imagined everyone was watching.

He left the pool area and walked up the curving path. The units he passed were gray with red trim, the roofs brown, the patios only slightly protected from the open space by gates and landscaped hedges. Elms had been evenly spaced on the undulating, manicured lawn.

Then he saw Chipper racing across the grass. The dog was chasing something Guy couldn't see, and he heard Warren calling, "Chipper! Chipper!" but Chipper didn't stop. He circled an elm tree and ran to where Guy was, and Guy grabbed him by the collar and picked him up.

Warren came out of the gate from his patio. "Oh, it's you. Thanks."

"Where's Janet?" Guy asked. He handed Chipper to Warren.

"She went back to Mississippi. She left me."

Guy didn't know what to say. "For a visit?"

Warren smiled. "You're as naive as I am. I don't think so. I came home from work Saturday, and there was a note. She's gone, gone, gone."

"I'm sorry," Guy said. "I thought she liked it here."

"She was always a little off, you know, from the accident. Giddy. Not quite there."

Guy shook his head.

"The plane crash. She was in the hospital when I met her. Her leg… I assumed she told you."

"She didn't tell me much," Guy said.

"She didn't tell me anything," Warren said. "So what's she going to do in Mississippi? That's what I'd like to know. I make plenty of money."

"Maybe she'll do what she did before," Guy said.

"Maybe. But what was that?"

"That's the trouble with the world," Guy said. "You don't know what will happen next."

That evening Guy poured himself a bourbon and called Peg. "Did you get everything you packed?" Guy asked. "Is Troy all right?"

"Thank you so much," Peg said. "Troy's a little tired still. He's got Edward's things in his room."

"Good."

"I meant to help you," Peg said. "You shouldn't be doing all that lifting."

"I'm fine," Guy said. "I'm in good shape."

"So now you've moved in."

"Now I've moved in," he said. "I was about to go out and look for birds. I'll call you tomorrow."

"You have a good time," Peg said. "I'm so glad you're busy."

He sat on the patio and finished the bourbon. The sky turned rose and darkened. In the distance starlings were coming to roost in the dead elms at the edge of the meadow—swarms of them now, thousands. They had spent the day ravaging the countryside, and now they were screeching and nattering, jockeying for position on the bare branches.

Guy went inside and drank another shot of bourbon, then rolled out the Oriental rug. He picked up the shotgun and loaded six shells into the magazine, wrapped the gun in his blue windbreaker. The sky, what there was of it, was violet, a little paler in the west.

He followed the path toward the noise, past the identical townhouses, around the enclosure of the swimming pool and the fence of the children's playground. He crossed the new asphalt road and the cement sidewalk that abutted the property where more townhouses were planned, and walked out into the meadow. Orange ribbons fluttered on wooden surveyor's stakes at the boundaries of the lots. Guy pulled these stakes as he passed them—five, six, seven—and tossed them into the high grass.

The starlings kept coming, filling the branches with black. They seethed, flapped their wings, all the time screeching and squawking. He cradled the shotgun under the windbreaker, lifted it, and without aiming, fired a blast into the trees. A few starlings fell, and those nearby exploded into flight. He fired again, and several more birds spiraled out of the blue-red sky. More birds rose into the air, whirled above him like dark memory. He jammed two more shells into the barrel and fired quickly. The horde of starlings burst from the trees and joined the others, screaming to themselves, a mass of darkness like a tornado against the fading light in the west.

WHAT SHALL BECOME OF ME?

That spring morning Alvie Drayton rode the school bus down Highway 14 toward Marion, Alabama. She sat over the back tires where the noise was so loud she couldn't hear the other children shouting. The girls up front talked and giggled about the boys, and the boys yelled at the girls, but Alvie gazed out the window where the sprigs of beech and laurel pressed from the drab background, and the dogwoods glittered like pink and white stars.

When the bus stopped to pick up Derrick McKey, the tire noise stopped too, and Winnie and Lavanna came flying down the aisle. "Winnie says Tyreese love her," Lavanna said. "You hear that, Alvie? Winnie says Tyreese tol' her that."

"He did," Winnie said. "I known Tyreese a long time, and he tol' me."

"Bull-*she*-it," Lavanna said. "You lie! Oh, you do lie! She lyin', ain't she, Alvie? What do Tyreese say?"

"Just because he's my brother doesn't mean I know about his love life."

"Tyreese be six years older than you, Winnie. He ain't interested in lovin' you."

The bus started up again, and Winnie and Lavanna went back down the aisle to their seats. Alvie pressed her forehead to the cool window. She felt the bone slide on the smooth glass as the bus vibrated and bounced. The tires sang again and drowned out the voices.

The woodland gave way to fields of green winter wheat, then the ugly stumps of a clearcut, and then the church. The church didn't look like the ones in Marion which had pitched roofs and steeples and were made of stones from the old quarry. This was a cinder-block rectangle by the roadside, crowned with a low roof. After the church were more fields plowed for cotton and the white gate of the Beaufains' hunting place, then a stretch of pinewoods again before the creek.

The creek was Alvie's favorite place. The bottomland was a brushy tangle, and every day she anticipated seeing the water. The bus tires changed pitch over the bridge, and then the creek was there: black water with the sun and shadows dancing through the branches. From the middle of the bridge, her favorite sycamore tree was visible for a second, canted over the slow current at the bend, as if it were about to fall into its own wavery reflection. Its bark was pale gray-green and splotched, peeling from the trunk like human skin. Alvie longed to touch that tree, to climb into its low branches, and to look at herself in the flowing water.

The worst thing about ninth grade was getting people to leave her alone. Alvie didn't mean her friends—Lavanna and Winnie, or Derrick McKey, who was so shy he could barely speak. She didn't mean, even, the older boys who pestered her at her locker. "Hey, Alvie, can you shoot a basketball? Do you dribble between your legs?" She dismissed their rudeness as sad. She meant the teachers, especially Miss Ferris, whom she had for English and homeroom. The other teachers let her sit in the back because she was so tall, but Miss Ferris put her up front in the left-hand row by the windows. "Come on, Alvie," she kept saying, "you have to share what you know."

Sometimes Miss Ferris let her tutor the slower readers like Derrick, and Alvie liked that. She liked Derrick, and she got to sit in the cool hallway where the fluorescent lights hummed and the corridor diminished into a comforting, hazy grayness. But Derrick struggled so much with the words. *Business* in his mouth was *binnah* and *going* was *gwan*. "Don't you ever watch television?" Alvie asked him.

Before he left to work in the new automobile plant in Tennessee, her Daddy used to throw a football with Tyreese every evening until it got dark. Sometimes dinner got cold on the table, and Mama said grace over the slap of the ball going back and forth in the yard. "God bless this food to our use and that football to Tyreese," she said.

"Amen," said Lofton, who was a lineman, and that only because her Daddy made him play.

Once her Daddy came all the way from Tennessee to see a game, and every time Tyreese carried the ball, the crowd cheered. And every time they cheered, her Daddy got more silent. Afterward he had stood on the field waiting for Tyreese and Lofton, staring up into the banks of lights where the moths careened away into the darkness. "What are you so keen on?" her Mama asked. "We beat them Selma boys, and Lofton got to play. Tyreese scored three touchdowns."

"I taught Tyreese to play quarterback," her Daddy said.

But the coach and God had made Tyreese a running back, and when her Daddy went back to Tennessee, Tyreese didn't see anything wrong in being a hero. He drove around in their Daddy's Mercury as if he owned it, waving to all the people who knew he played football. He called himself "The Car Man" and Lofton "The Dirt Man" because Lofton drove a tractor for the Beaufains after school and on weekends.

Then one night Tyreese had an accident. He broke his leg and the doctors put two pins in it, and football and basketball were over. He healed all right—there wasn't much of a scar and no limp—but there was a slowness that wasn't there before, and he was out in the Mercury till late at night after everyone else in the house was asleep.

Brian Beaufain was the smartest boy in Alvie's class. In laboratory science he did all the experiments without mistakes, and in English he'd have answered every one of Miss Ferris's questions if she'd have let him. What bothered Alvie most about him, though, was he watched her all the time. He stared across the classroom and spied on her after school at the bus stop. It wasn't right for a white boy to stare at a black girl, and Alvie felt as if Brian knew she was hiding something.

One Friday morning Miss Ferris dreamed up a spelling match. She put Brian on the Wordsmiths and Alvie on the Spellunkers, and Miss Ferris selected words without going in any particular order. She gave Lavanna the word *careful* and Brian the word *disproportionate*, and in that way Miss Ferris manipulated the score so it was close. Near the time for the bell, when it was Alvie's turn, the Spellunkers were behind by one point. Miss Ferris gave Alvie the word *preposterous*. Alvie's team moaned and groaned. Brian Beaufain wrung his hands.

"Preposterous," Alvie said. "P-R-E-P-O-S-T-U-R-O-U-S."

The Spellunkers all cheered, but Brian Beaufain looked disappointed, and Miss Ferris smiled sadly. "Oh, Alvie," she said, "why don't you want to try?"

Sundays their family went to church. Tyreese and Lofton dressed up in white shirts and ties and dark jackets, and Alvie thought they looked so handsome alongside Mama and her on the bench. The Golden Harmonizers sang "Haven't You Heard the Lord Today" and "When I Arise," and Mama and Lofton sang the hymns loudly as if they meant every word. Alvie listened and only sang sometimes and watched everything that went on. Tyreese had the evil eye on Winnie.

After the hymns, the preacher stood up and shouted. "Are you a sinner?"

"Yes, oh Lord, I am a sinner."

"You gotta stop."

"Yes, oh Lord, I gwan stop."

"You promise me?"

"Yes, Lord, I promise."

"Now, you all know the ways of sinning."

"Amen."

"You know sinning keeps you from the Kingdom of Heaven."

"Amen."

Alvie didn't shout with the others. She drifted on her own thoughts. Sometimes she asked God questions directly, "Am I cursed or am I blessed?" Or, "Should I have spelled that word right?" Or, "If I can keep my secret, why shouldn't I?"

But God never answered.

"Pray, now, Brothers and Sisters," the preacher said.

Alvie prayed. She prayed for her Daddy in Tennessee and for her Mama and Tyreese and Lofton. And she prayed to get answers to her questions.

One afternoon Miss Ferris handed out scripts for a play. "Read these tonight," she said, "and tomorrow we'll talk about the parts. Tryouts will be Monday. Everyone will have a chance, and the ones who don't make it can make costumes and do stage design."

The next day Miss Ferris wrote the names of the characters on the blackboard in yellow chalk. "Alvie, which part are you interested in playing?"

"None," Alvie said. "I forgot to take the play home with me."

Miss Ferris looked around the room. "How many of you have read the play?"

A few hands went up, including Brian Beaufain's.

"You all have to do this," Miss Ferris said. She looked at Alvie and sighed. "All right, I'll give you through the weekend to read the play. Alvie, I'd like to see you after homeroom."

That afternoon after school, Alvie watched the floor where the dim reflection of the fluorescent lights blinked on and off. The talk and laughter of her classmates dissipated, and she heard Miss Ferris's footsteps come down the aisle toward her.

"Stand up, Alvie," Miss Ferris said.

Alvie stood up.

"Look at me."

Alvie lifted her head. She was as tall as Miss Ferris, and she looked right in Miss Ferris's blue eyes. Miss Ferris was pretty in a frail way. Her blond hair was short, and her skin freckled like wheat.

"You like me, don't you, Alvie?"

"Yes, ma'am."

"Do you trust me?"

"Yes, ma'am."

Miss Ferris nodded. "Does Winnie Cobb live near you?"

"Across through the pinewoods by the old quarry."

Miss Ferris paused. "What do you think Winnie's chances are?"

"Her chances for what?"

Miss Ferris lifted the top of Alvie's desk. Inside were the books Miss Ferris had lent her for tutoring Derrick McKey and the playbook. "Will you read the play?"

"Yes, ma'am."

"Do not say 'Yes, ma'am' to me. Say 'yes.' Will you read the play?"

Alvie nodded.

"Good." Miss Ferris smiled. It wasn't a real smile but a patient one. "You are smart," she said. "I don't know how smart. Winnie Cobb doesn't have this advantage. She's going to be in Marion or Selma all her life."

Alvie didn't know what to say, so she kept quiet.

Miss Ferris turned and walked back up the aisle. "I can't decide whether the lead role in this play is a boy or a girl, white or black. There is one boy who could play the part, and one girl." Alvie expected Miss Ferris to go on, but instead she gathered her schoolbooks and walked to the door. She paused and looked back. "Maybe you'll know," she said, and snapped off the lights.

Alvie got up early the next morning and made a fire in the stove. She heated water and, in case her Mama yelled at her to eat something, made grits. Out the window, sunlight spread out through the pinewoods.

"You gotta sweep today, child," her Mama called.

"All right, Mama."

But her Mama didn't get out of bed. Alvie ate her grits and drank some tea and then went outside. She surprised a redbird near the stoop. Dew was on the grass and on the windshield of the Mercury. Tyreese was asleep on the front seat.

Alvie climbed quickly up the embankment to the highway. From there the sky was wider—gray and white and pale. She started walking.

Compared to riding the bus, the fields moved by slowly. Winter wheat was up a good eight inches, and the furrowed fields, ready for soybeans or cotton, lay in perfect rows. Why had Miss Ferris asked that question about Winnie's chances? How did Alvie know what would happen to Winnie? Nothing would happen. Winnie would quit school and get a job and get married, or maybe not get married. Probably she'd have children. So what if she lived in Marion or Selma?

Alvie passed the Beaufains' gate. They didn't live on the land, so no one was there that early. She thought of going to the creek that way, along the main driveway, but just then a doe stepped up the embankment and tiptoed across the road. Her hooves clicked like stones on the pavement, and she dropped down on the other side into a thicket. A fawn followed, but it stopped in the middle of the highway. It stared in Alvie's direction as if it smelled her but couldn't tell how far away she was.

A car was coming from behind, its windshield flashing in the early sun. The sound the car made changed as it crossed the bridge over the creek. The fawn didn't move, and Alvie ran forward and clapped her hands until the fawn turned and skittered back down the embankment where it had come from. The car screamed past, and the driver honked.

How would the fawn get to its mother? Alvie walked backwards till she reached the bridge, but neither the doe nor the fawn appeared again.

At the bridge she stood for a long time and let the sun warm her hands through the metal railing. The sycamore tree had leafed out into the thick green calm, and as the sun burned away the haze, its light made the leaves shimmer over the black water. Alvie tried to see a way she could get to the tree, but the water was high along the steep bank. It would have been hard to get through the brush, and who knew where there would be snakes?

That afternoon, Alvie swept the house. Tyreese and Lofton had driven Mama to work at the Woolworth's in Selma, and Alvie whisked the broom over the wood floor. Whenever she was alone in the house, she felt her Daddy and her old Gran around her. Her Gran was dead, but her love was like a gentle scent in the room. Alvie saw her in the chair by the window where she always sat because she was blind and gravitated toward the light.

Alvie stopped sweeping and watched the dust motes float in the sunlit air. She remembered the night in February when it was so cold outside, and the wind had come right through the pinewoods and into the house. She was eight then and had been washing greens in the sink. Tyreese was at basketball practice and her Mama at work, and Alvie couldn't remember where Lofton was. Her Gran asked to be moved closer to the stove, and her Daddy had carried her over to the heat, chair and all, as if she were nothing.

"Read me some, can you, Alvie?" her Gran had said. "I'm so hard to see."

"She can't read, Mama," her Daddy said. "You know she won't ever read in school."

"Oh, she can read," her Gran said.

"I've got to wash the greens," Alvie said.

"Get the Bible," her Daddy said. "I don't believe you can read."

Alvie knew he was teasing, but she dried her hands on her shirt and got the Bible. She pulled a chair up beside the stove so there was heat on one side of her and cold on the other. Her father pretended to look out the window into the dark back yard.

"What do you want to hear?" she asked her Gran. "You want to hear Job again?"

"Read me something new," her Gran said.

Alvie skipped through Exodus and Job and landed on the First Book of Kings.

Now King David was old and stricken in years; and they covered him with clothes, but he gat no heat. Wherefore his servants said unto him, Let there be sought for my lord the king a young virgin: and let her stand before the king, and let her cherish him, and let her lie in thy bosom, that my lord the king may get heat.

Alvie read in a voice more from the TV than from her friends, and every time she paused, her Gran said "Amen."

She read all the way to the third chapter, where the two prostitutes came before Solomon with the one child.

Then said the king, The one saith, This is my son that liveth, and thy
son is the dead: and the other saith, Nay; but thy son is the
dead, and my son is the living. And the king said, Bring me a sword.

Her Daddy moved from the window and went outside. Her Gran
heard his steps and the door open and close.

Alvie stopped reading. "Doesn't he want to hear?"

"He don't want to cry," her Gran said.

Alvie stared at her Gran for knowing such a thing. Her face was all lines
and wrinkles, as if her whole life had healed right there around her eyes.

"Start again," her Gran said. "I want to hear it again."

Alvie looked out the dark window for her Daddy, and when he didn't
come back, she turned back to the beginning of the book.

Now King David was old and stricken in years...

She paused a moment and looked at her Gran listening with her
whole heart, and Alvie put the Bible face down in her lap and spoke the
words just as if she were seeing them written in silver in the air. She said
all the names and places and everything that happened without ever once
looking at the book.

On Sunday after church, Mama and Lofton unfolded chairs for a
wedding, and Alvie had to ride home with Tyreese. The ground in the
parking lot was white with dust from cars pulling out so they couldn't
roll down the windows, and the inside of the Mercury was hot from
sitting in the sun. Tyreese had his tie off and his white shirt unbuttoned
halfway down the front. They turned right onto the pavement and
accelerated, and both of them wound down the windows fast. Alvie took
a deep breath and felt the wind on her forehead. Tyreese drove so fast
across the bridge Alvie only got a glimpse of the sycamore tree.

"Is that the place you used to fish?" she asked.

"Uh huh. Me and Lofton, we used to sneak in at the gate. You want to
go fishing?"

Tyreese passed three cars and barely got back in line passing another.

"What're you in such a hurry for?" Alvie asked.

Then she saw the old Dodge ahead and Winnie in the backseat waving to Tyreese.

When they got home, Alvie put some okra soup on the stove. Tyreese threw his jacket and tie into his room. "I got to watch basketball in town," he said. "When's the soup ready?"

"When it's hot. Mama wants some wood in."

"Yes'm." Tyreese went right out back.

Stirring the soup, Alvie watched him out the window. Tyreese took off his shirt, and his thick arms whipped the axe through the air as if he were going to hurt somebody.

Alvie went and changed out of her own white dress and hung up Tyreese's jacket and tie. When she came back, Tyreese wasn't there anymore. The axe was wedged in the chopping block and shirt over the handle. Pieces of pine littered the ground around the steps.

Alvie turned off the soup and went out into the yard. "Tyreese? Soup's ready." She picked up two or three pieces of wood and tossed them inside the screen door.

Then she followed the path to the garden and went through the honeysuckle hedge into the pinewoods. The path joined the abandoned quarry road, and before she'd gone too far, she heard Winnie's voice and then Tyreese's. They were arguing about something, and Alvie ducked behind a bush.

"I got a bet on," Tyreese said. "Hawks and eight points."

"How much?"

"Hundred dollar."

"Where you ever get a hundred dollar?" Winnie asked.

"I'm a working man," Tyreese said. "In a week I make more'n that at the cigar factory."

"What you gwan buy me when you win?"

Alvie looked out through the bushes. Tyreese and Winnie were standing next to the rusted car at the edge of the quarry. Winnie still had her pink church dress on, and she barely came up to Tyreese's bare shoulder.

"Don't know yet," Tyreese said. He smiled and lifted Winnie onto the fender of the car.

Winnie put her arms around his neck, and he worked his hands under her dress. Alvie didn't want to watch, but she couldn't help it. Tyreese's thick arms held Winnie tight as rope, and his face was glazed with sweat. Winnie unfastened Tyreese's belt buckle and drew down the zipper of his trousers. Then she shifted her legs a little so her dress rode up higher.

The next day Alvie said she was too sick to go to school. Her Mama sat on the bed and laid her palm on Alvie's forehead. "You ain't got no fever."

"It's my stomach." Alvie said.

"You got the month blues? We all done it and get by."

"Mama, it ain't that kind of sick."

A car horn sounded out on the highway, and her Mama gave her a kiss and pulled the sheet up. "I got to run. You take good care of yourself."

Alvie got up as soon as her Mama was gone.

She'd only skipped school once before, when she and Winnie hitchhiked to Selma and stole some candy and cigarettes. Alvie had looked behind her that whole day. "What you so scared about?" Winnie had asked. "If we get caught, what are they gwan do?"

Alvie knew her Daddy would have done something about skipping school, but this time he wasn't home. Anyway, she felt a different scared—all nervous. She roamed the house for a while and then went out back and sat on the steps. There was weeding and hoeing to do in the garden, but if she did it, her Mama would know she wasn't sick, so she sat and listened to the cars hiss by on the other side of the house. The sun shone off the white clapboard and warmed her bare arms. She tilted her face to it and closed her eyes and touched her shoulders which were like hot silk. The heat swarmed in her skin. She slid her hands from her shoulders and across her breasts and down between her legs where the scared ached in her something terrible.

That lunch Alvie read the play. It was about a girl who loved music. She wanted to listen to music all the time, but she couldn't because the government of the country where she lived wouldn't let her. It didn't say why. The girl didn't have a name, either. The script called her YOUTH and her friends were FRIENDS.

Naturally the girl got into trouble over the music.

FRIEND: You can't turn it up louder. They'll hear us.
YOUTH: I want to listen. What good is music if you can't hear it?
FRIEND: You have to listen to it silently.
YOUTH: That's not good enough. (YOUTH turns up the radio much louder.) I want to hear the notes.

The script didn't say what kind of music it was. Alvie guessed it was Taylor Jethro or Prince, but for all she knew it was a symphony. Of course the girl and her friend got caught. They were brought into court for a trial, and the radio was presented as evidence.

YOUTH: It's just a box with some wires in it.
PROSECUTOR: Were you listening to it?
YOUTH: What if I was? The radio broadcasts lots of things.
PROSECUTOR: When the agent found you, what were you listening to?
YOUTH: (After a pause) Music.
PROSECUTOR: You admit you were listening to music?
YOUTH: I was listening. My friend wasn't.

Alvie wondered why the girl didn't say she was trying to find a station with a baseball game on it, or maybe a speech by one of the politicians. Telling the truth got you into trouble. She remembered the time she and her Mama had been in the Lancasters' store. Mr. Lancaster was ringing up the items and chatting with Mama about Tyreese. Alvie noticed the prices he punched in on the register weren't the ones on the shelves—ten cents more for milk, four cents a pound more for cornmeal, three for soup.

"Mama, he's not doing the prices right," Alvie said.

Mr. Lancaster smiled at her. "What are you talking about, child?"

"Soup's twenty-seven cents on the shelf, and you charged thirty-one."

"Hush up, now, Alvie Drayton," her Mama said.

Mr. Lancaster rang up the rest of the groceries right, and her Mama paid ten dollars on her account, as she always did, because she couldn't read. When they got outside, her Mama took good hold of her arm. "Don't you never do that again. What if he don't give us no more credit? What if he gets in trouble with some folks and closes the store? You hear me?"

Alvie heard, but anyway, she didn't see why the girl in the play didn't lie. She and her friend got convicted and sentenced to a work school. They had to make clothes for people in the army, and while the girl worked she made up music and sang to the rhythm of the sewing machines. Then one day the electricity went off, and the machines stopped. The girl was singing loudly.

She was sent to another factory where they made license plates. Alvie expected the girl would escape from the factory and go live with a rich uncle who made violins, or maybe fall for a boy who had a secret room where he played the guitar. But instead she went deaf. The noise from the license-plate factory broke all the tiny bones in her ears. Alvie wondered how the play could end that way.

She was thinking about this and about what it would be like to be deaf, when she heard the screen door open.

"Alvie, you here?"

There was a pause.

"Alvie?"

Winnie came into the room.

"I was pretending I was deaf," Alvie said.

Winnie smiled at her. "You ain't sick, are you? You don't look sick."

"I am. I'm scared."

"Miss Ferris said I should bring you some books," Winnie said. She dropped three books on Alvie's bed.

"Did you try out for the play?" Alvie asked.

"Nobody did. Miss Ferris put it off till you be there." Winnie looked at herself in the mirror over the bureau. "You see Tyreese today?"

"I heard the Mercury this morning. I guess he went to work."

"You know if he won that bet?"

"What bet?" Alvie asked.

"He's gwan buy me something. I been thinking about him all day. Real close, you know what I mean? You ever think of a man, Alvie?"

"If he won a bet," Alvie said, "I'd have heard about it."

The tryouts for the play began the next morning. Miss Ferris gave the class a choice between reading the prosecutor's tirade asking for the girl's conviction or the girl's soliloquy about how music made her feel. Everyone stood up and read aloud.

It was painful for Alvie to hear Hope Johnson slur her words and Derrick McKey mumble. How could any of them be in a play? And all Miss Ferris did was nod. Brian Beaufain read the soliloquy about music. It startled Alvie to hear the part in a boy's voice, and Alvie could see how Miss Ferris might think YOUTH *was* a boy.

After Brian sat down, the class was quiet. The next in line was Winnie.

Winnie folded the script in her hands. "I can't," Winnie said.

"Why can't you?"

"I lost my voice."

The class giggled. Winnie smiled.

"Why don't you stand up and try a few lines?" Miss Ferris asked.

Winnie shook her head. Miss Ferris waited. The room tightened up, and, to avoid a scene, Miss Ferris called on Arthur Davis.

Arthur was a plump white boy with almost no hair. He rolled his eyes and raced through the prosecutor's speech in a loud voice, the words coming out half-formed and garbled. Alvie wanted to yell at Arthur to slow down.

Then it was her turn. She stood beside her desk and didn't say anything.

"Alvie?"

"I'm not going to read a part," Alvie said.

The class laughed and whispered, and Alvie looked around the room. Brian Beaufain was staring at her.

"What are you looking at?" she asked across the room.

"You," Brian said.

Miss Ferris stood up from her desk. "Alvie, why don't you…?"

Alvie walked over to Miss Ferris's desk and handed her the playbook. Then Alvie turned around and stood in front of the class. Everyone quieted at once. Alvie hesitated.

"Let me tell you why I love music. It's not, as people say, because it's the language of the heart. What do I care about that? What I love is that it's the language of the imagination…"

Alvie spoke clearly and slowly in the voice she had used reading to her Gran. She saw all the words like silver in the air, and no one in the class said anything when she finished.

The next Saturday, Alvie got up early again. She was going to sneak through the Beaufains' gate and find the back way to the sycamore tree, but there was a note on the kitchen table in Tyreese's illegible scrawl. She tilted it to the pale light from the window.

Alvie, I got to talk to you. Don't go nowhere.
Tyreese

She crumpled the note in her hand. She wanted to get to the gate before anyone else came, before it got too hot. And whatever Tyreese had to tell her couldn't be good.

She looked into Tyreese's and Lofton's room. Lofton was asleep. He looked as though he could sleep forever, tired out from farming, but Tyreese had flailed off his covers and breathed as if he were dreaming of something frightening. Almost as soon as Alvie's shadow got to the doorway, Tyreese jerked wide awake.

"You got something to say?" Alvie asked.

Tyreese pointed toward the door. "Outside," he said. "Wait for me."

Alvie slipped past her mother's room and opened the back door. The sun was low in the spidery trees to the east, and she walked out to the garden. It was coming up in the rows, one left empty for luck. Alvie kneeled down and plucked a few weeds around the beans and listened to a Bobwhite calling from the hedgerow.

Then Tyreese came out. He turned over a bucket, sat on it with his long legs splayed out, and watched her for a few seconds. He took a cigarette from his shirt pocket and held it in his mouth without lighting it.

"Winnie told me," he said.

Alvie kept on weeding. "Told you what?"

"About the play...What you did."

"So?"

"You remember when me and Daddy used to throw that football?"

"Sure, I remember."

"I think about it all the time," Tyreese said. "I wonder where Daddy is right this minute."

Alvie leaned back on her heels. "I never knew you thought about anybody but yourself."

Tyreese smiled, but the smile had the same slowness as his leg. He lit his cigarette, and smoke curled above his head. "I guess he's sleeping," Tyreese said. "I hope he is. But I know this. He don't want you to be no running back. He wants you to throw the ball."

Tyreese's face was crisscrossed with the shadows of the trees, and he looked so tired. He looked to Alvie as if he were going to cry. She saw all those hours he had thrown the football in the yard and all the ones he would throw it with no football and no field. She thought of all the hours at the cigar factory—not the ones he'd already worked, but the ones he hadn't worked yet. She got up from the garden and kneeled down in front of him. She put her arms around him, and he put his arms around her. She could feel Tyreese shaking. He said, "Alvie, oh Alvie," as if it were the end of the world.

She didn't go to the sycamore tree that morning or the next morning either. Sunday she had to go with her Mama and Lofton and Tyreese to church. Her Mama shouted as she always did when the preacher spoke, but Alvie was silent. When it was time for praying, she didn't pray. She watched Tyreese watching Winnie, though now and then Alvie gazed up into the high clear window where the sun came through.

After that Sunday, she didn't have time to go to the sycamore tree. Miss Ferris had given her a lot of new books, and she had the play to do, and she was too tired. One afternoon, though, she left school early without telling anyone and walked home. The sky was low and white, and the air so humid all there needed to be was a noise to set the rain falling. As she walked, she sang a hymn her Daddy had sung to her, "Oh, God, I am the little one. What shall become of me?"

She didn't know how long she stood on the bridge. The sycamore tree wasn't so noticeable anymore now that the woods were full of leaves. The black water swirled sluggishly under exposed logs where turtles slept, and, in the shallows, a heron twitched nervously, waiting for a minnow to swim close. Once a hawk called from the deeper woods—KEE-AH, KEE-AH. It sounded like a child's cry. The hawk rose from the green leaves into the white sky, and Alvie watched it soar until it disappeared.

The couple across the way in the Airstream had been parked for a week and had barely been outside. Julius had admired the way the man had leveled the trailer so precisely on the pad, detached the Ford truck, and, smoking a cigarette, hosed down the truck and the skirting of the trailer. He was tall and lean, silver-haired, wiry in the arms. He wore a white undershirt, blue jeans, and the kind of pale blue sneakers that were sold in K-Mart. His skin was very pale, which Julius interpreted as corroboration the man and his wife had just arrived from up North; the trailer and the truck had Wisconsin plates.

"They just sit inside," Julius said. "No walks, no horseshoes, no social life. He changed the oil in the truck the first day and hasn't seen the sun since then." He stopped pacing and looked at Valerie, who was mending a red and yellow quilt under the awning of their Vacationeer. Julius shook his head and drank from the beer in his hand.

"How do you know they're sitting?" Valerie asked.

"What do you think they're doing, dancing?"

"Maybe they're playing Scrabble," she said. "Or cards. I wish you'd play cards."

"That's sitting," Julius said. "Same thing." He squinted at the Airstream and then beyond it to the row of palm trees along the highway where the clustered fronds made a descending line toward the levee in the distance. "And I don't see why you have to mend that quilt. Why can't Lynn sew her own things?"

"It's a favor," Valerie said. "Surely you don't begrudge your daughter a favor."

"I don't begrudge anyone who works a favor," Julius said. "I'll buy any orange picker a beer. But why doesn't she get a job? Isn't that what women do these days when their husbands leave them?"

Julius had always worked. He'd had a scholarship job in college, went into the army, and then owned a small printing business in Minneapolis. He'd put in fourteen-hour days doing the design, typesetting, sales, and bookkeeping. When he sold the business, he and Valerie were able to retire comfortably, if not extravagantly. They spent winters where they wanted to. They'd tried Florida and Arizona, but South Texas was best, Julius thought—less crowded, not too dry, the ideal temperature for short sleeves.

Besides it was less civilized. Texas was a state of independence, the only one that, at one time, had been a separate country. And South Texas practically spoke a foreign language. Julius had enrolled in a Spanish class in McAllen so he could get around in the grocery store.

Valerie would have been happy anywhere. She sewed. She watched the birds at her feeders—orioles and green jays and chachalacas. She drank iced tea, and every now and then ate a chocolate chip cookie from the moisture-proof bag she kept beside her on the table. Forty years ago, when they'd met at an officer's club dance, she'd been a striking woman. He hadn't been able to keep his eyes off her. And, besides her beauty, he trusted what she said, believed her gaiety was enthusiasm and her silences signs of love. Not that she ever lied to him. Her honesty was real. But, with the years, he'd expected more than a comfortable house and a yard. He'd wanted trips to Alaska and the Yukon—a cruise up the Inland Passage to Glacier Bay. He hoped for an excursion to the Far East where he'd been stationed during the war. But she preferred to visit relatives in Atlanta, or to see what the Epcot Center looked like, or to spend the day shopping over in Madison.

Julius set his beer on the table and stepped from the shade into the warm sun, which glanced as if from a mirror off the corrugated tin roof of a farm building in the orange groves across the road. He positioned himself so the glare twisted in the fronds of the nearest palm. Every morning he walked on the levee that carved a straight line of yellow and green in front of the tangle of the floodplain. The levee was a raised track, patrolled occasionally by the border police, and Julius liked the view to the north over the plowed fields and orange groves and to the south over the tangled trees and vines toward the river. Mexico was only a few hundred yards away.

The Airstream was a medium to small one, much smaller than the Vacationeer. It looked to Julius like the World War II airplanes he had ridden in, with rivets visible in each scaly silver sheet. He couldn't imagine what it was like inside, but it had to be cramped. How any two people could survive each other for a week in such a small space was a mystery. Their names were Elaine and Harold Stanton. Julius had found this out from the manager of the RV park who'd showed him the register. LaCrosse, Wisconsin, was their hometown, and they'd paid in advance for January and February.

He'd seen the woman twice, though he wasn't always there to watch for her. She'd gone across the highway once to Zaragoza's store, and Julius had followed her at a respectable distance. Many of the women in the park had let themselves slide—Valerie among them—because what was there in old age to keep fit for? But Elaine Stanton had trim hips and a nice walk and no saggy skin in her upper arms. Traffic on the highway kept her from crossing, and he'd caught up with her at the edge of the pavement. She looked considerably younger than her husband, with salt-and-pepper hair cut so short it molded to the roundness of her head. Her skin was smooth, too, and not so pale as her husband's. It was weathered, Julius thought. She must have gardened and raked the leaves in their faraway yard, while her husband went to a factory or to an auto repair shop.

Julius had meant to speak to her—to ask how she liked McAllen, what the weather was now in Wisconsin, how old her children were, if she had any—that's what people talked about in the park. But the traffic was noisy, and something in her demeanor kept him at bay. She'd glanced at him but hadn't smiled, and he felt in her expression an odd intensity he couldn't decipher. He pondered her message, if it was a message, and when he scanned down the highway to check for a break in the traffic, she darted across between two cars, leaving him there at the side of the road.

When they came south, Valerie brought with her a number of projects— mending Lynn had accumulated during the spring and fall, crosswords Valerie had saved from the Sunday papers, two or three Reader's Digest Condensed Books she wanted to read. Valerie was always writing notes to Lynn, as if Valerie were Ann Landers. She told Lynn of the virtues of politeness in the laundromat, how to keep men friends, what moral position to adopt on the question of aged animals. Julius read these notes sometimes when Valerie took her afternoon nap.

Lynn was forty-four and had learned long ago to ignore advice. Sure, it wasn't easy for her when Peter left. She'd had to make adjustments. Like her mother, Lynn was pretty, and she'd had more chances in life than those less attractive, but looks could be isolating, too. People were afraid to approach you, and your standards were higher. Other people wouldn't admit pretty people suffered.

Still, the divorce wasn't what Lynn had made it out to be. Peter had been fair. He'd given Lynn the house and the better car and a good share of the cash. Peter knew how it looked to the neighbors—that he'd left for no good reason—but afterward Peter confided to Julius he'd left because Lynn was having an affair.

Julius hadn't told Valerie this detail. Valerie saw Lynn as the blameless victim, and to have informed her otherwise would have caused her grief beyond measure. What good could it do? Valerie would have examined the subject endlessly, but nothing would change.

Since the divorce, Lynn had become a fitness freak—a runner, aerobic dancer, even a weight-lifter. Julius thought her obsession was atonement for her infidelity, productive from the standpoint of physical health but enervating psychologically. He felt sorry for her. What she should do, he thought, was to move to another city while she was still young, get a job, and leave the past behind her.

The Orange Grove RV Park was on the east side of Farm-to-Market Road 2062. It was a dollar a night cheaper than the state park, and the trailer sites were larger. Valerie liked the modern showers and the social hall, where every night there was bridge, a lecture, a slide show, or dancing. Julius liked the orange trees. At the back of the park and all around it were so many orange trees he couldn't begin to count them, each with hanging fruit. The smell of oranges permeated every breath of air.

Julius had never been able to sit still. He'd towed the VW Jetta from Minneapolis and had gone on the nature tours at Santa Ana and Laguna Atascosa National Wildlife Refuges, had scouted out McAllen and Harlingen and Padre Island and the dams at Falcon Lake and Anzalduas. He dragged Valerie to Laredo one day, and another time to Brownsville, where they crossed the border to shop in Matamoros. Once they'd gone to the beach, all the way out to Boca Chica, where the Rio Grande emptied into the Gulf of Mexico, and he drove for miles on the sand.

It was a natural extension of his curiosity to want to know more about the Stantons. "Don't you wonder what they're doing?" he asked Valerie. "Two people come down from Wisconsin to be in warm weather and never see the light of day?"

"Leave them be," Valerie said. "If they want something, they'll ask for it."

"Something isn't right," Julius said.

He ran his hand over his smooth cheek to make certain he'd shaved that morning, smoothed the thin wisps of hair on his head, and tucked the bottom of his T-shirt into his shorts.

"Don't interfere," Valerie said. "Julius, can't you be still?"

"It isn't interfering to be friendly," Julius said.

He crossed the empty space between the two trailers and knocked on their door. Elaine answered.

"It's you," she said. "What do you want?"

"I thought your husband might want to throw some horseshoes," Julius said. "Is he here?"

"He's not my husband," the woman said. She turned from the door without opening it wider. "Harold, do you want to throw horseshoes?"

"Horseshoes?" Julius heard the man say. "No. Who's that?"

Julius peered through the space between the door and the jamb, and his eye caught the kitchenette, a tiny alcove where water was boiling on the stove. Dirty dishes were piled on the counter, along with a nearly empty half-gallon of Ancient Age and an ashtray full of cigarette butts. He could hear the man and the woman talking behind the door.

Finally the woman looked out. "He isn't feeling well," she said. "Maybe another time."

"Anything I can do?" Julius asked.

"No." The woman started to close the door, then hesitated. "Wait a minute." She again engaged the man in conversation and came back. "There is something. Do you know the shops around here? Are you going anytime soon to McAllen?"

"I can," Julius said, "and I speak Spanish."

"He needs a notebook."

"A notebook? What kind?"

"Is that what you want, Harold?"

Julius heard movement inside, and Harold appeared at the door. A thin wash of white whiskers covered his jaws, and his eyes were narrow and reddish. Julius smelled alcohol.

"A notebook," Harold said. "I need to get some things down."

Julius glanced at Elaine, standing behind. She shrugged and looked away.

"A small one?" Julius asked. "A school-sized lined one?"

"A movie wouldn't do it," Harold said. "If I made a movie... but I'm not about to do that. We weren't a family to take movies. Not videos, either. Not even photographs. My sister died last year. And her children, they all moved to Seattle. Who's going to keep track of all these people?"

Harold's eyes looked tired. Julius thought he'd maybe been drinking and had been awake for days. "You want to write a history, is that it? Something about the family?"

Elaine looked back at Julius. "He's never mentioned this," she said. "Where it comes from I don't know. He's been sick, and then, out of nowhere, he gets this energy."

"And the dreams," the man said. "All these dreams I have. We're old. We have things to tell."

Julius knew of a shopping center not far down U.S. 83, but he stopped first at a supermarket. He refused to go to Walmart. The market had about what he expected—tablets, notepads, ring binders, spirals. What did the man want to write about his family? Anecdotes? Sporadic memories? A chronology? If Julius had had more of an idea who the man was and his education, he'd have been able to pick out an appropriate notebook.

Anyway, to write took spelling, grammar, the right vocabulary. The man seemed determined, though, and, Julius supposed, you could communicate with mistakes, too. If you wanted to do something badly enough, you'd find a way.

He bought a spiral notebook with a soft yellow cover, a lined pad, and a six-pack of Bic pens. A school notebook wasn't what he'd have bought for himself. He'd have wanted a hard-cover writing ledger with plain paper. But a grocery store didn't have one of those.

He went to a new-and-used bookshop in the Don José Shopping Plaza, but all they had was bestsellers and how-to books and a slew of cheap paperbacks, many in Spanish. He bought one old hardback called *Las Flores de Mejico*, which intrigued him. There were no notebooks.

The center of McAllen was low-slung stores and bumper-to-bumper traffic. Winter was the season of snowbirds, but the town was mostly itself Hispanic. The Mexican influence was everywhere—taquerias, Electronicos Las Palmas, Eglesias de los Todos Santos. He found a stationery store on Avenida Reynosa that had notebooks—leather or cloth covers, bound, lined or with plain white or beige paper. They weren't cheap: twelve dollars for a pocket-sized one, twenty for the medium-size, and over forty for one with eight-and-a-half by eleven pages.

Maybe Harold Stanton was crazy, Julius thought. He looked a little off-kilter and frenzied, though maybe drink had something to do with that. Elaine had made that ambiguous shrug behind his back—what did that mean? Old people got confused and couldn't remember where they'd put their glasses or their car keys. They talked to themselves, or to people who weren't there, got exhausted walking around the block, and drifted into reveries. Harold had seemed vigorous and intelligent when he'd first arrived, washing the trailer and changing the oil in the truck, but what could one tell from appearances?

Harold and Elaine weren't married, for example. That was an interesting twist. How had the Stantons met? What had each seen in the other? Why had they come south together? Maybe they were having an adventure away from their spouses back home. Or they were widow and widower newly connected. Maybe they were brother and sister, registered under the same name.

People were supposed to be what they professed. That's what Valerie would have said—no secrets, no deceptions, nothing clandestine. He wondered what she'd have said about Lynn's affair.

He studied the notebooks, measured their weight, assessed the designs on the covers. He liked the craftsmanship of leather and thread, the texture of fine paper. He selected, finally, the most expensive book, with a cowhide cover and a gold edge. He bought a Parker pen, too, and three ink cartridges.

On the way back to the RV park, Julius stopped at a cantina on the corner under the overpass of U.S. 83 and had two or three beers, more like four, with some Hispanic men who worked at the fertilizer plant in Westlaco. He bought the pitchers of beer. Their wives were pickers in the fields or in the groves or worked in one of the industrial parks spawned by NAFTA near the border. Their children went to school, but, when the crops came in, they were let out to work. That was the gist of what Julius understood. He hadn't got every word because they spoke so fast.

On the straightaway to the RV park, he let the Jetta run up to sixty. Groves of avocados, limes, and orange groves on both sides of the road flashed past. Up ahead the arc lights of the trailer park shimmered under the fading sky.

Orange trees made him think of the tropics—lush, fragrant, soft but forbidding. He pulled the Jetta up beside the Vacationeer, turned off the engine, and heard the cooling fan click on. No lights were on in the

Airstream. He sat for a moment to see whether Valerie would come out to greet him or glance from the window, but she didn't do either one. Finally, he coiled the plastic shopping bags around his hand, extricated himself from the car, and walked to the dark Airstream. Valerie would say leave them be, but he'd had a few beers and wasn't ready yet to go inside.

The arc light above cast the Airstream in lavender, and Julius perceived it as a solitary outpost in the lush world of flowers. He saw no reason to be afraid or secretive, but he felt oddly uncomfortable. Let Harold write whatever was so important to him to get down. But if they were sleeping, he didn't want to wake them.

Julius paused and looked back to see whether Valerie had come to the window, but she hadn't, so he climbed the single step to the silver-lavender door and was about to knock when he heard voices inside. The voices were muddled through the metal, the woman's urging, anxious, the man's rougher, but tempered with sighs.

"Please," Elaine said. "Oh my God."

"Wait for me," Harold said. "I'm about there."

"Please, please, please."

"Oh, Jesus," Harold said.

"That's so good. Hold me."

Julius pressed his ear to the cool metal door, holding the notebooks tightly to his chest.

Julius stepped away across the grass and ducked into the orange grove. He'd seen movies and watched television and had heard similar voices, but that was *pretending*. This was real. He'd never heard the demands, or cries, or the careless talk of love. He was ashamed, not because he'd eavesdropped—how was he to know what they were doing in the darkness?—but because what he'd heard was foreign to him. Valerie, in their lovemaking, had never evinced such pleasure, never instructed him of her desires, if she had them, never begged for anything with such helplessness or urgency. He'd never inspired her to such joy as he'd just heard through the metal wall of the Airstream.

He walked away from the light and picked his way among the dark trees. A low moon splintered through the branches, and in minutes he was lost in the grove. All around him was the scent of oranges. He walked faster and, after several minutes, came to a fence which he followed toward the levee. At the corner, he slipped through the barbed wire and came out at the edge of a plowed field, a wide swath of dark earth ready for planting. To the south, the moon floated above the tangled floodplain.

The levee curved away from him in both directions, and he climbed the embankment to the road. The surface was caliche, nearly white, and he sat down on the berm. Lights from the farmsteads shone above the dark earth, and farther away the city of McAllen glowed above the horizon. A faint glimmer of pink still remained in the sky, but the floodplain was black. All through the trees the frogs and insects had begun their territorial warnings and displays, and beyond the trees the Rio Grande churned its way toward the ocean.

He took out the leather notebook and opened it. Moonlight creased the page, a white luminous rectangle. If it were his, what would he write in such a book? Would he start with his mother and father who had endured the Depression in North Dakota? They nearly starved, and their caution ever after had been the source of his own repressed fears, his long life of working. Or would he start with his own birth, after his parents fled the farm to Minneapolis? Is that where his own family began? What facts would he describe? He supposed he'd tell of his success at school. He'd describe St. Olaf, his working in the dining hall, that he hadn't made the football team and dropped out to join the army. After that, the days coalesced into marriage, Lynn's birth, and the long slide into the printing business.

Who'd disagree if he said he'd lived a good life? The facts were what you said they were. Valerie was a good person, kind and conscientious, but he'd never loved her. Should he write that? But if he thought of his life as a true story, he couldn't lie.

He stared at the shimmering page. What he wanted to write was his dreams. He knew what Harold had meant. They were old. What Julius would write, if he could be precise with words, would be the ache, the hollow, the gradual loss. He was never going to visit the places he'd have liked to see—Alaska, California, Mexico so close. The flower book he'd bought for the flowers he'd never identify. What was there to live for now?

A mockingbird sang in the dark orange grove behind him, and in the floodplain below him a heron squawked in a dark resaca. A slight breeze came across from the river and cooled his skin.

Maybe, Julius thought, it would be better to write nothing at all.

He closed the book and was about to get up when he heard beneath him, splashing in the resaca, the breaking of branches. At first he thought it was a javelina tearing through vines, or maybe a bobcat pursuing prey in the shallows. He lay down flat in the grass at the edge of the road. His heart jumped in his veins, echoed in his ears. This was the border, and Mexicans crossed the river all the time. Julius could not look: he listened. He heard twigs snapping. He imagined a man breaking free of the thorny brush, pushing his way through cattails. For a few minutes it was quiet, and then Julius heard the swishing of grass, a sound like sighing, as a man climbed the embankment. Julius stayed still for a long time, imagining the man crossing the white road and running then in the moonlight across the plowed field.

DITCH RIDER

Earlier that evening my nephew Scott had gone up to check the weirs and to make sure water was coming down the ditch. He had a date with Kim afterward, so he'd put on clean blue jeans and a plaid shirt, and instead of rubber irrigating boots he'd worn his blue and red leather cowboy boots, hand-stitched. He'd even combed his hair. Then he'd taken my dirt bike up the county road with a shovel across the handlebars.

That had been at six-thirty and still light. I hadn't noticed whether there was water until after dinner when I went out to piss and to settle the calves. It was dark then, and the wind had stopped. A few thin clouds rolled above the dry piñon mesas to the west. Chimney Peak and Courthouse, two granite blocks above the ranch, were slick with moonlight. It was bright enough not to need a flashlight. The ditch was empty. I could hear it was empty. But there had been water earlier, because a sheen of mud reflected moonlight, and water stood in the low spots.

One of the calves had pneumonia, and by the time I finished doctoring and got back to the house, it was after ten. I called Kim's house to see whether Scott was there and what he'd done up the ditch.

Kim's mother answered. "I haven't seen him," she said. "They all went to the movies."

"Did Scott go?"

"I don't know. Which one is Scott?"

She sounded drunk. "This is Jack Lindstrom," I said. "Scott's uncle."

"I'll tell Kim you called." And she hung up.

The summer had been real dry. A chinook blew most of June, and with the wind, the snowmelt was too quick in the mountains. By July, the creek that fed the ditch was lower by half, and now, in August, it was barely a quarter of what it had been at high water. Even when clouds boiled up over the mesa, they spilled off to the north without leaving moisture.

Some days I got a foot of water on my alfalfa, some days nothing, then half a foot. It was Pie Reynolds and the Leukers stealing my water. Water was scarce in that part of Colorado, almost as valuable as gold. Scott and I spent a portion of every day walking the ditch to make our presence known, but that hadn't done much good. What we really needed was a ditch rider. In the old days, a man on horseback made himself a decent wage riding a half-dozen to a dozen ditches and keeping the water running. He was judge and enforcer. There were no court or monkey-suit lawyers or the requirement of proof of damages. People who paid him got the water they had a right to.

I'd talked to Pie Reynolds a number of times, and Pie was most agreeable. Yes, he knew my property was the original homestead and had senior priority on the ditch. Yes, three feet were coming in at the weir at the creek. Yes, water had got onto his pasture somehow, but that was an accident. Muskrats undermined the ditch bank, or a diversion had washed out, or his wife had done the irrigating. He was sorry. It wouldn't happen again. But the next day, a foot of water was running into his meadow.

Jared Leuker wasn't so friendly. When I knocked on the door of Jared's trailer, he didn't come out. And we had an encounter a couple of weeks earlier, when I found him and his son Harry putting my water on their alfalfa. I asked what they were doing.

"What's it look like we're doing?" Jared asked.

"Irrigating with my water."

Harry stopped shoveling. "Go to hell," he said. "And get off our land."

"I have a right to walk the ditch."

"So walk the ditch," Jared said. "We're borrowing your water for a while. We ain't letting our crop burn."

I cut their water back at the places they'd already cut away the bank, but as soon as I'd gone, I know they diverted it again. The next time I came up the ditch there was a barbed-wire fence at their property line.

I was thinking about this, lying in bed, halfway expecting to hear Scott drive in any minute on the bike. I didn't relish calling the sheriff on Pie Reynolds or the Leukers, either. I was a peaceable man. I only wanted what was right, and notifying the sheriff—even if he wouldn't do anything—would only make them angry at me.

When I'd taken the job on Trinket McCormick's ranch, I knew nothing about cattle. My ex-wife and I had run a restaurant in Sedalia, Missouri, and after she left me for a salesman in Hannibal, I came out to Colorado to flyfish and figure out what to do next. I'd known for a long time my wife was playing around. I gave her ultimatums, but she switched from one man to another. She liked turmoil. One day she cared about me and promised to settle in, and the next she'd throw a glass at me across the dinner table. She kept me in limbo that way, until I started spending more hours at the restaurant. I made a pretty good business of it, too, but when I sold, she got half.

That summer I slept in the camper on the back of my pickup. With varying skill and luck, I fished the Yampa and the Gunnison and the Animas, but the time on my hands made me edgy. In the fall, I hired on with Trinket as a jack-of-all-trades master-of-none. She was the last of the McCormicks in the valley. Over the years she'd sold off land piecemeal to live on, each time deeding away water, but keeping the original priority in the homestead. I cooked her meals, did errands in town, chores around the ranch—fed cattle, doctored by a vet's textbook, irrigated the alfalfa and timothy. In November she broke her hip on ice in the driveway, and her niece took her to Denver and put her in a home.

That winter I learned the symptoms of pneumonia, how to administer sulfa drugs, the various ways cattle were stressed by wind and cold. I experimented with feed additives, got common sense tutoring from the bulls themselves about which bulls liked which others in the same pen. I read about marketing and transport, strategies to build up a weak herd, which was what Trinket had left, how prices depended on more than the demand for beef. And I learned raising cattle was more work than I wanted, because, no matter how you played the odds, you had no margin for error.

The other hired man, Dave Jenkins, left that winter, and I thought about bringing Scott out from Missouri. My sister's husband had been in poor health, mostly through his smoking and drinking, and Scott was not the easiest kid to have around. He was in trouble in school and maybe with the police—my sister never told me exactly—and it occurred to me he might like the ranch as a change of scenery. Having him help out would take the pressure off me, and I'd heard of city kids sometimes did surprising turnarounds when they were around animals. Or maybe I'd seen that in the movies.

"He's unruly, Jack," my sister Gail said on the phone. "I wouldn't wish him on anybody."

"I'm not anybody," I said. "And you're not wishing him on me. He can help."

"He won't be a help. I'll tell you that right now. He used to be a good boy, but I'm at the end of my rope with him."

"Then what can you lose sending him out here for a few months?"

"Don't say I didn't warn you," my sister said.

Scott wasn't so bad as Gail let on. He was more unmotivated than wild. He slept too much, didn't cut his hair, didn't eat right, and I admit he could be exasperating. Once I took him over to the San Miguel to teach him to flyfish, but he wasn't interested. He carried two cans of Coors in his creel, and after he'd drunk those, he'd gone back to the truck and listened to music on the radio.

I made him do chores, of course—mostly feeding cattle and watching the calves. He was good with the calves. He had a gentleness that surprised me, but I wouldn't say he enjoyed the work. He minded tending the calves less than he minded other work. He moped, but he wasn't sour, and he didn't whine. It was too bad he got no pleasure from a job well done.

What he liked least was ditch work. He hated wearing rubber boots and shoveling, checking the water in the weirs, cutting back willows. He didn't like walking the ditch to see who was stealing water. But he liked riding the dirt bike. That was my hook in him.

The phone rang. I'd dozed off a moment, and when I got my bearings, I thought it must be Scott, and I answered.

It was Kim. "Is Scott there?" she asked.

I looked at the clock beside the bed: it was a little past midnight. "I thought he was with you."

"I just got back from the movies," Kim said. "The bastard. I'll bet he's with Donna."

"Who's Donna?" I asked.

She hung up the way her mother did.

I lay there with the phone in my hand. Scott's curfew was twelve sharp, and he'd been pretty good about it. He'd missed one or two, always with some explanation or lie I could live with. Scott had never mentioned Donna, though he wasn't one to offer a lot of information.

An accident was the first thing I thought of. Scott wasn't home because he'd crashed the dirt bike. It was the kind of situation I dreaded—having to hope bad things weren't true. I thought of calling the state patrol, but it was early for that. The best thing that could happen was nothing.

So what I did was get up and put on my work boots and my dark windbreaker. Riding around the county looking for a motorcycle was a waste of time, so I thought I'd go up the ditch and make sure nothing had happened to him. I threw the shovel into the back of the truck and got wire cutters from the shed.

On impulse, I went back into the house and got my .22 pistol.

It had been hot that afternoon, but at that altitude, it was cool at night. I pulled the windbreaker to my throat and snapped the cuffs. The moon was higher, farther away it seemed, but still bright enough to see snakes in the road. I had a flashlight in the glove box to read the weirs.

I drove up a mile on the gravel and parked on the berm on the west edge of Trinket McCormick's land. I hefted my shovel out of the truck bed and slipped the wire cutters, a flashlight, and the .22 into a waist pack. Then I walked up the road.

From the top of a rise, I saw the arc light at Pie's yard, and beyond it several other lights shone in the dark. The ditch made a visible line across the contour: above it was sage and yucca and piñon, and below it alfalfa and buckwheat and timothy that grew on the slope down to the billowy cottonwoods along the creek.

A half mile farther, the road angled toward the mesa. Scott probably rode the dirt bike to the headgate because it made sense to check that first. Sometimes a log got jammed in the weir, or someone downstream cut us all off for the sake of another ditch. It was best to make sure the ditch was running before you started accusing people. In my experience, though, it was safe to assume the general case, which was that someone was taking my water. And I'd rather walk up the ditch than down.

Night was the best time to irrigate because the wind died off and the air was cool. Surface water didn't evaporate so fast as when the sun was out. Plus, it was easier to steal water when everyone else was asleep.

No water was running at the McCormicks' property line. The next two lots, each a hundred yards wide, belonged to an investor back East who was going to build an A-frame and sit on his deck and drink gin till his liver gave out. He didn't care about water. I walked his dry ground to the edge of Pie Reynolds's place where I found bike tracks on the gravel. But I couldn't tell when they'd been made or who made them.

I listened for a minute. A semi moaned on the highway two miles away. The Leukers' dog barked. Then it was quiet. I heard water trickling into Pie Reynolds's forty acres.

Not much water was in the ditch for Reynolds to steal, but he was taking all of it. I filled in the holes he'd dug in the ditch bank.

Magnussen's was next. He had second priority and usually was honest about what he took. But water was running onto his ground, too, so I shut him down. Three feet should have been at the weir coming into Magnussen's property, but in the flashlight only a foot and a fraction showed on the gauge. Three feet were supposed to be coming through the cement box, but instead it was one foot and a fraction.

Above the weir was where the Leukers had erected the new barbed wire fence—five strands of barbed wire strung so tightly I couldn't squeeze through. Scott had bitched about the fence, and I didn't blame him. I cut all five strands of wire and walked through.

The Leukers had an elaborate array of underwater hoses to siphon water under the ditch bank. I plugged the inlets with clumps of grass, tore out a board which shunted water through a cut, and dammed up another diversion with dirt. I did this quietly to keep the dog from barking.

The farther I worked up the ditch, the madder I got. What was going to stop the Leukers? I pulled another hose all the way through the bank.

Finally I came over a little rise and in sight of the trailer. The Leukers' dog heard me or got my scent and started barking from the porch. It was a Shepherd mix, big and broad-chested. It braced its legs on the top step, and its breath steamed in the moonlight.

I edged around in the alfalfa along the circle of light and stepped back into the darkness. I figured being that far away the dog wouldn't leave the porch, but Leuker might come out to see what the ruckus was.

And I was right. After a few minutes of barking, the light came on in the trailer, and then the porch light. The door opened, and Jared peered out in his undershirt and loose pajama bottoms. His dark hair and dark beard made him look like a crazy man blinded by light. He scanned for a moment and didn't see me and finally swore at the dog.

The dog stopped barking. Leuker closed the door, and the light went out.

I waited another five minutes. The dog lay down against the door where, from my vantage lower in the field, I couldn't see him. The light didn't come on again.

I felt underfoot the wet earth. Water was running everywhere around me. Something about the way the dog had barked and how Leuker looked worked into me. Or maybe it was my own sneaking into his field. But why was I hiding? I couldn't explain it exactly. Maybe it was not knowing where Scott was, or that what he'd done that afternoon against his will had been for nothing. What we both did on the ditch was nothing.

Leuker had cut a diversion right in front of his trailer, and the moment my shovel sucked wet ground, the dog barked again. He leaped down the steps, this time onto the hard uphill of the ditch bank. Now that he saw me, his bark was more savage. He came on toward me and stopped, and I raised the shovel to fend him off. He barked, snarled, and snapped at me, and I knew Jared would be up again.

I drew the pistol and, almost from point-blank range, shot the dog between the eyes.

The dog yelped once and fell forward into the ditch where he shuddered in the water and lay still.

Then I did something I didn't expect of myself. Instead of running away, I jumped the ditch and scrabbled up along the porch to the dark side of the trailer. The door opened, and the barrel of a shotgun protruded from behind the screen door. It was quiet in the yard. No barking. No sounds of trucks. No airplanes. The only sound was the murmur of water flowing in the ditch.

Leuker came out slowly, barefooted, still in his undershirt and pajama bottoms. He lifted the shotgun to his shoulder.

I waited until he was in the middle of the porch, several steps from the door.

"Leave it there, Jared," I said. "Point the gun at the ground. Don't even look around."

"That's my dog," Jared said. He gestured with the shotgun toward the ditch.

"*Was*," I said. "Put the shotgun down."

He hesitated, then bent over and laid the shotgun on the wooden deck.

"Now keep on toward the steps."

He took three or four slow steps and turned and shielded his eyes from the porch light. "Is that you, Lindstrom?" he asked.

I stayed in the shadow of the trailer. "Is Harry in the house?" I asked.

"No."

I aimed above Jared's head and squeezed off a shot. "Tell him to come out."

Jared glanced at the door. "Come on out," he said.

A woman opened the door and came out in a black slip. She was heavy-set and wore her hair short. I'd never seen her before.

"Tell Harry to come out, too," I said.

Harry followed the woman out onto the porch. Harry had a dark swirl across his cheek and a gut that ballooned under a white tee shirt.

He had on a pair of jockey shorts.

"What're you going to do?" Harry asked me.

I didn't know what I was going to do. Nothing, maybe. I was going to scare them. But seeing them like that in the light made me think these were people you couldn't scare. "I'm going to kill your daddy," I said.

"Bullshit," Harry said.

"I'm the ditch rider," I said. "You're stealing water, and I'm going to see you don't."

Harry laughed. "So who's going to stop us?"

I came out from the corner of the trailer into the light. "The punishment is what I say it is." I held the pistol straight out with two hands. "Now I want you to step down from there, Jared."

I motioned Jared forward, and then the woman and Harry after them. They went down the steps into the dirt yard. I picked up the shotgun and checked it. There were four shells in the magazine and one in the barrel.

They walked to the ditch where the dog was lying in the water. Water was backed up behind the body and flowed through the diversion cut onto the field. Blood curled up from under the dog's jaw.

I touched the woman's shoulder with the shotgun. "Get the dog out of the water," I said. Then I leveled the shotgun at Harry. "Harry, I want you to go down into the field."

"What for?"

"You walk thirty yards down in there and lie down. You hear me? Lie down on the ground and start talking real loud so I can hear you. Say, 'I ain't going to steal water no more.' *Say it.*"

"I ain't going to steal water no more," Harry said.

"If you stop saying it, I'm going to shoot your daddy like I shot your dog there."

The woman waded into the ditch and dragged the dog up onto the bank and sat down, breathing hard. She was shivering.

"Get going, Harry," I said.

Harry walked down into the alfalfa about where I had been. "It's cold," he said.

"You haven't felt cold yet," I said. "Lie down and start talking."

I held the pistol to Jared's head, and Harry disappeared into the alfalfa. That's what it took to be believed. Harry, at least, believed me. He started talking loudly.

I turned to Jared. "Now pick up that shovel, Jared. Close off the water."

Jared picked up the shovel and drove it into the earth, lifted a heavy load of sod, and tamped it into the opening. All the while the woman was muttering to herself and rubbing her arms. Harry was yelling and moaning down in the dark field.

When Jared finished, I took the shovel and pushed him up the ditch toward the headgate. He walked in the water because he didn't have on shoes.

"My nephew was up here this afternoon," I said. "You see him?"

"I ain't seen him," Jared said.

"He was here."

"Maybe he was," Jared said. "So what?"

Harry stopped yammering. He was crawling backward deeper into the alfalfa.

I fired a shotgun blast into the air, and Jared ducked.

"Keep talking, Harry. I can't hear you."

Harry started jabbering again.

"Louder," I said.

"I ain't going to steal water no more," Harry yelled.

I turned back to Jared. "What's the truth? You see him, or didn't you?"

"He was up here on a motorcycle," Jared said.

"And?"

"Nothing. He cut us back."

Ahead of us the creek was louder, and I shone the light across into the willows. The stream had a fair flow, and the weir was open. We stopped beside the cement box.

"How much water, Jared?" I aimed the flashlight at the gauge, past where Jared was standing.

"Three feet, a little more."

"You understand arithmetic?" I asked. "There's three feet coming through, and I'm supposed to get two feet at the end."

Jared didn't say anything.

"You see what I mean?" I asked.

"I get it," Jared said.

"I don't think you do," I said. "You get the arithmetic part. You understand the words. But you don't get the rest of it."

"Fuck you," Jared said.

I wanted to explain the rest of it to him, but I wasn't sure how. "I want you to kneel down," I said.

"What?"

"You heard me. I want you to kneel down right where you are in the ditch."

"You ain't going to do nothing," he said. But there was some doubt in his voice, and maybe a little fear.

"I'm thinking about it," I said. "Kneel."

He knelt in the water. His pajama bottoms were already wet and dragging low around his waist, and when he got onto his knees they drooped lower over his ass. The water ran fast around his thighs.

"I want you to pray," I said. "I want you to pray my nephew is safe, which he'd better be. And I want you to pray you're going to change yourself, so I won't have to come up here another time."

Jared closed his eyes. I could see his lips moving, but he might have been swearing at me and probably was.

I turned away and walked back down the ditch. I passed the dead dog and the woman sitting numbly on the bank rubbing her shoulders, and Harry who was still out in the field gibbering in the darkness. I cut the Leukers' fence down, and Pie Reynolds's fence, and I left the Leukers' shotgun stuck barrel down in one of the mounds of earth at Pie Reynolds's property line.

Scott was at the house when I got back. The dirt bike was parked out by the shed, its chrome fenders gleaming in the moonlight. I put the shovel and the wire cutters away and stood in the yard for a few minutes and watched the moon float above the mesa. The clouds had dissipated in the cold air, and stars were everywhere. Music thumped from Scott's room, strong and hard against the quiet. His windowpane rattled.

I guess I felt a little satisfied. I didn't expect things would be better with Pie Reynolds or the Leukers, but they wouldn't be the same, either.

I felt good about that. We'd have to wait and see what happened next.

And it would not be the same for Scott. The dirt bike was easy: I'd keep the key. The curfew, though, the lies—those were harder to fix. I'd heard enough lies in my life, and I wouldn't hear any more from him.

The music stopped, and the light in Scott's room went out. I heard cars on the highway, a hum that wasn't engines, but tires. From the mesa, somewhere in the trees, a coyote sang—a yap and a howl that never failed to thrill me. I yapped and howled back at it, then grinned at myself, and went over and sat on the leather seat of the dirt bike to wait for the water that, pretty soon, had better be coming down the ditch.

TWO MINUTES OF FORGETTING

The woman sat motionless in the cushioned chair staring toward the light coming through the window. Her name was Carla. That was almost all DuPree knew about her, except she'd been at her brother's house more than a year. DuPree spoke to her—it seemed the thing to do on meeting a person for the first time, especially one who did nothing all day but sit. She was facing the window, and DuPree stood a little to one side of the chair. The woman's expression didn't change, though from DuPree's absorption of light, a pale shadow fell across her features. Out the window DuPree noticed the gray sky, a lawn, a pond, trees heavy with the leaves of late summer. A few people strolled along the sidewalk at the edge of the yard. It looked as if it would rain.

DuPree asked how she was. He mentioned the weather, because he assumed at some time in her life Carla had experienced rain and snow and sunburn. He talked about the cars passing on the street, the wind moving through the trees—things he could see plainly. Since he could see them, he believed Carla could see them, too, though her eyes didn't move. She gave no sign she saw anything or heard what he said.

Her face had a pretty shape. Her nose was finely molded, and her eyes were light blue, flecked oddly with yellow. Her skin looked dry and weathered. Her reddish-brown hair was cut short, easy to care for, no doubt, for reasons of hygiene. DuPree fixed in his mind how Carla looked at that moment before the rain, before he started to play the piano.

Carla was the sister of a businessman DuPree had met at a weekend party on Long Island where DuPree's band had provided the dance music. That was what DuPree's life had come to—the dilution of his talent for the amusement of the rich, although he admitted the rich paid generously to be entertained. DuPree was not old—only forty—and he still had ambitions of composing great music. But times were difficult. The dot.com collapse had made money tight, and government subsidies for composers and artists had dried up. Orchestras had to play popular works to draw audiences. Risk and experimentation, always dangerous, were even more so now, and DuPree had resorted to private tutoring, which he hated, and had put together a dance combo with a percussionist, a bass, a cornet, a sax/clarinet, and a piano. All the musicians moonlighted.

Carla's brother had approached DuPree at a break and delivered a friendly, sad confessional fueled, DuPree knew, by alcohol. "It's my sister who makes me unhappy," the man said. "I know she'd like your music." "Does she dance?" DuPree asked. "No, no, she doesn't go out." DuPree imagined the woman as a cripple. "She's sick," the man said. He had gone on to tell DuPree more about his sister than DuPree cared to know. She'd been a graduate student in anthropology and was curious about the ancient peoples of the western United States. She'd been on digs in Arizona and New Mexico, and one summer had fallen in love with a professor who, when the dig ended, had abandoned her. DuPree had feigned interest. He'd been to New Mexico once.

A few days later, the man telephoned. "I spoke with some acquaintances in the city who know you," the man said. "One was particularly complimentary about your work. He said you were an excellent musician, but stubborn, selfish, arrogant, and not always agreeable to work with."

DuPree laughed. "I'm agreeable," he said, "if I'm not dealing with idiots."

"I'm not an idiot," the man said, "and neither is my sister."

DuPree was hired to play for Carla an hour a day. The room contained a chair, an oriental rug, a piano, and a bench. The piano was a baby grand, by no means a concert instrument, but it was tuned well and had a good sound board. DuPree, at the money he was being paid, had no cause to complain. He arrived at the man's house with his music at four o'clock and was let in by the maid. The first few days DuPree played show tunes, ragtime, and dance selections, thinking he was supposed to cheer Carla up. He played Cole Porter, Scott Joplin, and Gershwin. It wasn't his job to notice Carla's responses, but now and then he looked over to see whether she recognized the particularly famous pieces from *West Side Story* or *Fiddler on the Roof.* Carla sat impassively.

The second week was like the first. Carla gave no indication she knew he was there. DuPree played swing. He played jazz. He stumbled through a few Bach preludes and fugues and tried Brahms's shorter works as a way of listening to the techniques of the masters. He liked Schubert, too, particularly the lyrical parts. He murdered the music because he hadn't played those pieces in so long, but Carla didn't notice. She faced the window. Her posture was the same. Her breathing and her barren expression was the same. The only difference DuPree detected was the intensity of the light on her face. When the sun went under a cloud, the muted gray light made her eyes grayer-blue, and when the sun shone, her eyes were cerulean.

After a few weeks, DuPree called Carla's brother. "I've been there every day," DuPree said.

"I know you have. How's it going?"

"All right."

"You're having second thoughts?"

"Not exactly." DuPree didn't know how to say what he felt. It unnerved him to play for Carla. It was like playing for himself, yet it wasn't. He was as demanding as ever of his own ability. He felt the notes as keenly as when he played in his own apartment. He conjured up the stars and the wind and landscapes of diverse beauty. But he didn't know whether she heard him. That made the playing vastly different.

"She hasn't clapped?" Carla's brother asked.

"It's not a joke," DuPree said. "I've played a variety of classical studies, Broadway show tunes…"

"You shouldn't expect her to respond."

"I don't even know whether she *hears* it."

"Mr. DuPree, I'm not paying you for therapy."

"It seems as if it should matter," DuPree said.

"It's enough that you're there," Carla's brother said. "I'm satisfied with what you're doing, and I'm the one paying you."

DuPree kept on with the dance band because he didn't know how long Carla's brother's largesse would last, but he gave up his private lessons. He no longer advertised for students he knew ahead of time he wouldn't like, nor called friends who might know of teaching vacancies he didn't want to apply for. Instead he was able to idle away his mornings on his own compositions. "Idle" was his own term for what he thought of as luxury.

He composed two minutes of music at a time: that was how he worked. Two minutes was a long stretch, and it took hours, sometimes days, to finish one segment. Then he began another, weaving the first into the second, and so on, continuing the motifs, building on them, leaving them and returning again. It was tedious, but exhilarating.

At one o'clock, exhausted from his morning's work, he got ready to go to Carla's brother's house. He showered and shaved, put on a clean shirt and tie and a worn leather jacket. It was a twenty-minute subway ride to the train station, then thirty minutes by train out of the city, and another twenty-minute walk from there. In the warm weather, he enjoyed the fresh air. A park was en route, and the river path allowed a view across to the houses on the far shore. DuPree thought about what he had accomplished that morning, the new ideas he'd had, the thousands of scribbles he wanted to make tomorrow and the day after. Sometimes, as he walked, he jotted down phrases and chords. At the end of the park, he cut over two long blocks and was at the house.

DuPree had not inquired too diligently into Carla's illness. It wasn't his business why she was catatonic or why she wasn't in a hospital. He knew from the maid Carla was fed intravenously and that she had physical therapy for her arms and legs and internal organs. He'd read about catatonia, too. It was a choice the mind made over the body. The onset could be a single trauma or a gradual disintegration or weakening, so that a relatively small event could trigger a massive withdrawal. DuPree thought it better not to ask too much.

At the same time, he didn't ignore Carla's condition. She was in the room with him, after all, and he found himself theorizing about her psyche. He knew she'd been a brilliant student, that she'd suffered from love, and he imagined an interior drama to which she had responded *in extremis*. She was a cliff eroded by wind and rain, or a tree collapsed under the weight of snowflakes. Pandering to these notions, DuPree made up themes for his hour's music. He thought of picnics under stormy skies, sunlight on a beige landscape around Albuquerque, snow squalls in Taos—whatever struck his fancy. Usually the moods were upbeat, but sometimes, depending on what the weather was outside or how his work had gone that morning, he delved into contemplative ideas or melancholic motifs. Carla didn't notice.

In September, the cold rains came. Time acquired an eerie inconsistency—cold sun, gray, bursts of rain. Sometimes, instead of walking from the train station, DuPree took a cab, and when he didn't, he noticed people more than landscapes, as if the weather made him more aware of sadness. Near the train depot, women stood under awnings with their net bags and old men hid in doorways. Where would these people go when the snow fell? Fewer people visited the park, and DuPree felt sympathy for the women who watched their children on the swings or the maids who walked their employers' dogs.

Each day DuPree arrived at the house at the same time. The piano was in the corner. The oriental rug collected dust under Carla's chair. Everything was the same except the light. The light winnowed toward the winter solstice, but DuPree had never been so conscious of it. Each day, dusk came earlier; each hour he played, a little less light came into the room.

DuPree's programs dissembled. He started out improvising freely with thoughts of a summer lake, but he ended up on a dirty street outside his apartment in the city. Once he began with a sudden inspiration from Schubert and stopped abruptly, thinking of a flourish he had composed that morning. He played two minutes of his own music and stopped again, confused by the emotions which swirled through him. "What I try to do," he said, "is to compose two minutes at a time. Do you understand? What I just played was my own composition."

Carla didn't move.

He played the same two minutes and another two, then paused and made notations on a piece of paper. "Perhaps it's not so clear after all," he said.

He smiled at himself for speaking aloud.

One week in October all the leaves fell from the trees. DuPree noticed this walking through the park after a heavy rainstorm. The houses across the river on the palisade weren't shrouded anymore by the foliage, and he could see all the way through the park to the big estates that loomed on a distant hill. DuPree decided right then to quit the band. He hadn't thought of it before, but as soon as it occurred to him, he knew he'd wanted to escape for a long time. He had no assurance Carla's brother would keep him on, but why wouldn't he? Playing for Carla was like emptying the sea—it could go on forever.

That afternoon, DuPree called Carla's brother. "I'd like to change the routine," he said. "I'll still go everyday, but at different hours. Do you mind?"

"It's fine with me," Carla's brother said. "I'll see whether she agrees."

"You mean you can tell?"

"She's improving," Carla's brother said.

"How is she improving?"

"'Improving' is perhaps the wrong word. She's changing. Her posture is better. Her heart rate is up. Her muscle twitch is stronger. I'm speaking relatively, of course."

"That's good," DuPree said.

"The doctor isn't certain whether it's good or bad. We'll see."

The next day DuPree went at two in the afternoon. The following morning he went at eleven, and the next afternoon at three. He gave advance notice to the maid, and Carla, as always, was waiting in the room when he arrived.

He played Mozart and Schubert and Brahms, but he also he tried out his own composition. Why not? Carla didn't mind. Besides, the classical pieces didn't convey what he was after. The notes were smooth and sweet, but too long and too much like floating. DuPree wanted teeth. He wanted edges, broken spaces, sharp tones. In this he imagined a conspiracy with Carla: he thought she understood. Music was a language. He was talking to her. He didn't know exactly what he was saying, and Carla was hearing, though DuPree didn't know what.

In mid-November, with the holidays closing in, DuPree felt the financial squeeze of not working in the band. At the same time, though, he felt unbridled relief. He had no dreary parties to drag himself to, no car rides with the percussionist and the cornet player who talked about ice hockey and the latest insipid movies, no phony Christmas dance music to pretend to enjoy. The backlash of unhappiness DuPree usually felt didn't strike him at all.

Every day he woke early, made coffee, and sat down at his piano. The struggle with his work was the same—it went so slowly!—but energy surged through his fingertips. The neighbors complained about the banging on the piano, and he promised to be more considerate, but he couldn't help himself. He went on working day after day.

The hour he spent with Carla became an extension of the morning's work. While he rode the subway and the train, he played the music over in his mind, and when he was with her, he played on the piano the studies he'd done. He compared them to what he'd done in the previous weeks. "Right now these are separate incidents," he told her, "but I'm trying to make them interrelated, like a collage. In this section, I want to give the impression of chaos. Listen."

He played for several minutes, then paused. "The fundamental motif begins in the second part, clandestinely at first, then more dramatically. There's a shifting over, not necessarily toward order, but toward light. Light contains all the colors. I work by imagining certain objects like an iris, say, or a red boat, and then I try to separate the color from the flower or the boat and transmute that into notes. Do you see? It's not complicated."

He played what he had written of the second part.

"Now in a later part, I'm thinking of…" He stopped, realizing how pedantic he must have sounded. "No, I won't tell you. I'll play it for you when I'm finished."

He got up and carried the piano bench over to the window where Carla was sitting. He put the bench beside her chair and sat down. He gazed toward the street. It was snowing lightly, but the sun had broken through the clouds, and the air was peculiarly alive. Light glanced from the branches of the trees. DuPree said nothing. He simply breathed in and out in the same rhythm as Carla and stared into the hazy sunlight.

In January, with a cold gray sky hovering outside his apartment window, DuPree sat at his piano composing the first two minutes of the last part of the work he had called "Revelations." He was having a terrible time because the last part was to be light itself. He played combinations and sequences, but none sounded right.

At mid-morning the telephone rang. He assumed it was his neighbor complaining again, and he didn't blame the woman, but it was Carla's brother. "Mr. DuPree, I want to thank you," Carla's brother said.

"You're welcome," DuPree said. "What did I do?"

"You've been loyal to Carla."

"I've been to the house every day," DuPree said. "Even during the holidays."

"But it's a new year, and the facts are hard," Carla's brother said. "I've spoken to the doctor."

"Is she better?"

"He thinks she's upset by the change in her regimen."

"So we should go back to the regular time?"

"Or it could be the music itself," Carla's brother said. "Her neurological functions are markedly altered."

"She likes the music," DuPree said. "You've said so yourself. I know she'd forgotten how to respond to it, but…"

"On the contrary," Carla's brother said. "She remembers. She remembers everything. The disease is remembering."

DuPree was silent for a moment.

"At any rate, I'm calling to inform you I've encountered some personal difficulties. My wife has seen fit to purchase, without my knowledge, a townhouse in the city. The country, as you must be aware, is sinking into recession. Interest payments have mounted at a time when cash is short."

"Without your knowledge?" DuPree couldn't imagine anyone's secretly purchasing a townhouse in the city.

"The family's in flux," Carla's brother went on. "Such things happen. I'm very sorry."

At first DuPree didn't grasp what Carla's brother was sorry about. Was he getting divorced? Then he thought of Carla. "You're not putting Carla in a hospital?"

"No. Carla will stay here. I'm not deserting her. But I simply can't afford her the luxury of private music."

DuPree was stunned. "So it's me you're sorry for?" He took the receiver from his ear and laid it gently in its cradle.

That night DuPree had a fitful night's sleep. He knew he'd dreamed, but when he woke he couldn't remember what. It was unusual for him not to recall. He struggled to find clues to the dream—pathways, insights—but nothing came to him except the notion that the dream was something he needed to remember. He took a shower in hopes the hot water would coax the dream to consciousness. He could feel it was there, but he couldn't remember it.

He sat at the piano in his bathrobe but worked only sporadically. He kept jumping up and pacing. What would Carla think when he didn't appear? "She won't notice," he said aloud. Then, "Of course she'll notice." He sat at the piano and played several bars, but left off and got up and paced.

He couldn't fault Carla's brother. The stipend had been exceptionally good, and DuPree had been able to put aside a little money. It wasn't enough to rescue him—he had rent, utilities, food to buy. The savings would get him through a month or two at most. What then? Would he become one of the homeless who lived in alleys and doorways and disappeared in the winter?

But even worse than the future was the thought of the empty time. Going to play for Carla had taken three hours from his day—an hour's train ride and walk on either side of the hour he played for her. What would he do with himself?

The next day he woke late, sluggishly. He got dressed and went out for a newspaper. He had to look at the want ads. He had to plan, to set something up. He had to think about tomorrow. It was a cold morning, snowless, but icy. His breath feathered into the air. Habit led him to the subway station, but he passed the entrance and continued to Zeno's corner store where he took a paper from the stack and went in to pay.

"I haven't seen you around, professor," Zeno said. "How ya been? You been in love or what?"

"I've been around," DuPree said. "I'm not in love." He fingered one of Zeno's homemade cinnamon rolls and plucked an orange from the pyramid in the case. He laid the pastry on the newspaper on the counter and held the orange in his hand. It seemed odd to DuPree he could exchange something as worthless as money for something so beautiful as an orange.

Zeno rang up the items. "Looking for a job again, huh?" Zeno asked.

The thought of looking through the want-ads made DuPree's blood run cold. "I'm not looking for a job," DuPree said. "In fact, I don't want the paper."

"One-sixty, then," Zeno said. "You want a sack?"

DuPree ate the cinnamon roll on the subway. He licked his fingers clean. But he didn't eat the orange. He kept it in his coat pocket.

When he disembarked from the train, he walked slowly through the park. Almost no people were there—a family dressed up and hurrying along a path, perhaps to a funeral, and an old man walking a gimpy mongrel. The river was ice, and the houses on the palisade looked far away in the frigid air.

The maid answered the bell. "Mr. DuPree, what are you doing here?"

"I came to see Carla."

"But you can't."

"Why can't I? What's she doing?"

The maid looked confused. "Should I call her brother?"

"Call him," DuPree said. "Tell him I'd like to play for her. I'll do it for nothing."

The maid closed the door. DuPree waited on the porch. The lawn was yellow. Off to the left was a pond with a weeping willow barren of leaves bending toward the frozen water. Then DuPree remembered his dream. He had been out West—no exact place, but high in the mountains. He had climbed to a snowfield where the reflected heat and light were so strong he was burned. How could such white cold—ice, really—create such warmth and illumination? He turned away from the snowfield and saw only black, as if he were blinded.

The door opened. "Carla's brother says it will be all right," the maid said. She opened the door wider. "I've taken the liberty of wheeling her into the music room."

Carla was in the same chair facing the window. DuPree was certain her posture was stiffer than when he had seen her the last time. She stared straight ahead.

"I know. I wasn't here yesterday. I'm sorry."

Carla didn't move.

"I can be sick, too," he said. He took the orange from his coat pocket and put it on the top of the piano. Then he sat down on the bench and gazed at the keys. How familiar the whorls in the ivory were! The grain of cherry wood! He looked over at Carla. "No, I wasn't sick. I won't lie to you." He paused and extended his hands. He took a deep breath and began to play. Chaos reverberated through the soft air like stones falling from the side of a mountain. Then, overlaced, came the light, gradual at first—a sunrise expanding outward, DuPree thought. He imagined a stream cascading from an invisible source above him—the shining water, the sound of water rushing over rocks. That was what he was after. Each drop of water from the snowfield he couldn't see shone in the music.

Suddenly he left off. "Now you," DuPree said.

Carla's expression didn't change.

DuPree got up. He moved Carla's chair so he could see her more directly from the piano, and she could see him without moving her head. "You're going to compose your own music," DuPree said.

Carla stared straight ahead. The sunlight from the window caught one azure eye and made shadows of her nose, her other eye, and the slope of her cheek.

"I'll play the notes," DuPree said, "and you'll tell me whether they're the right ones. Let me know however you can. I'll play a single note and then another, and we'll put them together. Do you see?"

DuPree played an F. Carla didn't move.

"Start with the orange," DuPree said gently. "The color is like the sun or a neon sign." He played an A sharp. "Just two minutes is all. It will take us a long time. We'll have to practice." He played an A. "Perhaps the orange is fire. Perhaps it's the clouds at sunset. There's no hurry. You can tell me what you want to forget."

FUGITIVE COLORS

It was an ordinary Friday morning in Colorado Springs, late September, and I was in the back yard digging up clumps of iris. Eric and Millie were in school. I'd already potted asters, bleeding hearts, and coreopsis, dismantling my prolific flower garden, and imagined the distant spring when I'd plant a new garden at another house not yet found. We'd had several cold nights, and though the sun was warm on my back, a chill lingered in the dark earth. Even with gloves on, my hands were cold, and I rubbed them together to get the blood moving.

I carried the cardboard box of irises to the shed, then culled seeds from dead hollyhocks, larkspurs, and marigolds. My mother was picking me up at ten, and before that I had to check the children's overnight bags for their weekend visit with their father. Eric was twelve and packed what he needed, but Millie, at nine, was more scattered than she should have been. Sometimes she put in five shirts and no shoes, or, if Keith were taking them hiking, she packed dresses instead of long pants. Last week I found six Milky Ways and an entire package of Oreos inside her birding cap.

The kitchen was dark, or seemed dark, coming in from the bright sun. I poured a cup of coffee and carried it upstairs. I'd moved Eric to the room in the basement where the dartboard was so Millie could have privacy, and with his bed and dresser gone, Millie had created a bigger mess. Her bookcase was crammed with birds' nests and the walls were covered with pictures of soaring hawks, flights of cranes, flocks of shorebirds. I turned the page of her calendar from May to September, from a singing warbler to a Snowy Egret.

Her computer was on screen-saver, and her CDs were scattered over her desk. I collected them into their covers, put her dirty clothes in the hamper, and stacked her books. On principle I refused to make her bed. Her overnight bag was crammed willy-nilly, and I folded the clothes and packed them neatly. She'd put in everything except underwear and socks.

I got three pairs of panties from her top drawer. As I sorted through her socks, a flash caught my eye and something fell onto the floor. It was an earring—not a kid's bauble of tin and rhinestones, but an emerald tear-drop with old-fashioned screws. I found the mate and held them up to the light. The stones looked real to me; so did the gold. My mother wore studs, but she made a fuss over any gift she gave Millie, so they must have been from Keith's mother's estate. She'd worn an assortment of earrings. But why hadn't Keith told me he'd given them to her? Why hadn't Millie?

Millie was no beauty queen and didn't want to be. She had short brown hair cut above her ears, brown eyes set wide apart, skin flawed by two moles on her chin. When she was vexed, as she was frequently, she made an awkward sideways pursing of her lips. She was an endearing child, but often imperturbable, sometimes volatile. Even before the separation, she'd had tantrums for no apparent reason, and she was a frequent dreamer. In school she stared out the window or read her own books. Last year in science, she'd got up from her desk, fetched an encyclopedia, and read aloud to the class about churches in the Middle Ages.

I put the earrings back in her drawer and went into her closet to find a jacket in case Keith took them to the concert in the park. Pulling apart the hangers, I noticed a blue dress I'd never seen before. It was expensive, new or almost new, from Saks Fifth Avenue—taffeta with a white collar and lacy sleeves. It couldn't have come from Keith's mother's estate, or from Keith, either, whose tastes ran to blue jeans and turtlenecks. Immediately I thought of my father.

He and my mother had relocated from Seattle—he'd been an engineer for Boeing—and they'd bought a Santa Fe-style adobe near the Garden of the Gods. Before his retirement, my mother had tried to coax him into a hobby, but he wasn't interested in photography or woodcarving or golf. Enter Millie. He was calm with her, and she responded by being calm. They went for walks. She showed him magpies and scrub jays in the piñon-juniper foothills, chickadees in the scrub oaks, Red-tailed Hawks circling above the mesa in front of Pikes Peak. Millie was his love, the one star in his sky.

I found Millie's red windbreaker, laid it on top of the overnight bag, and added her toothbrush and vitamins to the books in the side pocket.

My mother arrived a little after ten in her green Pathfinder, and I slid into the passenger seat with my hairbrush, my head wet from a shower. "What's your problem?" she asked. "Were you fiddling in your garden again?"

"It's not fiddling," I said. "You look nice, Mom." She had on beige slacks and a pink shirt, and her hair was puffed and frizzed a shade of blonde I hadn't seen before.

"I should. I spent ninety dollars at the hairdresser's."

In Seattle she'd had "associations," as she called them—friends she had lunch with and an artsy group that took courses in ceramics, weaving, and silkscreening. She thought I needed to get out more, so she'd signed us up for a painting class at the Fine Arts Center.

"How is Keith?" she asked when we were driving.

"All right, I guess." I pulled my hairbrush through a wet snarl.

"I worry about him."

"Don't. You have Dad to worry about. Is he still exploring on the Internet?"

"Your father's your father, only more so."

"Has he been buying stuff for Millie on eBay?" I asked.

"Like what?"

"Like, maybe, earrings or a new dress?"

"Not that I know of. But he sits in front of that screen for too long. At least I know where he is."

She stopped behind several cars at a red light.

"Maybe you don't," I said. "He could be chatting with a twenty-year-old."

My mother stared at me. The light changed, and cars behind us honked.

The instructor, Luis Mendoza, was a man of small stature but great vigor. He wore the same green pants and a red-and-white striped shirt to each class. Usually, during the first half-hour, he made us draw quick sketches of one another with charcoal. Using a blunt instrument and a single tone gave freer expression to the hand, he said, which was the medium through which the eye and the emotions conspired. After that, we painted a model, if he had one, or a still-life. That particular day, after the sketches, Luis arranged a drinking glass with water in it, together with an orange and an apple and a sprig of leaves, but I chose to copy a landscape by Corot. I had copied other paintings, or rather photographs of them, to try to absorb the artists' color tones, moods, and compositions. I'd tried a Turner landscape, "The Lacemaker" by Vermeer, and a Velasquez miniature queen.

My mother pooh-poohed this effort. "What do you want to copy for?" she asked. "Why not participate in the class? See if you can do better than I do."

"We're not in competition," I said.

Luis roamed among us, answering questions, pointing out how shadows were defined, how to mix colors, the different ways to use perspective. After a while he came over to me. "Very nice," he said. "Good colors. Why Corot?"

"I don't know," I said. "Today I like gray."

Keith and I had met sea-kayaking in the San Juan Islands north of Seattle. I'd finished my degree in English at UW and was visiting friends on Lopez, and he was with a biodiversity class from graduate school at Colorado. I had nothing more in mind then than traveling to China and the Far East, seeing other cultures, looking around, and Keith assumed from this I was smart and adaptable. We were married thirteen years, and neither of us had committed any particular sin. Our separation was amicable. We'd split the liquid assets and credit-card debt.

His environmental consulting firm wasn't making much, but he paid modest support. He saw the children weekends and for special events like Eric's tennis tournaments or a birthday party Millie went to. I'd never had the complaints about Keith I heard from my friends about their husbands. He gave me space, if not permission, to take a Spanish class at night or help on the library committee. We had biking and skiing in common. He actually cooked a meal now and then, too—not frozen pizza, but shrimp pasta with mushrooms and garlic or a roast beef. He remembered birthdays and anniversaries, even my parents'. Our life together was okay, nothing was wrong, but I was uneasy. I didn't want to be, but I was. Like suspicion or curiosity, it weighed on me. I felt I had to do more or see what I hadn't before, though I couldn't put a name to my emotions. When, finally, I said I wanted a hiatus in our lives, Keith was astonished.

"Don't you love me?" he'd asked. "What about Eric and Millie?"

"I love you," I said. "They'll adapt."

"You're being selfish."

"Maybe I am. I can't explain it even to myself."

"Is there hope?" he asked. "Or is this permanent?"

"We'll have to see."

He had no choice but to move out, and after all that time together, we settled into a routine of puzzlement and sorrow.

Saturday, after Eric and Millie had left, I worked in the garden and played doubles with some women friends from the neighborhood. I took a long bath, ate a salad, and watched *The English Patient* on television. Sunday was cloudy. I read the paper and did the Jumble. At noon I went to my parents' for an early dinner of roast pork.

When Keith dropped off the children that evening, I greeted them on the porch and, as he always did, Keith waited a minute in his van to see whether I'd talk. Usually I had nothing to say, but that evening I walked over. "Did you give Millie any presents?" I asked. "Did your mother leave her a pair of emerald earrings?"

"My mother was buried with her jewelry," Keith said. "You know that."

"Right. So you didn't buy her a new dress, either?"

"What kind of dress?"

"Any dress."

"Millie was strange on the hike today," he said. "She talked about going to the Cave of the Winds."

"She's petrified of the dark," I said.

"At dinner she ate everything on her plate including the salad."

"Maybe she's coming into a phase," I said.

"Or leaving one. Watch her, and see what you think."

At bedtime, Millie was quieter than usual. She took a bath, brushed her teeth, and laid out her clothes for school. As was our ritual, I came in at eight to sing or read to her, but she was in bed with the lights out.

I cleared books from her chair and sat down. "I gather you'd like a song," I said.

"Can we not do anything tonight? Will your feelings be hurt?"

"We can choose what we do," I said. "Should I play you a tape?"

"I want to be quiet," she said.

I stood and pulled up her blanket and turned on her nightlight.

"Not that, either," she said. "I'm not afraid of the dark anymore."

"Are you all right, sweetheart?" I put a hand on her forehead.

"I don't have a fever," she said. "I'm fine. Why wouldn't I be?"

The whole next week Millie was odd, which is to say she was more like other children. She finished a project on whales a day early, and when her grandmother called she spoke politely instead of handing the phone to Eric. Thursday after school, she went home with her grandfather, and when I fetched her that evening he reiterated Keith's observations. "Usually she's more full of beans," he said.

"In general, I'd like her with fewer beans."

"We went to the bird refuge," he said. "We had quite a conversation about spirits."

"What kind of spirits?"

"I asked if she meant alcohol, and she said, 'No, like ghosts.' I thought maybe she'd been reading a scary story. I said ghosts didn't exist except in books, and she said, 'I know that, but what about the soul?'"

"What did you say to that?"

"I told her that, in addition to the body, some people thought living things had a part called the soul. No one could see it, so you had to believe it existed. She asked whether I believed, and I said I didn't, that I trusted science. In my opinion, the soul was a construct psychologists and religious leaders invented in order to have work."

"That's the cynic's view," I said.

"Did I say the wrong thing? What proof is there for the existence of a soul? Anyway, Millie thought about it, and then she asked, 'What sort of work?' 'Saving souls from eternal damnation,' I said. 'Oh,' she said. And that was that."

"She didn't wonder what eternal damnation was?"

"No, an owl flew through the cottonwoods and we went to look for it."

At dinner Eric asked a riddle—What gets older, but doesn't age?—and Millie scoffed at him. "That doesn't make sense," she said.

He ignored her and looked at me.

"I give up," I said.

"A rock," Eric said.

"That's not true," Millie said. "Rocks do age."

"They don't show it."

"Getting older and aging are synonyms," Millie said.

"Are aging and maturing the same?" I asked, trying to avert an argument. "What about maturing and ripening?"

"A fruit ripens," Eric said. "People get more mature."

"Not you," Millie said. "You're a boy."

"Maybe I'm ripening," he said.

"You are, but Mom isn't. She's already ripe."

"Thank you, Millie."

"You can't help it, Mom," she said. "You ripen to a certain point, and then you start to rot."

"Mom's not rotting," Eric said.

"You don't have to use that word," Millie said, "but she is."

The next morning after the children went to school, I sat in the kitchen with a cup of coffee and contemplated rotting. Normally I listened to NPR and conversed with the ficus tree in my solarium, but that morning I sensed the shadow from the neighbor's house and muted light through the elm tree in the side yard. I felt permeated by an inexplicable grief.

Mid-morning, the telephone rang. I assumed it was my mother because she'd talked about going shopping.

"Is this Kristen Stover?" a woman's voice asked.

"It is so far," I said. "Who's this?"

"Renee Taft, Greta's mother." There was a pause. "I'm concerned about Greta in all this. I don't know whether to be angry or sympathetic, but I want to know what you're going to do."

"Back up, Renee," I said. "What am I going to do about *what*?"

"The school didn't call you?"

"Why, has Millie done something?"

"Millie didn't do anything," Renee said. "But I thought—"

"For God's sake, Renee, tell me what's going on."

"Greta was *very* upset when she came home yesterday. I don't know Mrs. Allworth well, but apparently she said—this is what Greta told me… "

"What did Mrs. Allworth say?"

"She told the class Millie was her daughter in a former life."

I took a deep breath. "I'm sure she wasn't serious."

"Imagine how the other children felt. I consoled Greta as best I could. Millie hasn't said anything about it?"

"No, she hasn't."

"Well, what are you going to do? Shouldn't you complain to the principal?"

"I'll call Millie's father," I said, and I hung up.

I sat for a moment. My child. Millie, sweetheart. I wondered, *Who was Mrs. Allworth?*

I told the receptionist in Keith's office we had a crisis with one of the children, and in ten minutes Keith called me back. "Is Millie all right?" he asked.

"How do you know it's about Millie?"

"I'm in a meeting about clean water," he said, "but I'll cancel my lunch plans. What happened?"

"Millie's teacher claimed Millie is her child from a former life. This happened yesterday. What could possess someone to think such a thing, much less to say it to a third-grade class?"

"How did you hear about it?"

"Greta Taft's mother called. You don't think this is an emergency?"

"I do, if you do," he said.

"I'll go to the school board," I said, "but what should I say to Millie? I don't want her to think she had another mother, then or now."

"I wouldn't go crazy just yet," Keith said. "Let's talk about it at noon. I'm sure there's an explanation."

"You always think there's an explanation," I said, and I slammed down the phone.

In the garden I transplanted daisies into pots. The sun was hot, and I sweated. After a half-hour, I went inside and made Millie a tuna fish and sweet pickle sandwich and put it in a bag, along with carrot sticks, a juice box, and Oreos and took it over to the school.

The brick school had been built in the twenties and upgraded with modular classrooms for science and computer tech. The playground was a hodgepodge of spaces. I signed in at the office, walked down a dark hall, and continued up the stairs to the third grade. Mrs. Allworth's name was on the door of one of the rooms, and I approached and listened.

"Is that all Claudia wants?" Mrs. Allworth asked. Her voice was flat, Midwestern.

"She wants her brother to like her," a girl said.

"Why does she want that?"

"So he won't pound on her," said a boy.

I moved closer and looked in. Mrs. Allworth was about fifty, heavy-set and dark-complected and she wore her brown hair short—a wig, maybe. Among the heads and desks I picked out Millie, slouched in her seat, looking out the window. Several hands waved in the air, but not hers.

"Greta?" Mrs. Allworth said.

Greta was tall and sat in back. "Being liked is better than being hated."

I identified several other children I knew—Marianne Lowe in brown pigtails, Matt Carswell with bright red hair, no bigger than a minute, Dara Whitelow. I didn't see why any one of them couldn't have been Mrs. Allworth's child in a former life.

Mrs. Allworth glanced over and I stepped into the doorway. "I brought Millie Stover her lunch," I said. "May I speak to her a minute?"

Millie crossed in front of the class. She had on the plaid skirt and print blouse she'd laid out the night before and two unmatched socks, one pink and one green. I drew her into the dim hallway.

"Are you all right?" I asked.

"You can see I am."

"Why do you have on those socks?"

"I like them." She made a sideways twitch with her mouth. "You're all dirty, Mom. Your pants are a mess, and look at your arms."

"I was working in the garden."

We looked at each other for a moment.

"I brought you this," I said, and handed her the lunch.

"Mom, why are you here?"

"Because I love you," I said.

"Thanks," she said, and again she twitched her mouth sideways. She took the lunch and walked back into the classroom.

When I got home Keith was talking to my parents on the porch, and as I walked up, my mother rushed down the steps. "Keith called us," she said. "We decided we should come over, too."

"It was a false alarm," I said.

"Were you at school? Did you talk to the principal? What'd he say?"

"He didn't know about it, but I learned Mrs. Allworth taught in

Kansas before she came here."

"They teach creationism in Kansas," my mother said.

"They used to. As the principal said, the school is not the FBI. They had her *vita* and recommendations. He asked whether I had a particular complaint, and I said not yet."

I eased past my mother and climbed the steps. My father was sitting in a wicker rocking chair. He was gray-haired and weathered, and in the sunlight he looked old. "How's Millie?" he asked.

"She was a little surprised to see me. I took her a lunch. But that's the right question to ask."

"You can't ignore this, Kristen," my mother. "I won't let you."

"I'm not ignoring it. If anything's wrong, I think Millie should tell me about it."

"That sounds reasonable," Keith said.

"Thank you," I said. "I wouldn't want to go crazy just yet."

I went into the house and closed the door.

Carrots, lentils, beef, onions—I simmered them on the stove. I glanced at the newspaper. I turned on the television, watched a soap for five minutes, and turned it off. I read in the dictionary about reincarnation—*a rebirth in new bodies or forms, esp. a rebirth of the soul in a new human body; a fresh embodiment.* I took a walk around the block.

It was no wonder Millie had asked my father those questions, or was the idea of an earlier life merely a curiosity to her, like rain from a blue sky. Did she really think she had another mother before me? That Millie had asked my father and not me was disturbing. It meant she was aware of the delicate nature of the circumstances. Was I to consider Mrs. Allworth a rival? If I behaved badly or watched Millie too closely, would I push her to Mrs. Allworth? On the other hand, if I didn't pay enough attention to her or gave her too much freedom, she might go to Mrs. Allworth on her own.

And what about Millie's mental health? I didn't want her to get preferential treatment in class or to be persecuted by the other children for being the teacher's pet. Ah, so *that* was where the gifts had come from!

Millie's hiding the gifts (and not hiding them well) was confirmation of her insecurity. She understood the gifts created a distance between us. I felt it best not to confront Millie directly, but rather to ascertain the depth of Millie's involvement. The only way I could think of to do that was to search her room.

Millie, of course, would be furious if she found out, and rightfully so. Packing her clothes for weekends was one thing, but snooping was different. I wasn't after anything so criminal as drugs or a handgun. What I wanted was information. Without knowledge, how could a parent care for a child?

In her closet was a CD player I'd never seen, a white cotton nightgown she hadn't worn in my presence, and under the mattress I found a set of Louisa May Alcott books, a fancy edition of *Wuthering Heights*, and a brand new Harry Potter. In her desk was a calligraphy set that no one I knew had bought her.

Keith and I had settled in Colorado Springs because he was a native Coloradan and he'd found a job doing environmental inventories for Abecedarian, Inc., a developer of housing tracts east of the city. (It was Keith's idea that he could best work from the inside to prevent damage to the fragile prairie.) We rented the first year, but when Keith got a raise, we bought a starter house with the idea of reselling it when Eric and Millie outgrew it.

Now the neighborhood was in limbo. Light rail might be coming. The land along the creek where Millie explored for birds could become condominiums. Frito-Lay had bought vacant land near the school. How would a potato-chip factory impact our lives? An RV repair shop in an aluminum warehouse wanted to expand.

That afternoon I drove south on 21st Street, past fast-food franchises and Wal-Mart and the mazes of planned-unit developments that littered the landscape. Cheyenne Canyon was where I was headed. It was an eclectic mix of modern cheap—bungalows, refurbished summer cabins, and two-bedroom houses. Farther south on the mesa was the Broadmoor—ritzy homes of the wealthy, which afforded it the best school district in the city.

I drove up and down the canyon and wrote notes on the houses I liked—one with a wrap-around porch and a turret (out of my price range), a remodeled cabin, a fixer-upper on the west side of the canyon that had trees in the yard. I jotted down the phone numbers of the listing brokers.

In painting class I drew with charcoal the whole four hours. I sketched every person in the room, including Luis, but mostly I focused on my mother. I drew her from behind, from sitting on the floor and looking up at her, from a stepladder looking down. Luis thought my drawings were a breakthrough. "They're wonderfully odd," he said, "and you're not copying."

"She's not painting, either," my mother said.

"But she's captured a likeness, a deeper person."

"Why is she drawing me?"

"In twenty years, the daughter becomes the mother," I said. "I want to find out who you are." I was in the midst of drawing her profile. "Did I tell you I've been house-hunting?"

"Why didn't you call me? I'd have gone with you."

"It'll be my house," I said. "I want to make my own choice."

"Does this have to do with Keith? Are you getting divorced?"

"It has to do with the children. I want them to be in a better school."

"You can't escape memories," my mother said.

I finished the drawing with a couple of lines of her hair and tore it off the page. "Of course you can. You make new ones."

She looked closely at the sketch I'd done. "This doesn't look anything like me," she said. "Anyway, you've always been more like your father."

Millie and Greta Taft weren't close friends, though from time to time Greta's name came up in connection with a class trip or a project Millie had to cooperate on. I'd met Renee at PTA meetings, and the year before we'd sat beside each other at parents' night, our legs scrunched under the children's desks. A week after she'd called me, I called her back. "It's Kristen Stover," I said. "I was wondering how Greta's doing."

"Oh, hello," Renee said. "Greta's all right. She was upset for a while, but she's calmed down. How's Millie?"

"I wanted to tell you I talked to the principal."

"And?"

"He hadn't heard about it."

"Are you insinuating Greta made this up?"

"Not at all. I was only wondering whether Greta heard the story right."

"Greta doesn't lie," Renee said. "If you're so curious, why don't you call Mrs. Allworth?"

There was another moment's pause, and Renee hung up.

"I think I will," I said, though no one was there.

A couple of days later, I picked up Eric and Millie from school and took them to look at a house I was thinking of buying. The real estate broker was meeting us, and on the way over I told the children what we were doing. Eric was sitting in front, Millie in back. "We've outgrown our place," I said, "and I'm concerned about your school. If they add any more modular classrooms, the playground will be gone."

"There's the park," Eric said.

"Frito-Lay is taking it to build a potato-chip factory."

"What's wrong with potato chips?" Eric asked.

I looked in the rearview mirror to see whether Millie was listening. She was staring out the window.

"From this new house, the high school is within biking distance," I said. "It has tennis courts. And, Millie, the yard has lots of trees. I brought your binoculars so you can tell us what the birds are."

Millie heard, but she didn't react.

The house was a white stucco across the road from Cheyenne Creek. The front yard had tall maples, two white firs, and a willow near a frog pond. Louella, the real estate woman, was already there and let us in. Eric warmed to the place immediately. He liked the idea of having a room he could close the door to, especially one with its own bathroom. Millie's room would be at the front where she could see into the yard, but she said nothing.

Louella showed me the garden the owner had neglected and the lawn her dog had ruined. I imagined where I'd plant iris and coreopsis, where the roses would go. Millie sat in the side yard with her binoculars, but she stared at the ground.

Driving home I explained about buying a house—what the agent did, how the buyer made an offer, which the seller could accept or reject or make a counteroffer. "I'd still have to talk to the bank about financing," I said. "We'd have to borrow money." I explained what a mortgage was and the lending rate, and all the while Millie glowered in the backseat.

In the middle of this, coming down a hill, I was struck by pale yellow sunrays angling down from windswept gray rain clouds. "Look, Millie," I said. "The rain's like a gray curtain being pulled down over the foothills."

Millie went nuts. She screamed at me and yelled and flailed her arms and legs so violently I had to pull off the road.

When I stopped, she jumped out of the car and ran. Fortunately, we were beside a greenbelt. She bolted through a picnic area, and I chased her, dodging the tables and firepits. I caught her on a hill a little way past, but even then she fought me. She kicked and swung wildly with her fists, but finally I pinned her arms and spanked her hard on the rear. She was stunned and stared at me as if I'd deliberately cut her with a knife. "I hate you," she said. "You've ruined my life."

"Millie, sweetheart, it's not the end of the world to move from one house to another."

"You don't know anything about me."

"I've lived with you nine years," I said, loosening my grip. "I know you a little."

"You think you do, but you don't. You don't know my soul."

"Maybe you could tell me about it."

She glared at me a moment and then took off running again. This time I let her go. I jogged behind her up the trail and down into a gully and up to the next ridge until she tired. We walked back to the car in silence.

What I liked about Keith—what I still liked about him—was his gentleness. He believed in local action, that one voice put with another was the essence of power. Despite the evidence, he thought good triumphed over evil because, without trust in such a notion, there was no hope. For that reason he listened to what people said, watching their eyes and nodding, as if spoken words were of the utmost importance. Maybe they were.

This diplomacy worked well in the marketplace of environmental consulting where people wanted to hear reasons for doing good. They needed to feel the small territory they controlled was important in the broader scheme, whether they owned a few acres behind a housing development or a huge marshland along a river. Preservation of land was a virtue; when it was developed, it was gone for good, like an extinct species. The problem was the cost. Keeping land as it was had no measurable value.

Keith had not been so calculating in our family interactions. His dinner table conversation with the children was all over the map—the demise of big cats, the depletion of the Oglala aquifer, the mental problems of the homeless. He explained about Muslim culture, Cinco de Mayo, and the travesty of grazing on federal lands. He talked in a soft, reasonable voice. In private he commiserated with me without recounting an experience of his own more substantial or serious. When I discovered a wrinkle, for example, or a gray hair, he might say, "You could never have too many wrinkles for me," or, "Your hair could fall out, and I'd still love you."

It was hard not to like someone like him.

After seeing the other house, Millie was sullen, obdurate, and private. Of her own volition she stayed later at school; at home she kept to her room; she rarely spoke at dinner. After the first few days of her coming home late, I picked her up in the car. She hated that, but said nothing.

One night, out of sympathy, I cooked shrimp pasta Millie particularly liked and Eric set the table with my grandmother's bird china.

"I don't see why we have to be nice to *her*," Eric said. "Appeasement never worked with the Germans."

"She's going through a hard time."

"So am I," Eric said. "I have Millie for a sister."

At dinner I asked Millie the usual questions. "How was school? What did you do at recess?"

"I stayed in."

"I thought you had to go outside for recess."

"I went outside, then I came in. What difference does it make?"

There was silence.

"How's the shrimp?" I asked.

"Good," Eric said.

"Not as good as Daddy's," Millie said.

"How's Mrs. Allworth?" I asked.

More silence.

"I heard she's strict about homework."

"I don't do homework."

"Is that like not doing windows?"

Millie stared at me.

"It's a joke," I said. "Cleaning people say they don't do windows."

Millie didn't laugh. She got up from the table, went upstairs, and slammed the door to her room.

On a Monday at noon, Keith and I met at a café near his office. "She's angry, and she's becoming unmanageable," I said. "Is she like that on weekends?"

"Some up, some down," he said. "I guess she's over the nice phase."

"She won't talk to me."

"Did she ever?" he asked. "She's never communicated very well."

"She communicates she's miserable."

Keith sipped his Coke and looked at me. It was more than a look; it was analysis. "You're not telling me something."

"What am I not telling you?"

"Why don't you admit it, and we can talk from there?"

I set down my sandwich. "Since when are you the determiner of my reality?"

"I'm not," he said, "but you're being just like Millie."

"It has to do with that teacher," I said.

"You said no other parents complained."

"They haven't. But there are presents—those earrings I asked you about, the blue dress, a nightgown, a calligraphy set… "

"Why didn't you tell me all this?"

"I thought Millie would confess. A couple of days ago she had a fit in the car. When I stopped, she ran away, and when I caught her, we fought. I mean, knock-down, drag-out. She told me I didn't know her soul."

We were quiet a moment, not eating. Finally Keith said, "I don't want my daughter to be in pain."

"I don't want her to be in pain, either," I said. "I'm going to talk to Mrs. Allworth."

Sex is the physical expression of love, but it can be less intimate or more. One's body is naked and compared to others' bodies from magazine pages and movies. My body was the one Keith chose, but I was never comfortable with it. Growing up, I'd had colds, earaches, knee pain. I grew too fast and was awkward. I took up kayaking and bicycling because coordination didn't matter.

Every night we were married I went to bed before Keith. I undressed in the bathroom, put on a nightgown, and slipped under the covers. Keith never noticed. He came into the room while I was reading, undressed, and went naked to the bathroom. Making love, when that happened, was in darkness.

Tuesday morning my mother called to say she wasn't going to painting class. "Your father's not well," she said. "He has a cold and didn't sleep much last night. I don't think I should desert him."

"Should he see a doctor?"

"He was on the Internet doing research till late. I don't know when he came to bed."

"What kind of research?"

"Let me talk to her," I heard my father say from the background.

My mother gave him the phone.

"Your mother's driving me crazy," he said. "She can't let five minutes go by without saying something inane."

"What were you doing up all night?"

I heard a door open and close. "I'm in the den now." He paused. "I was researching the soul. There were forty-eight sites relating to it— As the Soul Speaks; a Lost Soul's exposition; the Timia Group to assist humanity in discovering love, peace, and happiness through self-discovery; Richard's Gallery of Pathetic Human Regret; and several photo essays of spiritual places. Each of them assumes the existence of the thing that must be proved."

"And you want... what?"

"I want confirmation," he said. "There are two alternatives, yes or no. You'd think it would be easy for someone to make a choice."

"Put Mom back on," I said. "I'll tell her you're fine, and she can go to the painting class."

Thunder rolled and lightning flashed out the window, and Luis made us watch the storm move through. He talked about flat light and the way it spread out the images and merged one object with another. "Certain colors diminish from within," he said, "reds especially, but sometimes blues, too. They're called fugitive colors. Over time they fade."

"How does that happen?" I asked.

"Why is one storm different from another?" Luis said. "It's not possible to know."

When the storm passed, I tried the still-life Luis had assembled—a straw hat, two red shoes, and an empty birdcage with a green satin cloth pulled over it askew. I mixed my paints carefully on the palette—the pale background tones first, on which the other objects would be defined. Luis came up behind me as I was applying the first brush strokes to the canvas.

"It's a difficult collection," he said.

"It's not as if I'm really an artist," I said.

"But you might be," Luis said. "You have a good eye."

"I'm too old."

"If you're too old, what am I?" my mother asked.

"I mean, in time we might execute a likeness, but what is form without substance?"

"You have to paint what you feel," Luis said. "At least you're not painting what someone else feels anymore."

I painted the background and then struggled to gain even a pathetic image of the red shoes.

A warm afternoon a day later, nearly five o'clock—Eric was at soccer and Millie had gone home from school with my father. I found Mrs. Allworth's address on MapQuest. Her house was in one of Keith's hated subdivisions east of the city, and on the way over I planned what to say. I was going to be serene and issue no ultimatums. Millie was at stake, but I had my rights and wouldn't be intimidated.

The neighborhood was treeless, pastel houses one after another. Hers was green. A white Saturn was in the driveway. I walked to the door and took a deep breath before I clacked the faux-brass knocker.

I wasn't prepared for the woman who answered, not Mrs. Allworth from the classroom. This woman was in her twenties, slender, with long blonde hair. "We don't want any," she said, "whatever it is you're selling."

"I'm looking for Mrs. Allworth."

"Are you a Jehovah's Witness?"

"I'm Kristen Stover, Millie's mother."

The woman laughed. "Oh, I'm sorry," she said. "So many people sell vacuum cleaners and magazines that I've learned to be gruff. I'm Mrs. Allworth."

"You're not the person I saw in Millie's classroom."

"Was it last week? I had the flu." She put out her hand, and I shook it. "Come in, won't you? You know, this is odd, but I was about to call you."

She held the door open and I went into a living room dimly lit and furnished with heavy things—an oak sofa, a rectangular wooden chair, a stone lamp.

"We're renting furnished," Mrs. Allworth said. "I make that disclaimer whenever anyone comes in. Would you like tea? I was about to have some."

I followed her into the kitchen where papers and books littered the dining table. Out the window was a postage-stamp back yard and a view of Pikes Peak over a redwood fence. "Excuse the mess," Mrs. Allworth said. "I do my schoolwork first thing so when my husband gets home we can go to the gym." She put on the teakettle and got down two cups.

"Why would you call me?" I asked.

"Millie has this notion I'm related to her in some way," Mrs. Allworth said, "like I'm her mother or something. I don't know where she got the idea, but in class it's had negative repercussions. I don't want other pupils to think I play favorites."

"Of course not."

"I gather from other students she's made no secret of her relationship to me. Can I be frank, Mrs. Stover? The other girls think Millie's a little daft."

"She's prone to dreaming," I said.

Mrs. Allworth put tea bags in the cups. "On the other hand, children know things we don't. Every day I'm astonished how much freer their minds are than ours. Would you like sugar?"

"No, thank you."

"I mean, we adults think language is so liberating, and yes, it separates us from the so-called lower animals. But it's limiting, too. There's a whole realm beyond words, don't you think?"

"You mean the emotions?"

"We believe we can express in words what exists, but what if we can't? Does it follow that what we can't express doesn't exist? Why can't there be other worlds we're unable to talk about?"

"Like former lives?"

The kettle boiled, and Mrs. Allworth poured the water and set one hot cup on the table near me.

"I don't know about former lives, but let me tell you what happened in class. We were doing our multiplication tables, and Millie asked, 'Could you have been my mother?' Just like that, out loud. I'm afraid I didn't take her as seriously as I should have. I said, 'Millie, we're doing seven times seven,' and she said, 'But could you have?' And I said something off-hand, like 'in another life, maybe.' After that she started hanging out with me after school."

"So it was Millie's idea?"

Mrs. Allworth sat down with her tea. "What happens is they forget," she said. "As they grow up, they learn words and *think* with words, and they assume, as we do, their lives are getting bigger and better. But it's as if—and this is what I see in class—the more words they know, the more they forget what they knew before, and they replace these things with darkness."

"You're saying you didn't buy her those presents?"

"No, of course not. I wouldn't buy anything for a student. Millie tried to give me a pair of earrings once, but I didn't take them. Don't get me wrong, Mrs. Stover. I think Millie's a great kid. I'm sure you're proud to be her mother. But I want my own child."

I drank my tea. "What does your husband do?" I asked. "What do the two of you do at the gym?"

Millie and I made a tacit agreement that if I didn't embarrass her by picking her up from school, she'd come straight home. This arrangement suited her purposes—she determined the meaning of 'straight home'—and mine because I wanted to give her sufficient latitude while knowing where she was. She had the illusion of freedom, and I had the illusion of control.

Millie was still gloomy and silent, but my new knowledge that she was the instigator of the crisis altered my perceptions. For instance, the imperative of buying a new house dissipated. So as not to let Millie think her tantrum had changed my mind, I went ahead and listed our house anyway and showed it several times when she was home. I set the price unreasonably high.

The mystery of the gifts was easy enough to solve. The bank where Millie had her savings account was only two blocks from her school, and her passbook reflected several withdrawals over the past six weeks, nothing huge, but enough to have purchased a pair of fairly expensive earrings and a blue dress. The proprietors and clerks of several shops

nearby knew Millie—the thrift store people, the old women in the
Dollar Variety, the bookstore owner. Millie had bought the emerald
earrings for $45 from a grizzled Vietnam vet in a pawnshop.

Beyond the gifts, though, was the greater mystery of why she'd
bought them, why she had felt the need to claim Mrs. Allworth as her
mother. What was deficient about her own? In my self-examination,
I wondered about the soul and whether, as Mrs. Allworth suggested,
Millie knew something I didn't.

In the garden I was most aware of physical reality—the greening,
the growing and blooming, the dying away. Flowers at that altitude had
short, brilliant lives, and I loved the colors. What I wanted most was
to be within this tangible world, to experience my own blooming, but
I understood gradually that being in the garden was an escape. Tilling
the soil, fertilizing, watering, planting seeds, and transplanting—what I
created would not have existed on its own.

During the next several weeks, I went to painting classes twice a
week, the beginning one with my mother and an advanced one Luis let
me come to, though I was nervous about it. "What's advanced?" Luis
said. "The point is to go forward from where you are."

In the advanced class, we carried our easels and paints outside into
the neighborhood of old houses and chose from among the infinite vistas
what to paint—a maple tree in a spacious yard, a gabled house, a stone
pathway that receded into someone's garden. Millie was with me in my
imagination the whole time. My hope was that, on her own, she would
come to recognize our need for her (I included Keith and Eric in this),
and hers for us. At the same time, I worried she wouldn't be able to.

When a week went by, I knew I couldn't sit by and wait for her to
disappear.

One Friday afternoon before Keith came to pick up the children, I was
reading in the living room when Millie came in. "Hello," I said. "How
was school?"

"The same."

"Do you have homework?"

"There's no homework on weekends."

"Right. Your father's picking you up at four-thirty."

She passed through the room, and I heard her footsteps on the stairs. In the hall above, her door opened and I imagined what she saw then—her clothes put away, the floor swept, her desk neatly arranged. I'd made up the bed with fresh sheets, but she wouldn't notice those. What she'd see was all the gifts she'd bought for herself laid out carefully on the bedspread—the earrings, the blue dress, the calligraphy set—everything in plain view, including the new presents—a small geode from the rock shop, a leather pouch from the thrift store, and a Tweety Bird watch from the Dollar Variety.

She made no sound, no banging or throwing anything, at least not that I heard.

A little after four, Keith pulled up in the van and came inside. Eric came upstairs with his suitcase. "What are you doing here, Dad?" he asked.

"I'm supposed to be here."

"I mean, usually you wait outside."

He went to the banister and called up the stairs, "Millie, I'm here." Then he turned to Eric. "It's been a couple of weeks. I wanted to see your new quarters in the rec room."

They clomped down the stairs—the two men—and I heard their voices and the thumping of darts into the dartboard. Millie didn't appear.

In a few minutes, Keith and Eric came back upstairs, Keith carrying Eric's jacket and a basketball. In the living room he tossed Eric the ball and climbed three steps toward Millie's room. "Millie, bring a jacket," he said. "Tomorrow we're going to the Cave of the Winds."

"We are?" Eric said.

"I thought it was time," Keith said. "Say goodbye to your mother."

Eric gave me a kiss. "Bye, Mom."

He went outside, and the basketball thudded on the porch. Keith and I waited a minute. Millie came out of her room dragging her duffel bag—*whump whump whump*—down each riser. She didn't look at me as she crossed the living room.

"Goodbye, Millie," I said.

"Goodbye," Keith said to me, and he left.

When they were gone, I went up to Millie's room. The door was open. Her room was as neat as before, but the gifts had been put away.

I did a load of wash, cleaned the oven, and went for a run along the creek. When I got back, my mother had left a message inviting me for dinner, and I called back and declined.

"You should be more social," she said. She stopped. "Never mind."

That night I slept badly and woke early, wide awake. I had coffee and read the paper. At ten o'clock, I drove up Ute Pass to the Cave of the Winds.

I bought tickets in the visitors' center and waited until a little after ten-thirty, when Keith and I had agreed he'd be there with the children. They ambled in, Eric in jeans and a Broncos sweatshirt, Millie in blue tights under pink shorts and a skimpy T-shirt. Keith was holding Millie's hand.

Eric saw me first.

"I was in the neighborhood," I said. "Hello, Millie."

"This isn't a neighborhood," Millie said.

I handed Keith the tickets. "You're going to be cold in the cave, sweetheart," I said. "It's only fifty-four degrees."

"Mom, go home," Millie said. "This is our time with Dad."

"The next tour's at eleven," I said.

"I'm leaving," Millie said.

"You can leave if you want to," I said. "It's a free country."

Keith squatted down to her. "We don't have to do this," he said, "but we're here. You've been brave about coming. You said you wanted to."

"I changed my mind."

"You're afraid," Eric said. He turned to me. "She's afraid, Mom."

"I'm not afraid," Millie said.

"Then prove it," Eric said.

I could have kissed him for saying that.

The tour guide was a young man with a crew cut, dressed in khaki pants, a navy blue blazer, and a tie. He explained how the Pickett brothers discovered the cave, that George Snider excavated the rooms, about its geological history, how erosion from limestone formed stalactites and stalagmites, cave coral, and frostwork. The group was about twenty people, and I stayed at some remove from Millie so she wouldn't think I was watching her. We walked through Fat Man's Misery and Tall Man's Headache and stopped in the Bridal Chamber. "People get married here," the guide said, "because they're already in the hole, on the rocks, and there's nowhere to go but up."

A titter ran through the group. Keith and I looked at each other. Millie didn't laugh.

Finally, in a loose line, we filed into the Majestic Hall, the guide first, then Millie and Eric and Keith and others close behind. I was near the back.

Someone asked the guide how deep the cave was. "There is no bottom," he said. "If we kept walking, we'd get to China."

"I doubt it," Millie said. "We'd burn up in the center of the earth."

"She has no sense of humor," Eric said.

We closed ranks and the guide stepped out from the group. "Here in the Majestic Hall we see the evidence of millions and millions of years of nose drip … "

Millie listened to the guide's banter as if she'd forgotten she was underground. I wasn't listening, particularly, but was watching Millie. Once she twitched her lips sideways, and I thought I glimpsed on her face a shiver of fear. Did I imagine it? What had the guide said? Then Millie turned suddenly toward me, aware I was watching her, and I averted my eyes.

I focused on the guide, who was walking to a panel on the wall. "Now please be quiet," he said. "Most of us are already in the dark, but now we'll really know what it's like."

We were all looking at him.

"Ready?" he asked. He smiled and pulled the switch.

We were plunged into a blackness so all-encompassing and powerful I was stunned. An involuntary sigh escaped me. To have light in one moment and then to have such darkness—it was like death. And it was quiet, too. No one made a sound.

What to think of? The blackness, of course, the inability to move because of it. I swept my hand through the air, but saw neither hand nor motion. I thought of the soul. And what about Millie? Though I heard nothing, I felt her crying and didn't know where she was. I couldn't reach her. She couldn't reach me.

"Millie?" I called out.

She didn't answer.

"Millie? My God, Millie, where are you?"

"I'm right here," she said.

I scrambled toward her voice, pushed other people aside. "Where?" I called.

"Right here."

I touched her shirt, grasped her arm, enfolded her body, pressed her to me with all my might. And she held me.

Then the lights came on again.

In November, I took the house off the market. Eric barely noticed and, though Millie didn't say anything, I knew she was glad to stay where we were. Over the weeks she had gradually become herself again, though perhaps she didn't return quite to the person she'd been. She searched for birds with my father, did her homework, even helped once to make a casserole for dinner. She was more mature, though not ripe yet.

Her packing for visits with Keith improved, too. She was more aware of what she needed for where she was going. The gifts disappeared from her room, or at least I didn't see them and didn't look. Once I went to the pawnshop and asked the man whether Millie had been in. "Oh, yeah, sure," he said, "she wanted to sell me back the earrings she bought." He pulled them from the case and set them on the counter. "She said they didn't work out, so I gave her the forty-five dollars back."

"That was nice of you," I said.

"She was a nice kid. I sold 'em cheap the first time."

"How much were they?"

"Sixty."

I got out the wallet from my purse. "I need them to remember something," I said. "It's the only time my daughter will be nine."

That winter I took a part-time job in a plant nursery, fertilizing, watering, transplanting. I had flexible hours so I was home when the children got back from school, and I could keep on with my painting classes. I even painted on my own. I bought a wooden paint box, a portable easel and chair and set them up in my back yard, or on my parents' deck, or even in my living room where light angled through the window. I felt I was moving toward something.

In January, my father had an aneurysm and was hospitalized. With miracle surgery, he recovered quickly and was back on his feet, but his illness took its toll on my mother. She thought my father was prone to overdo on Millie's account—he shouldn't spend so many hours walking trails looking for birds.

"What will he do if he doesn't?" I asked. "He isn't going to live forever."

"Maybe he will," my mother said. "How can you say that so coldly?"

"I didn't say it coldly," I said. "I love you both, but it's the truth."

"Let's not think of it then," my mother said.

"I'll think of it," I said. "It has to do with the soul."

During the spring, Keith and I met for lunch more frequently and talked about various things—the effect of the snowpack for summer irrigation, how his company was faring, and, of course, Eric and Millie. He didn't press me about what would happen next with us, and I didn't offer any explanations. I was happier, I think, than I'd ever been.

In April, on an unseasonably warm day when the leaves were starting, I took my oils down to the creek at the end of our street where Millie liked to look for birds. I set a canvas on my easel and sat with my paint box on my lap. For a long time I didn't paint. I didn't even mix colors. I looked and saw why Millie liked the place. Looking was what I hadn't done before. The darkness on one side of a tree trunk contrasted with the light on the other, with gradations of shadow in between. The edges of the dead leaves on the ground were bathed in gold. I saw the towhee Millie had described—black head and back, white underneath, rusty sides, red eye—foraging under the bushes. The stream was brown with white riffles from the sun that shone on the flowing water. No fugitive colors existed here, nothing that faded. The subtle greens emerging, the varying blue of the distant hills, the tans close in were what they were: a world not possible to describe in words, absolute in the moment, changing only according to the light and the air and what I made of it.

GALIMATIA

I was sixteen the summer she moved into the hogan in the shadow of the sandstone cliff. No one knew where she had come from, though it was from beyond Tuba City where I went to the Indian School, and beyond Kayenta even, from the far part of the reservation. A friend of Sam Lomatowama's brought her in a truck and left her off with her provisions. My mother said her name was Galimatia, and I remember thinking she must have made up her own name. Gah-lee-mah-tee-ah. It wasn't Navajo, but I liked whispering it aloud to myself.

Our house was closest to Galimatia's—across the dirt road that ran through the bare earth and mesquite between the highway and the cliff. I watched her every day. She was in her twenties, slender, long-legged for an Indian, and wore her hair shoulder-length and curled instead of long and straight like the other women. She did nothing extraordinary that I could see—fetched water from the common well, cleaned up the papers that blew in around the boulders near her house, and stared up at the red sandstone cliff that cast its long shadow over the village.

My family sold turquoise-and-silver jewelry at the turnout by the bridge where tourists stopped to look down into Marble Canyon. The river at the bottom flowed red. Each family had a lean-to made of boards and corrugated tin and decorated with German and French and American flags. Except for my father, we all had to sell, even my little brother and sister. My father worked mornings in the camper shell that sat on the ground behind our adobe house. He made belt buckles and bracelets and earrings, and my mother did beadwork in the lean-to. If we were lucky, the tourists stopped and looked, and we had to endure their questions. Were these earrings really made by Indians? Where does the turquoise come from? How much does the government pay you to do this? I hated the tourists and their cameras and the places they came from. I hated the heat and the hours of waiting.

As the days went by, Galimatia explored more and more of the terrain. She walked among the boulders at the bottom of the cliff, climbed up along the lower ledges, and then she found the path—a series of handhold and footholds the ancestors had made that led up a pitch of sandstone. My father had once taken me up part-way to where the rushing water from storms had eroded a deep cleft in the rock. Galimatia reached this place, too, and looked up the crevice toward the higher rock wall and then down below her where I was in the village. Finally she turned away from the abyss and came down.

One morning in late June, before the sun had warmed the room I shared with my brother, I was at the window, as usual, waiting for Galimatia to emerge from her hogan. When she came out she was wearing shorts and a tan shirt and carried a small blue backpack. She did not look at me—what would she see? She wound her way through the boulders at the base of the cliff, climbed the steep scree without using her hands, and found the ancestors' path hollowed out in the stone. She moved easily and steadily, now and then touching the stone to keep her balance. She circled an outcropping that in that early light was a shadowy bird and emerged higher up at the deep cleft. She did not hesitate there or look down, but rather jumped the abyss gracefully, as if there were no danger. On the other side, she braced her body into the stone.

From that point, she followed the narrow ledge upward, spidered up a steep pitch on all fours, and came out in the scooped-out bowl near the top. For a few minutes I couldn't see her in the bowl, but then she came into view higher up, on the curve where sandstone and white limestone formed layers in the cliff. She scaled the last few broken shards of limestone and disappeared over the lip into the piñon trees on top of the mesa.

I was plagued by idleness. That's what my aunts and uncles said. I was smart, but I dreamed. At the Indian School, I didn't listen to my teachers, and they tried to shame me in front of the other students. "Why don't you memorize?" my chemistry teacher asked. "You have the ability to go to college. Why must you fail at what you could do so easily?"

"If you spent as much time studying as you do looking out the window," my English teacher said, "you might become a writer. Wouldn't that be a surprise?"

The other students laughed.

The teachers tried to enlist my parents to help bring me around. "He doesn't try," my adviser told my father. He had called my father to his office. "We can't see inside him, and he doesn't tell us what he thinks."

My father glared at me. "I'll have it out with him," my father said.

"He's polite," my adviser said, "and he says the right words, but he doesn't mean them."

"He doesn't respect his elders," my father said, "and he's lazy. I'll make him not so lazy."

For a few days my father laughed about it with my mother. Then he got drunk, and he beat me. "Do you want to stay in the village all your life?" he asked.

"No," I said.

"You want to be a lousy silversmith?"

"No."

"Then pay attention in school. Learn a trade. Do what you're told."

But I drifted. I liked my nothingness. I liked dreaming about the colors of the land, and the way the clouds moved, and the light which fell across the red sandstone cliff, changing it according to the season.

That summer my father towed an old Chevy truck back from Kayenta, and in my spare time I worked on it. The truck had been rolled in a ditch but looked worse than it was. The front fender was junk and the tailgate was missing. It needed brakes and four tires and a new transmission—problems I could solve if I had time and money. I saved what I got from selling, and I bought parts piecemeal.

Most afternoons I tinkered with the transmission and got it close to perfect, but once in a while, after my hours at the stall, it was too hot to work on the truck. The sun had turned the rabbit brush pale gray and it was too dry for flowers. The garden had to be watered by hand from the well. One day on my way home, I stopped for a soda and listened to the men talk while they drank beer behind the store. A half dozen of them sat around a cable-reel table in the shade of a locust tree.

"She's an ice-hearted whore," my uncle said. He was thirty-five and still black-haired, but already his face was soft from drink. "I went over and asked her about Sam Lomatowama and she wouldn't tell me anything."

"They get that way when they hate their own people," Ray Yazzie said.

"Maybe she's deaf," my father said. "Maybe she didn't hear you."

"She knows Sam in only one way," Ray Yazzie said.

The men laughed, and then they saw me and got quiet. "That's enough," my uncle said. "The boy likes her."

My face burned suddenly in confusion and shame, and I walked straight home.

I couldn't think straight. I saw the cracked adobe hogan, the wilted garden, broken-down truck. Instead of going to my room—I heard my brother and sister there—I opened the door to the camper shell that sat on the ground beside the house. My father's tools lay on the bench, along with a necklace he was working on—turquoise beads on a string with a small silver heart in the middle. The materials were Navajo, but not the necklace. No Navajo ever wore a necklace with a heart on it.

I sat there for a long time wondering if that's what I would be doing with my life in a few years. Then I looked out the metal-slatted window. Galimatia was descending the footholds on the cliff. Coming down was not the same as climbing, and her body was troubled in a way I hadn't seen it before, as if she were weary. She canted differently against the rock; her steps were more tentative. Once she slipped, skidded a few feet down the stone, and caught herself on the branch of a piñon tree. She rubbed one hand with the other, brushed some dirt from her knee. It was not a place to fall from.

I didn't know that I liked her, but I didn't not like her. I worried about her. She climbed the cliff every day, and came down in the afternoon, and I did not understand what that had to do with hating her own people.

One hot mid-morning in July, I was with my mother in the lean-to when Galimatia appeared like an apparition at the bridge. She had no pack on, only cut-off jeans and a white, sweat-soaked blouse. She had climbed out of the river gorge. But how had she got to the river? There was no way I knew of to get from the mesa to the river, and from the river to the bridge was a hard climb—over a thousand vertical feet. She did not look at us, but everyone in the stalls looked at her, even my mother.

"It's an evil woman who has the money to do nothing," my mother said.

I'd never heard my mother say a mean word before. "But what's she done?" I asked.

My mother shook her head and wouldn't answer.

Galimatia passed along the highway.

That night, after my brother was asleep, I sat up and watched her hogan. A lantern inside was lighted and her body or the shadow of her body moved through the window frame. Then she came outside. A quarter moon rolled in the sky, so I couldn't see her well. She carried a flashlight, probably to watch for snakes, so I knew where she was. She climbed among the boulders behind her house and up onto one of them, where she turned off the light. She was a dark figure against the dark stone, but, watching her, I felt an eerie closeness, as if I shared with her a secret I couldn't put a name to. I felt the nothingness I'd never spoken of to anyone had at last become real.

The weather through July was clear and dry, but every day I hoped for rain. Mornings were cool, but by nine o'clock it was hot. The garden was burning up; the road to the lean-to at the bridge was dust; we sweated under the tin roof. Above the sandstone cliff, the sky was hard blue, and to the west the heat-haze made the Kaibab a gray-red slab on the horizon. In the afternoons, clouds rose, sometimes huge dark thunderheads, but they drifted off over the mesa.

Galimatia came up from the river gorge every morning. The others pretended not to see her, but I couldn't pretend. I watched her from the moment she came over the rim of the canyon. She walked the edge of the asphalt, turned onto the gravel road to the store, and passed the store and the men who sat there in the shade of the locust tree. Farther on, she stopped at the well and drank, turned left behind the abandoned smokehouse, and was gone.

Sometimes, anticipating her coming, I walked out onto the bridge to look for her. I measured my steps so as not to appear too eager to my mother, and I turned my gaze first downriver in the direction of the mountains, though they were too far away to see. A slight breeze drifted through the canyon. Then I crossed the bridge and scanned upstream. Galimatia's white blouse was easy to spot against the sandstone or against the muddy reddish-brown water.

One day I lingered on the bridge, looking toward the invisible mountains, and saw an eagle sailing in the sky. It steered south on great dark wings that never once moved, and it grew smaller and smaller until it merged into distance. Even when I couldn't see it anymore, I felt its weightlessness in my bones. My long hair swirled like feathers in the warm breeze, and I opened my arms and touched the wind with my fingers.

When I turned to cross the bridge to look for Galimatia, she was standing on the other side of the road. "Are you looking for me?" she asked.

I was so surprised by her voice I had no time to think of a lie. My silence was admission.

"You've been watching me," she said.

We held each other's gaze for a few seconds. I knew she wanted something of me.

"You are the one I must ask," she said. "There is no one else."

I could not speak, but I could not bear to be silent. Whatever the question, whatever favor she needed, I wished to say yes. But I knew I couldn't.

I was rescued by a tourist bus that came onto the bridge. It shook the pavement we stood on and swerved past us, spewing its exhaust. It braked and pulled off the highway in front of the stalls. My mother called to me and waved, and I ran back to the stall to sell beaded purses and turquoise necklaces with hearts on them to the people in shorts and T-shirts already stepping off the bus into the heat.

My disgrace in the village for Galimatia's talking to me lasted for days. I couldn't watch Galimatia climb the cliff each morning and I didn't look for her in the river gorge. When she appeared at the bridge and walked past the stalls, I pretended not to see her. At night, I no longer spied on her, though I knew she sat on the boulder near her house looking at the stars.

But not watching her made her power over me that much stronger. To keep my mind occupied, I worked on the truck. I replaced the two worst tires with recaps, relined the brakes, and rebuilt the clutch. One afternoon a couple of my friends came by and wanted to play basketball—three-on-three, it was my basketball. We went over to the court by the store.

But it was too hot, and they teased me about Galimatia—how I liked older women. We quit after an hour, and I walked home with Frank Yazzie, Ray's son, passing the ball back and forth. We were sweaty and tired, as if the heat and the dust weighted us down.

"You looking forward to school?" Frank asked. He was bored and wanted to see a girl he knew from Red Lake.

"I'm thinking I might not go back," I said.

"You mean stay here?" Frank stopped and held the ball.

I looked away at the hogans and the shacks and trailers.

"You can't stay here," he said. "You'll die."

"I'm dying in school," I said.

He passed me the ball and we walked on. The clouds had built up over the cliff and thunder sounded far away.

At the next dirt intersection, Frank turned off toward his house and I went on alone. I thought how basketball was the same as making a heart necklace, something I had learned about without wanting to. I dribbled the ball on the dusty track like a crazy person showing off for no one. I bounced the ball behind my back, between my legs, real low to the ground. The sweat rose again on my forehead. Then I stopped abruptly. Nothing moved: no birds, no lizards, no people. The sky was white. My whole body yearned for water. A silver current like lightning ran through the air and I fell.

I woke in the shade on the cement slab by the well with a wet cloth on my face. Galimatia knelt beside me, took the cloth away, and wrung it out. I heard the pump handle squeak as she wet the cloth again. I smelled her body, smelled my own sweat, the dry leaves on the ground, the wet cloth she put on my forehead.

"I was watching you," she said.

The favor was to drive her to Flagstaff. She had no other way to get there, no woman to ask who was not frightened of her, no man who did not want her. She chose me, she said, because I had chosen her. She knew the sacrifice I was making to take her: my parents would be angry and I would be teased and ridiculed. But she made no effort to hide her request or make it easier on me. And I couldn't say no.

On the day we agreed to go—Tuesday—she came over at eleven in the morning and climbed into the bed of the truck. I was still in the house and saw her. She had on a blue denim dress and a blue kerchief and silver earrings and turquoise bracelets and a squash blossom necklace nothing like the cheap ones my father made.

I pulled on a jacket and came outside. My father emerged from the camper shell holding a pair of pliers. "I'm taking her to Flag," I said.

"Not in my truck."

"She asked me to," I said. "It's *my* truck."

I got into the cab. The starter whirred and finally the engine caught, and I reversed out the driveway. I did not look back at my father.

We drove through the village and past the store, which was the only way to get to the highway. The men in the shade of the locust tree followed us with their eyes. At the highway the women in the stalls stared at us; I could almost hear them talking. We turned left, away from the bridge, into the desolate country of mudmounds and tan hills, eroded gullies and sandstone formations.

As I drove, I glanced now and then at Galimatia in the rearview mirror. She sat among the tools and car parts, still as stone, though her hair blew from under her kerchief. Her eyes were slitted in the wind and gazed out at the bleak landscape, but I had no idea what she saw or thought of the hills and the distance and the time, except I knew what she saw and what I saw were not the same.

I let her off in downtown Flag. We agreed to meet at six o'clock at the Safeway, so I scouted junkyards for a new ignition switch and, in town, drank a malt and looked in the store windows at sneakers, car accessories, electronic gear. At six, I pulled into the parking lot at the grocery store. Galimatia was waiting on the curb with sacks of cornmeal and flour and beans and a couple of boxes of canned goods. She didn't have her jewelry anymore.

We loaded her food in the back of the truck. It was cooler then, and with the truck bed filled and darkness coming, Galimatia got into the cab with me. We drove north out of town.

I thought we might have a conversation. She would ask what I'd done in town and I'd tell her about looking for parts and wandering along the main street. I'd ask where she'd gone, how she got the money for what she'd bought, and how she'd come to live in the village. But as we drove north into the pine forest, the sun fell to ashes, and the dusk and stars spread around us. I had never been so silent with anyone else before in that way. It was not the ordinary silence of my mother and me or the silence of boredom or of loneliness, but one full and rich and joyful, and I would not have broken it for anything in the world.

The next morning I woke early in the dark, before anyone else in the family, and I dressed and sneaked out of the house. At first light, Galimatia started up the cliff. She carried her pack and climbed as easily as a dancer. She half-ran, half-jumped from boulder to ledge; she trotted up the footholds in the stone with no hands; she leaped the abyss. In a few minutes she was high on the cliff. When I couldn't see her anymore in the bowl near the top, and she couldn't see me, I followed.

The one path started at an opening among the boulders and proceeded up the steep scree to the footholds the ancestors had carved. When I reached the cleft in the sandstone, I paused to catch my breath. I thought of the night before. When I'd got home, my parents said nothing about my taking Galimatia to Flag, but I understood their disapproval. And I knew I was different, that I'd done something important. Yes, it was my truck and my gas and my wasted hours, but I had conquered my fear of shame and had learned something I hadn't known before.

The cleft was wider than I remembered, but Galimatia had jumped it easily. I leaped and caught myself heavily on the rock opposite. I smiled and took a deep breath. Then I inched along the ledge and scrambled up the next pitch and the next, to the bowl beneath the mesa. From there, it was a short climb through shards of white limestone over the lip and into the piñon trees.

The mesa sloped gradually upward to the north. I found Galimatia's tracks in the dust and followed them. Judging from the footprints, she took a regular path. I walked quickly, feeling the pull of minutes.

After a half-hour weaving through the piñons, the path angled toward the river gorge. As I neared the canyon, the marks in the dry earth petered out into stone and I lost the trail. Trees grew in scattered pockets. I wandered through a maze of sandstone spires along the rim of the canyon. It was cool still and tiny, sun-lit insects and floating seeds swirled in the air. The tops of the rocks burned red in the new sun.

Near the rim of the canyon, I came out in a swale with a few tufts of grass and a single piñon tree. Water must have collected there when it rained. I closed my eyes for a moment and felt the breeze whirl in the grasses. The lilting song of a wren rose from the river gorge. I was part of this place, part of the wren's song and the sighing, moving grass, part of the warm sun and the piñon tree and the moving air.

I opened my eyes. Galimatia was standing before me on a narrow ledge. "Come with me," she said. "Speak no words."

She disappeared behind a sandstone spire, and though before I was by myself, now I was alone. She had ordered me, and I had no choice.

I climbed down to where she had been and followed the ledge for several feet along the precipice. The path narrowed so that, to pass on,

I had to turn sideways with my back to the stone and face the river. I looked straight down a thousand feet into the gorge to the water. The wren sang again right beneath where I stood.

A little way farther on, the path veered again into the rocks, and I saw Galimatia above me, scaling hand- and foot-holds to a place where the sun angled into a shallow cave. She stopped there and beckoned me, but did not speak.

I was afraid to climb to where she was. My legs shook, and my hands trembled. The wind made a haunting song curling into the stone. At the cave, Galimatia offered her hand and pulled me up the last step.

The cave was my height and only a few feet deep, but large enough for several people to sit or sleep. At the back of it, someone had drawn pictures of a running man and a woman holding corn in her hands. A handprint outlined in ocher had signed them.

Galimatia unfolded a blanket from her pack. spread it on the floor of the cave, and took out a reed flute. She sat down without looking at me. The wind moaned, and she accompanied it on the flute. Minutes passed. She stopped, and the wind went on. Then she spoke softly, though not to me, in a language she'd learned in the place she'd come from. The sun flowed into the back of the cave, passed across the pictures, and held them in its glow.

In the wake of the sun was a more brilliant light that shone from me.

Later, Galimatia led me down the ancestors' path to the river. The way was more treacherous than climbing the cliff to the mesa for no one except Galimatia had worn the path for a long time. The steps were eroded or absent, and there were loose rocks in the fissures and ravines. We took our time, but I was afraid every moment. At the bottom, near the river, was a spring where we drank clear water and washed our bodies. We talked of the sky and the clouds, the shapes in the sandstone and the birds we saw, and of the language of these things. And years later, when I was a writer far from the village, I remembered what I'd seen there and what I'd heard, and I whispered Galimatia's name to myself over and over.

THE TOUCHING THAT LASTS

More than one or the other, more
than all the regrets, more than the hand
    that touches,
it is the touching that lasts.

                              – Greg Pape, "Wijiji"

I.

It was November, and I was more than a year out of college and in crisis. My boyfriend, Alex, was leaving San Francisco to look for moonflowers in Venezuela and he wanted me to go with him, or at least to commit to a future together. I had applied to seven medical schools and, if I got into one, had to decide whether I wanted to go. My hypochondriac friend, Shirley, a classmate from Yale, was behind on her rent which I was covering for her—not easy on a substitute teacher's pay, especially since I never knew when I would work.

To add stress to crisis, my father showed up from Colorado. He'd heard on the national bird tape about a Mongolian Plover at Point Reyes, and he used this quest for a life-bird as his excuse to visit me and his little girls from his second marriage, my half-sisters Dorrie and Irene, who were eight and five. They lived in Berkeley. (I have a brother, Glen, at

Brown). My father spent a night in a sleeping bag in the bed of his truck in the warehouse district in Emeryville, and the next morning picked up Dorrie and Irene and was at my apartment in the Castro by first light, honking in the street, and shouting up, "Louise! Weezy! Let's go!"

It took an hour, four of us squashed in the cab, to get across to Marin County and up to Point Reyes. The plover was supposedly in a field near Mill Road and we left the truck behind a Land Rover from Texas—the license plate said WLD BRDR, confirming our directions. We girls were glad to get out, and my father, carrying the bird scope, forged ahead up the hill. Fog muted the green pastures on both sides of the road and a mist wet the grass already trampled down by cattle. The invisible ocean murmured in the distance against invisible seacliffs.

"I have to go to the bathroom," was the first thing Irene said.

"You'll have to squat down," I said.

"Here?"

"Where else is there?"

"Here is where we are," Dorrie said. "I'll show you how."

I handed each girl a Kleenex.

My father divorced my mother, or vice versa, twelve years ago, married Lynn, Dorrie and Irene's mother two years later, and divorced her, or vice versa, five years ago, and now lived alone near Steamboat Springs. Early in his life he'd quit graduate school in anthropology for freelance photojournalism, which gave him the opportunity to travel. He was a bird lister—a person who wanted to see as many different birds as he could—and growing up I'd learned the basics of size, color, bill shape, wing-bars, flight patterns. He was a fanatic and never failed to act as if the bird he was looking for was the rarest one on earth.

Ahead of us, he set the scope on the ridge and, before looking into it, scanned the pastures with binoculars. His long hair curled over his collar and luffed in the updraft. He was a silhouette of scattered colors, bits and pieces of shadow and light that didn't fit together.

"Doesn't he look old, Weezy?" Dorrie asked me.

"He's forty-seven," I said. "That is old."

"No, that *cow*," Dorrie said. She pointed at a cow on the other side of the road.

"A cow is a she," I said.

"I know, but some of them look like old men."

I studied the cow's wizened face and sad mouth.

"Will you carry me?" Irene asked.

"You're too old to be carried."

"She's too *heavy*," Dorrie said.

"*You're* too heavy," Irene said. To me she said, "If you won't carry me, I'll suck my thumb."

"Then your teeth will get crooked," I said.

"*More* crooked," said Dorrie.

"We're almost to the top of the hill," I said. "Let's race."

Dorrie, always earnest, ran ahead, her bell bottoms swishing in awkward stride. I took Irene's hand. "Come on," I said, "maybe we can see the ocean."

We got to the crest of the hill out of breath. Our father was looking through the eyepiece of the scope.

"What do you see?" Dorrie asked.

"A herd of Killdeer," my father said.

"I want to see the deer," Irene said.

"Killdeer aren't deer," Dorrie said. "They're birds named for the sound they make."

"Then why did he say a 'herd'?"

"Because he's silly," I said. "A Killdeer is a plover with two black stripes across its white breast."

"What's a plover?" Irene asked.

Our father lowered the scope and positioned Irene at the eyepiece.

"A plover is a ground bird," Dorrie said, "a little like a sandpiper."

"How do you know all that?" my father asked.

"I go to school."

"But have you seen one?"

"Experience, you mean?" Dorrie said. "No, not yet."

"I see it," Irene said. "You're right. It's a bird."

"You can't learn things in school?" I asked my father.

"The way to learn," my father said, "is to be curious and ask questions."

"So why did you get divorced?" Dorrie asked.

"I beg your pardon?" my father asked.

Dorrie gazed straight at him. "You said I should ask questions."

"Your mother wanted to live in a different place," he said.

"I mean from Weezy's mother."

My father smiled. "Louise's mother was a jackhammer and a Geiger counter," he said. "We had a hard time being together."

"What's a Geiger counter?" Irene asked.

She moved away from the scope, and our father drew Dorrie over.

"A Geiger counter is a machine that measures radioactivity," my father said. "Like a metal detector."

"Maybe Daddy was silver," Irene said.

"Or iron," I said. "Why did you marry her if she was a Geiger counter and a jackhammer?"

"She was adaptable," my father said. "She could camp out or live at the Ritz. She was a good mother to you and Glen."

"Was she the first woman you loved?" Dorrie asked.

My father's expression shifted perceptibly from ease to grimace. A gust of wind that blew the mist across the ridge. "Do you want to see the Killdeer?" he asked. He checked in the scope to see whether the bird was still focused.

"If you want me to learn," Dorrie said, "you have to answer my questions."

My father made way for her, and Dorrie looked into the eyepiece briefly, then moved the scope back and forth across the field, as my father had.

"Do you see what you want to see?" he asked.

The wind came harder, and the mist turned to rain. Irene nestled in closer to me.

My father raised his binoculars and scanned to the north. "There's the wild birder from Texas," he said, pointing at a man some distance away along the road. "I wonder if he found the Mongolian Plover."

Dorrie stood up. "Well, was she?" she asked.

My father lowered his binoculars. "No, she wasn't the first woman I loved."

"Were you married to the first woman?" Irene asked.

"Yes," he said.

I put my arms around Irene tightly. "You were married before Mom?" I asked.

"Three times?" Dorrie said. "You were married three times?"

He looked at me. In the rain, his hair stuck to his head and the back of his neck and drops of water fell from his chin.

We took refuge in a movie theater in Mill Valley, and after the movie we went to a family restaurant that smelled of steak and cheese. The early conversation stuck to traditional topics—the girls' school, their new brother, Irene's cat, Mouse, which had the previous week been killed by a coyote. "Coyotes have to eat, too," Dorrie said.

"They don't have to eat my *cat*," Irene said.

"Look at the menu," my father said. "Do you know what you want, Louise?"

"I want to know about your first wife," I said.

"That was a long time ago."

"Do you know her name?" Irene asked.

"Of course he knows her name," Dorrie said. "They were *married*."

The waitress appeared, an older woman in a black short-sleeved shirt.

"We have to order," my father said. "How about if you girls split a cheeseburger?"

"I want a turkey sandwich," Irene said.

"Where did you live?" I asked.

"In France for a while, then in Maine." My father looked at Irene. "Her name was Camille."

He handed the waitress his menu. "We want one cheeseburger, a turkey sandwich, and a chicken-fried steak."

The waitress wrote that down, then looked at me.

"Nothing," I said. "I'm not hungry."

My father slept on my floor that night and showed bird slides at Dorrie and Irene's school the next day. The weather cleared and I assumed he went to look for the plover again, so I didn't see him. My life resumed its frenetic indirection. I was called to substitute three days in a row, and Dartmouth and Stanford wanted essays to support my application and MCAT scores. Then on Wednesday Alex staged what he called a love-in in Shirley's and my apartment, claiming he wasn't going to leave until I gave him an answer about a life together. He brought a camp chair and a backpack full of vegetables, nuts, and fruit.

He was still there Friday afternoon when I came home from school. I thought he was sweet, but Shirley had a different perspective. "He smells," she said. "Your father was okay for one night, but Alex is weird. Get him out of here."

I dropped my book bag by the phone. "Look, Alex, I've just taught a sophomore unit on gastropods and I'm tired. Shirley lives here, too."

"All you have to do is say yes," Alex said. "I'll be satisfied with that."

"You have a pretty low threshold of satisfaction," Shirley said. "Why would she say yes to someone who eats five pounds of pistachios in two days?"

"Because I love her."

Shirley rolled her eyes. "I think I'm getting a rash." She stomped down the hallway and slammed her door so hard the walls shook.

"If you love me," I said, "why are you going to Venezuela?"

"Because that's where moonflowers bloom," he said. "It's only for six months."

"And I'm supposed to lock myself in the closet while you're away?"

"Are you planning to see someone else?"

"I'm not planning to, but I might."

He stood up, spilling pistachio shells on the carpet. He was tall, long-haired because he said long hair made him feel wild. "Now we're getting somewhere," he said.

I turned away toward the window. Across the valley, apartment buildings and houses stair-stepped up the hill, and I picked out the hospital where I wanted to volunteer to test whether my motive to go to medical school was sound. Behind the hospital, a piece of Oakland Bay shimmered in sunlight, and beyond the bay the Berkeley Hills bloomed with houses. I thought of Dorrie and Irene, contending now with our father's absence.

Alex came up behind me, as if to emphasize his attachment to me.

"I like you, Alex. I like sleeping with you and waking up with you. But you're abandoning me."

"I'm not," he said. "I want you to be my anchor and the center of my life."

"And what kind of anchor are you?"

"Don't you think you're being selfish," he asked.

"Selfish?"

"You either love me or you don't."

Shirley emerged from her room carrying her raincoat and umbrella. "I'm going out for Thai," she said. "You want to come?"

"Yes," I said. I didn't look at Alex, but I spoke to him. "You'd better be gone when I get back."

Parents are hidden from the child. Before the child is born, they've already had a life the child doesn't know. My mother grew up in Savannah, Georgia and intersected with my father on a cold December evening in Dover, Delaware. They slept together the first night—my mother told me this. It was in the sixties and people were looser then. The next spring, they camped all over the country looking for birds— Texas, Arizona, Colorado—and they happened onto a pre-ski-boom ranchette in Steamboat Springs where they lived for several years. My mother wrote features for the *Steamboat Pilot* and my father took photographs. He built a darkroom in the loft of the house.

I was born in Steamboat Springs, but I have no memory of being born. I have no recollection of the first three years, maybe four. When I was five and Glen was two, we rented out the ranch and moved to Savannah where we lived on a barrier island connected to the mainland by a causeway. My mother got a job with her hometown paper, the *Morning News*, and taught journalism part-time at the college.

I know these things from blurred memory and later conversations, but I don't know details. I heard stories people in and around my family chose to tell, gleaned what I could eavesdropping at dinner parties or at Thanksgivings with my grandparents or when my parents' friends visited. My mother, I gathered, had a history with men, but when she met my father, her party life ended. My father was teased frequently about how such an educated man as he had sunk so low, though he maintained if he'd been an anthropologist he'd be just as broke.

Their stories, though, never amounted to a life history. They were anecdotes, offbeat blips of information that didn't explain enough about who they were or why they stayed together. Were their lives simply a series of episodes? Were they together because neither of them had anyone else?

The truth was, growing up I didn't pay much attention to my parents. What I remembered during those early years was tangential to my own life. My mother got drunk and fell off a dock, but I don't know whose dock it was or whether she was drunk on liquor or sadness. Once at my grandparents' house, a rooster attacked me. My father saved me, but I don't remember how. On Christmas Eve—I was three—I was spinning like a ballerina out of sheer happiness, and I hit my head on a door jamb. I remember hitting my head, but not my mother's shrieking, or my saying to her, as legend has it, "It's all right, Mommy, Weezy will live." My parents argued frequently, but I don't recall their words. I remember catching butterflies, practicing soccer, getting lost once on a camping trip in North Carolina. I was conscientious in school, good at sports, pretty—I hate that word now. I was the victim of expectations which I met without thinking or trying very hard. I recall schoolmates—Doug Barberi, who later went to prison, Sharon Allison, Will Krider, my boyfriend in sixth grade. Once it snowed on the beach, and I can still see the snowflakes against the sea.

Alex was leaving the first week of December, but I hadn't heard from him since his love-in at my apartment. I hadn't called him. He'd behaved like a child and owed me the courtesy of first contact. I could behave like a child, too. The days were as anxious as waiting for a hurricane. I wrote my essays for med schools at a café on Noe Street, talked to the ER director about volunteering at the hospital, counseled Shirley about her imaginary menopausal symptoms. All the while, I charted the winds and movement of the storm.

One cloudy Saturday I drove over to Berkeley to see Dorrie and Irene and brought my binoculars, thinking we'd all start life-lists. I gave the girls the choice of Aquatic Park or the Berkeley Pier.

"Pier," said Dorrie.

"Aquatic Park," Irene said. "I've never been there."

"You haven't been to the pier, either," Dorrie said.

"Where is there more sun?" Irene asked.

"There's no sun either place," I said. "I'll pick a number."

"You'll cheat," Irene said.

"Why would I cheat?"

"You like Dorrie more than me."

I stared at her. "Irene, what a terrible thing to say. Do you think that?"

"She's manipulating you," Dorrie said.

"I asked Irene."

Dorrie had her own insight into the world, but Irene was the more social of the girls. She had dark hair and blue eyes and knew how to make others notice her in a way Dorrie didn't.

I knelt down in front of her.

"Okay, I'll go to the pier," she said.

"That's not an answer to the question."

"You like us the same," she said.

The pier was at the end of César Chávez Park. We drove down University, crossed above the interstate, and along the grass-lined causeway. Clouds were low over the hills and rain hovered in the distance over Mount Tamalpais. Straight ahead was the Golden Gate Bridge, and, to the left, the Bay Bridge and San Francisco. We parked and walked, staying close together because we had only one pair of binoculars.

I showed them Surf Scoters, Western Grebes, California Gulls on pier posts, and a Common Loon in dull gray winter plumage. Irene had first look at the grebe, so Dorrie got first look at the loon, and, to annoy Irene, she hummed a song and took her time.

"I want to see, too," Irene said, and she grabbed for the glasses.

"Here," Dorrie said, handing over the binoculars, "he went under."

Irene wailed. I measured Dorrie sternly.

"I didn't make the loon go under," she said.

"Sharing is a virtue," I said. I turned to Irene. "Let's watch. He'll come back up."

The girls stood on the lowest rail so they could see the water better. A flock of scoters with their heads buried under their wings rode the gray swells. Rain merged the bay with the horizon.

"Three gulls," I said.

"Where?" Irene asked.

"I get it," Dorrie said. "Do you get it, Irene? *Gulls*. We are three gulls."

"I *get* it, Dorrie," Irene said.

"That's called a *tern* of phrase," I said. "Do you get *that*?"

"There's the loon," Dorrie said. She pointed at a gray-and-white bird, heavy in the water.

I held Irene by the waist so she could use both hands on the binoculars. "What do you see?" I asked.

"A bridge," Irene said.

"Lower."

"Water. A boat."

There was a sailboat moving right to left toward the end of the pier. "Do you know how to focus?" I asked.

"Not exactly."

"She's hopeless," Dorrie said.

"I'm not hopeless."

"She's not hopeless," I said. "She's five."

"Yeah," Irene said, "I'm five."

I held her finger to the ridged camber on the top of the glasses. "Focus with this," I said.

"He went under again," Dorrie said. "Did you see it, Irene?"

"I saw lots of things," Irene said.

"That's what matters," I said.

We walked to the end of the pier and watched a man loft a red-and-yellow box kite. Two teenagers dressed alike in lilac shirts leaned into each other and gazed out toward the Golden Gate. A Chinese man showed us the fish he'd caught that were swimming in a bucket.

The girls wanted ice cream at Fenton's, but it was getting late so we headed home. When we drove up, their stepfather, Samuel, was putting up a trellis for roses and Lynn came out onto the porch. She was tall and pale, dressed in a blue-denim jumper. It was always weird to see her because she'd been my stepmother once.

"Did you have a good time?" she asked.

"Weezy took us to the pier," Irene said. "I got twelve life birds."

"We were three gulls," Dorrie said.

Irene wanted to show me her new kitten, the replacement for the one killed by the coyote, and she and Dorrie went inside to find it. Samuel wheeled the garden cart around the side of the house, and suddenly Lynn and I were alone.

"Did Dad ever talk to you about Camille?" I asked.

She looked surprised. "Not very much, no. Why?"

"I never knew he had a first wife. I mean, before my mother."

"I guess they had problems, but he wasn't very specific."

"You never asked him?"

"I thought if he wanted to tell me he would. I wasn't going to pry."

"It doesn't seem like prying," I said.

"Maybe I didn't want to know," Lynn said. "Anyway, that was before your mother, even."

Irene came outside with a yellow-striped kitten draped over her arm. "Do you want to hold him?" she asked.

"I'm not too fond of cats," I said.

"He's a kitten," Dorrie said.

"The trouble with kittens is they grow up to be cats," I said.

Irene handed him to Dorrie. "His name is Lion," Irene said. "Coyotes don't eat lions."

"Especially if we keep him inside," Dorrie said.

When was I aware of love? My parents said they loved me from the beginning. I said I loved them. They loved Glen. We were bound by blood and spatial co-existence, moving together through time. The summer I was fourteen, I drove with my friend Gigi and her family to their vacation house on Montauk, Long Island—two days in the car from Savannah, then two weeks there. We sailed, played cards, ate dinners in the dining room with a hundred windows. We spent so much time together singing and talking and reading and laughing that we grew close. We couldn't help it. I didn't love them exactly, but it was like love. In time, it would have become love.

But that wasn't the kind of love that concerned me. I was fascinated by physical love. When did I become conscious of it? Once when I was about ten, my father and I were waiting for my mother under a movie marquee in downtown Savannah. We saw her across the street—a striking blond, willowy, agile—and as she crossed over toward us, a man whistled at her from a pick-up truck stopped at the red light. She glanced at him, blushed, and kept walking toward us.

"Someone you know?" my father asked.

"He was a construction worker," my mother said.

"Construction workers do it, too," my father said.

"Not with me."

"Who does it with you?"

"Photographers," she said. She looked at me. "Don't listen to this, Louise. It doesn't concern you."

In junior high, I learned how males and females of various species copulated—butterflies, frogs, horses, human beings. My girlfriends joked about boys' anatomies (ugh) and laughed nervously about penetration. How could that ever feel *good?* The boys' teasing indicated their equally intermittent progression of knowledge. Awareness accreted over weeks and months until in high school sex was in the air like a scent.

The summer I was sixteen, I had sex for the first time. Gil Harcourt was home from boarding school and we did it in the back seat of his parents' Mercedes. The next week we used my bed, and a few days later we made love at the edge of a golf course in the rain. In those stolen minutes I understood what no book ever mentioned, what no teasing or innuendo could impart, what no friend had confided. The pleasure, yes, I'd grown up enough to expect that. And the joy of closeness, too. But I had never imagined the headlong rush-and-mystery of lust.

My parents must have known of this, but they never told me. They weren't demonstrative. I never saw or heard them in bed. I never encountered a closed door I might have sneaked up to or walked through with feigned innocence. To be sure, Glen and I were incontrovertible evidence, but even our existence was not substantial enough for me to believe they'd ever made love.

My father was often gone on assignments, and though he sent us post-cards from wherever he was, it was his photographs I remembered—a humpbacked whale's tail going down into the ice floes in Prince William Sound, hundreds of yellow umbrellas at a festival in Japan, the jeweled throats and frozen wings of hummingbirds in Costa Rica. The photographs confused my memory. These moments of stopped time made my father seem illusory, as if he were only in those places for an instant and otherwise he didn't exist. It never occurred to me to ask what he did beyond the photos. What had he thought about when his camera was still? Who was with him when the hummingbirds slept? What had he done at night when the yellow umbrellas were closed?

At home he re-formed himself: he was who he appeared to be. Sometimes he took me birding with him, though birding wasn't separate from his work. Once, when I was about Dorrie's age, we canoed up a tidal creek so he could photograph wild azaleas and dogwoods. I remember the glide of the canoe, otters swimming across the creek, alligators lying on logs in the sun. My father heard a buzzing song high in the canopy which he thought was a Bachman's Warbler and we drifted as he scanned the treetops with binoculars. I didn't know what a Bachman's Warbler sounded like, or looked like, but I remember the sunlight dappling the water and the songs of other birds around us shimmering in the shadows of the forest.

We camped on the bank of the stream, and in the morning we walked down a dirt track past a row of shacks. My father made conver-sation with the black people and asked whether he could document what he saw. I remember the word 'document' the way Dorrie remembers everything anyone says. I remember the third house where an old woman with gray eyes was sitting in a plywood chair in the doorway. She must have been ninety.

"Can I take your picture?" my father asked.

She nodded toward his voice.

My father climbed the rickety steps and walked around her, one side to the other, not taking pictures, but talking the whole time very politely about the weather and asking about her children and grandchildren. Finally he said, "Would you please just move a little this way?"

The woman looked confused, but she fumbled for her cane and pushed herself up from the chair. "This way," my father said. He touched her elbow and slid her chair to the right.

The woman gave a soft laugh, took several shaky steps, and with difficulty sat down again. My father stepped back and picked up his camera.

I was embarrassed he'd done that to her, and ashamed, and as he shot his pictures I looked at her again and saw how different she looked in the new place—how beautiful she was in the sunlight.

The night before Alex was to leave, he called and asked me over to his apartment. "I can't come to your place," he said. "Shirley hates me."

"With some reason," I said. "Maybe I hate you, too."

"I'll make scallops for dinner."

"Not good enough."

"Häagen-Dazs for dessert. Coffee."

"Is that your final offer?"

"We'll have privacy. My roommate's at a Dead revival."

"That's an oxymoron," I said.

"Please," he said.

I took the bus over. I felt I had to go because he'd telephoned me, and the least I could do was to accept his apology. I even bought him a leather-bound journal as a going-away present.

I knew we wouldn't say much. What was there to talk about? We'd have dinner by candlelight, play some Chopin nocturnes, do the dishes— Alex had to have everything organized before he could enjoy himself. I'd give him his present. I might tell him about the interviews I'd been invited for at Dartmouth and Stanford. Then we'd go into the bedroom.

Making love with Alex was like watching the sunset over the ocean—beautiful because of the clouds and the waves, but different every time. We'd endure that peculiar ritual of disrobing (we're the only species that does that), we'd lie down together skin against skin, we'd touch. The condom would be an awkward interruption, but finally we'd engage in the pleasant fervor we'd learned was the expression of love—the wetness, the pummeling, and the slow aftermath.

Alex met me at the door holding a piece of paper in his hand. His face was serious, dark, his long hair swirling at his shoulders, and he was dressed only in a thin pair of blue underwear. "I'm primeval," he said.

"What's the paper?" I asked. "I hope it isn't a contract for me to sign."

I smiled, but he didn't. He turned the paper so I could see it. It was a photograph of a white flower, iridescent, set against a dark green background. "For the next few minutes, I want you to think only about this," he said.

The petals of the flower were veined and so delicate they looked as if they were about to disintegrate to ash. In the center was a profusion of darker bristles, perfectly formed and unimaginably complex. I felt myself merge into the picture. I hadn't taken two steps into the room.

Then Alex set the picture on his trunk near the door and pressed his nearly naked body against mine. He kissed me and unbuttoned my blouse.

"Concentrate on the moonflower," he said.

He licked my nipples. I was surprised, not because it felt good—it did—but because I continued to envisioned the flower. The petals bled into my consciousness, and I emitted a soft moan. I imagined pistil and stamen, the white against the dark green. I felt my jeans loosened and pulled down. Alex knelt and caressed my bare legs, his face close between my thighs. White swam up before me. My body strove with the image of the flower, so delicate. I heard my own voice singing, "Don't stop, don't stop."

And then this miracle: my body tensed and shuddered, and I held my breath while my whole being—white white white—floated into the dark air.

Alex left at five the next morning, and I lay awake for a while in the semi-dark. I had not told him about my interviews, and I'd forgotten to give him the journal I'd carefully inscribed to him with an ambiguous message—*a door is an entrance or an exit*. I reviewed what had happened the previous night. After the greeting at the door, Alex sauteed scallops and made a Greek salad, and we had chardonnay with dinner. We left the dishes and ate coffee ice cream in bed. Then we made love again, but it wasn't the same as when I was contemplating the moonflower. That was the image I retained on waking—that whiteness shining.

I slept again, and it was bright sun when I woke up, too late to see whether I had a teaching assignment. I got up and made coffee. Alex had left a note, together with the photograph of the moonflower.

> *Weezy, I am with you wherever you are,*
> *and you are with me. Please.*
> *A+*

I drank my coffee, took the bus back to Noe Street, and called my mother as soon as I walked into my apartment. "Why didn't you tell me?" I asked.

"Tell you what?" my mother asked.

"About orgasm."

"I can't talk now," my mother said. "I'm meeting Walter."

"That creep? Are you still seeing him?"

"What do you want to know about orgasm? It isn't harmful, or so I've heard."

"Alex left for Venezuela."

"Ah," she said, as if Alex's leaving explained something. "How are you doing with that?"

"I've been expecting it for eight weeks."

"Nothing happens till it happens," my mother said. "You can't prepare for it. I hated it when your father went on the road because when he came home I had to live with where he'd been."

"But you knew what he was like before."

"When I met your father he was a speeding train and I had to decide whether or not to jump on."

"Did you know about his first wife?"

"I don't want to talk about her."

"Why did you keep her hidden from Glen and me?"

"We didn't hide her. We didn't mention her."

"You talked about ex-George."

"We ran into George at parties and your father wasn't jealous."

"You were jealous of Camille?"

"It was natural to be jealous of a ghost," my mother said. "She was there, but not there."

"How long were they married?"

"Louise, why don't you ask *him?*"

"Did she take 'Hamilton' as you did?"

"Parish, I think her name was. Louise, I really have to go."

"I'm curious," I said. "You don't have to get mad."

"Curiosity doesn't get you anywhere," my mother said. "If I were you, I wouldn't make a life's work of this."

"Perish the thought," I said. "Thanks, Mom. I'll talk to you."

We hung up. I wrote 'Camille Parish' on the phone pad.

Glen and my father looked alike: the same nose, the same eyes and shape of the face. They had the same mannerisms. Glen was tall and reedy, though, and my father was sturdy. I don't resemble my father much in the face. My ears were small-lobed like his, but I had my mother's thin mouth, her delicate cheekbones, high forehead. But I had my father's body. My shoulders were broad, my legs strong. I had breasts my mother didn't have that I must have got from his side of the family.

Still, it wasn't the physical attributes that intrigued me so much as the emotional ground my father and I shared. We presented ourselves as quiet. We were calm. When his photographs were taken for a gallery exhibit, there was little fanfare; when he won a grant, he was happy, but not giddy. Similarly, when I graduated from Yale, I didn't dance around or scream with joy; I was thrilled getting interviews to medical schools, but I didn't celebrate. When Alex left for Venezuela, I didn't break down or cry or wring my hands.

And, like my father, I kept the details of my life from others. When I got pregnant in college and had an abortion, I didn't tell anyone. When I applied to medical schools, I didn't consult my friends or parents or professors, except when I needed recommendations. When I moved to San Francisco, I scoured for an apartment and then afterward asked Shirley to share it with me. If other people didn't know what you were doing, they couldn't meddle.

What my father possessed and I didn't was patience. He must have learned this in his work, waiting for the moment of consequence. I knew the precision it took to set up his equipment, to ready his tripods and cameras, his lighting. And then to wait. He spent hours being alert for possibilities. How many hours had he spent waiting for the precise moment the hummingbird would appear? How many days had he paddled his kayak in Prince William Sound not even knowing what moment he was waiting for?

My interview at Dartmouth was December fifteenth, and, because Glen was letting me borrow his car, I flew to Providence. As the plane bumped down through the murky afternoon clouds, I drank a martini and contemplated vaguely what I would say to make a good impression on the medical faculty—how I was reading medical journals in my spare time, that I watched *ER* and *Chicago Hope*, that my roommate claimed she had beri-beri and mad cow disease. I laughed at myself. God, what was I going to say? And was that the future I wanted? Perhaps I should have gone with Alex, sacrificed my indeterminate ambition to his research on moonflowers. But I wanted my own existence apart from his so I wouldn't reproach him for my own failure.

The plane broke through the clouds and Providence appeared, gray with age and obsolescence, and I had the unsettling sensation of returning to darkness. I'd felt stifled in the East. I wanted the frontier, adventure, *uncertainty*. That was what my father wanted when he left academia to take pictures. That was why I'd moved to California.

Glen didn't meet my plane, but at least he had the courtesy to be home when the taxi delivered me to his doorstep. He gave me a perfunctory embrace. "I'm a student," he said. "I don't have time to waste in airports."

"I'm your sister," I said.

"Even more reason. You comprehend my assessment of the greater good. Besides, I have a midterm one of these days pretty soon."

"I appreciate your letting me use your car," I said.

"Only in return for lifetime medical care," he said. "Nothing is free."

"Then you'll have to live in the same part of Uzbekistan," I said.

"Perhaps I will," he said. "Where are you taking me for dinner?"

We ate at a student hangout, and a couple of Glen's friends joined us. The careless banter was familiar and comforting—I'd forgotten how easy college life was and how funny Glen could be. After dinner we said goodbye to his cronies and at a liquor store I bought two bottles of merlot which we took back to Glen's room.

For a man with a midterm, Glen was eager to open the wine. We sat in his living room littered with clothes and magazines and guitars, and talked about his girlfriend, Sikh, his class in modern cultural artifacts, and skiing—he was thinking of taking it up since our father still lived in Steamboat Springs. At Christmas, though, he was going to Savannah but apparently didn't appreciate Walter any more than I did.

"Mom's not evil," he said. "She just has bad taste in men."

"Are you including Dad?" I asked.

"I think I am." He gave a half-smile like our father's.

"Maybe Dad doesn't have good taste in women," I said.

Glen poured the last of the first bottle of merlot and I opened the second.

"I saw Lynn and the girls before I left," I said. "They said hello."

"Yeah?"

"You used to like Lynn," I said.

"I do like her."

"But you don't call her or the girls."

Glen drank and raised his glass with a flourish. "What's your point, Weezy?"

"My point is the girls are your sisters, too."

"They live in California," Glen said. "I live in the real world."

"Dorrie's word-smart and Irene's street-smart. They're good little kids. It would take you five minutes a week to stay in touch with them."

Glen poured more wine and gave me a withering look. "In what way do Dad's spurious children have anything to do with me?"

"They're not spurious children anymore than we are."

"What Dad did with Lynn doesn't make their children part of me."

"Anything Dad did is a part of us. It's our history."

"History tells us where we've been, in case we can't remember."

"So your exclusivity theory is based on the nature of love? We're the only true children because our parents fell in love with each other first?"

"What if it is?"

"Did you know he was married before he met Mom?"

He scoffed. "Is that so?"

"Her name was Camille Parish."

Glen didn't say anything.

"So we're ordinary," I said. "No better than Dorrie and Irene."

Glen's anger shimmered, and we drank our wine in silence.

Finally he got up and put on a CD—instrumental music with a sitar and a zither. "How did you find out Dad was married before?"

"We were in Marin County. Dorrie asked whether he'd loved anyone before Mom, and Irene asked whether they were married." I got up and turned off the music. "People aren't only biological specimens, Glen. You might be surprised to know they have emotions."

"No kidding?" he said.

"What I want to know is how Dad *felt*."

"To what end? We know who our mother is. We know who our father is. That's all we care about."

"If we don't know Dad, how can we know ourselves?"

"Cut the crap, Weezy. Dad left us a long time ago. We don't know anything about him."

"He calls and visits. He sends photographs from where he's been. I think he's kept in touch pretty well."

"So what are we supposed to do?" Glen said. "*Thank* him?"

I let the silence go on for a minute. Then I said, "They lived in Maine for a while."

"Yeah, how long ago? Twenty-five years?"

"She probably remarried and changed her name," I said. "Maybe she moved."

"Is that what you want to do? Find her?"

"I could look," I said.

"And what if you find her?"

"What if I *don't*?" I said. "That's what I worry about."

Dr. Delsing, a blond woman in a white lab coat, and Dr. Halvorsen, an elderly man in a tweed jacket, were my interviewers at Dartmouth. We sat at an oak table in an oak-paneled room and they asked me the usual questions—why I wanted to be a doctor, what experiences I had that were testimony to serious intent, where did I think I'd be in ten years. I recounted a month's assistantship in Kenya working with unwed mothers; envelope stuffing for Operation Smile, an organization that financed surgery on children's cleft palates in Third World countries; and, as variation, my tour of the great museums of Europe with my mother. I made the predictable, if tangential, connection between the artists' psyche and understanding the human soul. As I rambled, Dr. Delsing and Dr. Halvorsen scrutinized my expression and tone of voice for sincerity and early wisdom.

When I stopped, the room went soft.

"Talk a little bit about your parents," Dr. Delsing said. "What are they like? What do they expect of you?"

"I'm my own person," I said.

"I wasn't implying you weren't," Dr. Delsing said. "But parents influence our personalities."

I was coached to give myself time to focus an answer, to reinforce in the interviewer's mind a sense of seriousness, perhaps even create in the interim a touch of drama. But I ran with the question. "My mother's the city editor for the *Savannah Morning News*," I said. "She made her way through the good-old-boy network. My relationship with her is friendly. I live in San Francisco, but we e-mail and talk on the phone." I let that sink in. Then I said, "My father is dead."

Dr. Halvorsen bounced the eraser of his pencil on the table. He looked at my file. "Your application says your father lives in Colorado."

I stood up as if I were offended. I unfastened my hair and pulled it loose. I paced. "My father and mother married two years before I was born. They were together fourteen years, and had two children. They divorced when I was seventeen, and my father married Lynn Arendt, and *they* had two children, Dorrie and Irene. My father and Lynn divorced five years ago."

Dr. Delsing raised her hand to get my attention. "We're not interested in a chronology, Ms. Hamilton—.

"—Besides my mother and Lynn, my father had a first wife," I said.

"What's so terrible about a first wife?" Dr. Halvorsen asked. "I've had one for thirty-eight years."

I stopped pacing. "I'm sorry to have taken your time," I said, and I bolted from the room.

I was troubled afterward, not because I'd ruined my chance at Dartmouth Medical School—did I want to spend four interminable years in that cold, grim countryside?—but because I'd let my emotions rule my head. I hadn't been patient. Instead of answering calmly and saying what they wanted to hear, I had blurted out my pain and suffering.

After the interview I'd planned to tour the medical school and spend the night in Hanover, but now I had the afternoon free. I drove south on I-89 toward Concord and already the idea was in my head: I was not that far from Maine.

The map showed a double-lane highway to Portsmouth. Why shouldn't I look for Camille? Judged by logic, my quest was improbable, but so was finding the Mongolian Plover at Point Reyes. So was the surfacing of a humpbacked whale in front of my father's kayak in Prince William Sound. I exited for the Seacoast and turned on my cell phone. The way to learn was to ask questions.

I found fifteen Parishes in Maine—no Camilles, but one C. The C was

Carla in Bar Harbor, a dressmaker who worked at home. She wasn't related to any Camille Parish in Maine or anywhere else. At three numbers no one answered; at four others I left a message to call me on my cell if anyone there knew a Camille Parish. I talked with seven other Parishes briefly, but none knew Camille.

I dialed my own number to inform Shirley of what was going on.

Alex had called. "He didn't know you had an interview at Dartmouth," Shirley said.

"Where was he?"

"Caracas. He was about to leave civilization for the jungle. I told him he'd never been in civilization."

"Did you tell him I loved him?"

"Weezy, I'm not your emotional secretary. How was the interview?

"I walked out."

"What do you mean you walked out?"

"They asked about my father and I got upset."

"Weezy, how could you walk out?"

"I couldn't think straight."

"Johns Hopkins called. They want you to call them. And your father—let's see, I wrote it down…He said he's off to Florida to, and I quote, 'photograph the infiltration of the indigenous ecosystem by parrots, walking catfish, and Australian pines,' unquote. He asked if I wanted to go with him."

"What?"

"He meant it as a joke," Shirley said. "Unlike other people I know, I have to work every day."

"But, if you could, you'd accept?"

"Weezy, he's forty-something. But cute. I might have."

"You're sick."

"He's lonely, Weezy. Don't you understand that?"

"God, you're all sick," I said, and I slammed down the phone.

Shirley and my father! I took a deep breath. *Shirley!* Another breath. An exit came up and I turned off and stopped. My father was lonely. That had never occurred to me. He traveled, he had who-knew-how-many women friends. I'd never thought of him as lonely.

I pressed the button on my cell and dialed his number.

His answering machine came on. "This is Ray Hamilton," his voice said. "I'm on assignment, but I'll pick up messages every few days."

The machine beeped.

"Daddy, this is Louise," I said. Another breath. "I love you."

Within limits, trial-and-error is a valid scientific method. If I knew Camille Parish had moved from Kittery to Bath, say, or that her name was Camille Hamilton, or where she and my father had lived, I could have pursued any of those leads. But there was no point in driving to Maine and asking blindly about Camille somebody on every street corner in every neighborhood in every town. Besides, I was tired, sad about missing Alex's phone call, and discouraged about my future.

I drove back to Providence. Glen's apartment was empty. I drank the dregs of the second bottle of merlot, scrambled three eggs for supper, and called again the numbers I hadn't reached in Maine. Two people were home—a man who wanted me to see his chain-saw sculptures and a woman whose husband was dying in the hospital. Neither knew Camille.

By midnight Glen hadn't come back, so I assumed he was staying with Sikh and I slept in his bed. In the morning, I had toast and coffee, scribbled a note of thanks for the use of his car, told him not to expect lifetime medical care, and got a taxi to the airport.

At the United counter, I changed my flight. I wanted a stopover in Denver on my way to San Francisco. When that was arranged, I called the last number in Maine. Still no answer. Nothing happens till it happens. Some mysteries remain mysteries.

My father must have kept evidence of Camille, so my plan was to rent a car in Denver, drive to Steamboat—the road over Rabbit Ears Pass was plowed—and arrive in daylight. I hadn't been to my father's house in five years, but I knew where his key was hidden. I meant to search his correspondence, check his telephone records, and look up names in his computer. But, as I said, things never work out as we imagine them.

My father's house was west of Steamboat on a gravel road that ran up a valley maybe half a mile wide, roughly parallel to a willowy stream bed where in several places hot springs seeped up. On either side, glacial moraine petered out into aspens, and, higher up, aspens merged into spruce and pine. Snow had fallen a few days before—the meadow was still white, but the south-facing slopes had melted back to yellow grass.

I coasted into the driveway. My father must have left his truck with a friend, or driven it to the airport, because the yard was empty. I turned off the engine of my rental Ford and sat for a moment. The farmhouse was still beige, two stories, but smaller than I remembered it. The four apple trees he'd planted in the front yard were bigger—one for each of us children when we were born. Two trees were grown now and the other two were six feet tall. They were leafless and made the house look forlorn.

My father had sixty acres back to the creek, though it had not been a working ranch since I'd known the place. I got out into a cold breeze and stood among the apple trees. Behind the house were the corrals—nails pulled from the posts, broken rails, gates hanging open. The eaves of the shed were lined with swallows' nests, abandoned for the winter.

This was what my father chose—the sky and the mountains and the sage hills with snow in the shadows. He chose the meadow and the corrals and the house seven miles from town on the county gravel. If he chose this, he also chose to be lonely.

A shadow drifted across the ground and stirred me—a raven sailing westward toward the diminishing sun. I found the house key above the beam of the porch.

The living room smelled of ashes left in the woodstove. He hadn't been gone long. Razor-like gold sunlight entered through the curtains on the west side of the room. I walked through the adjoining dining room to the tiny kitchen, got a drink of water, and sat at the table. The snowy meadow and the red willows along the creek were bathed in bluish shadow. A few tufts of grass poked up through the snow, and in the low spots vapor rose from hot water.

It was my purpose to be where I was, though I got edgy sitting there. My rhythm was the city's pulse—San Francisco, Providence, Denver— jagged, hurried—but I made myself wait in the quiet, in the deepening dusk. Shapes diminished, and stars appeared randomly in the blue light. Then a stillness I had not imagined possible came over me, as if the translucent light entered me, and I experienced what my father knew, what he felt when he was alone in his house. A coyote materialized by the side fence; an owl flew low across the meadow, and following its flight, I saw elk on the far hillside. They came out of the dark spruce, and, one by one, silhouetted themselves against a tongue of snow as they descended toward the creek bottom and disappeared into the willows.

The stillness unnerved me, and I rose and turned on a light, then turned it off again. I could not let myself be afraid. I walked through the house to the stairs to my father's loft.

When we visited, we children were not allowed to go up these stairs, and my father trusted us not to trespass. He took me up to the loft once so I wouldn't be curious—it was where his darkroom was. I remembered the confusion of enlargers, trays, bottles of chemicals. Prints were strung up on crisscrossing wires. But his work meant nothing to me then—I was eight, maybe. What I recall most vividly was the acrid smell of developer.

I climbed the stairs slowly in the dark, as if what drew me upward also held me back. The loft was one room with a skylight filled with stars. At the top of the stairs I turned on the light, and the room burst open to me.

Along one wall, squeezed in beside the gabled window, was a desk and computer. In the far corner was a bare sink and toilet—no need for privacy in a place no one else was allowed. The darkroom was a cubicle built under the eaves, with a superfluous red light above the door. It was the same as I remembered it. Unframed prints were tacked everywhere on the walls, pinned to wires.

It was the same, but like the apple trees, not the same. And I was different.

Photographs were everywhere—a child in a rice paddy with gray smoke rising in the distance, an avocet dancing in a pool of otherwise still water, a stark cityscape muted by haze, Asian kids at a parade, a black girl dribbling a basketball on broken asphalt, a Sharp-shinned Hawk devouring a waxwing. I expected the bird photographs but was surprised by the children. The more I looked, the more children there were—a Latino boy standing beside the body of a man on the side of a red-clay road, Dorrie and Irene at the beach, a Japanese girl dressed in a red kimono with her eyes closed.

These images inspired more questions. They were fragments of his life. Yet the questions themselves told me something: even if I asked and asked and asked, my father could never have shared with me everything I wanted to know.

I studied the children's faces, their eyes. Each child's eyes were curious. Did I imagine this? Every child's eyes asked, *What will happen next? Will I be all right?*

Above his desk was the only framed photograph—the one I'd been witness to years before of the old black woman sitting on her porch in the plywood chair in the sunlight. The light struck her like magic, transformed her, and made her alive.

Headlights scattered through the gable window onto the ceiling. A car was coming down the road —probably a rancher who lived farther on, but I switched off the light. The car was still a ways off, its headlights moving along the gravel, illuminating the weeds and the fenceline at the side of the road. A half-moon had risen, and its radiance brightened the pale snow.

The headlights slowed at my father's driveway and turned in, and I saw it was a truck. The lights swept over the rental car and the shed and corral. I went downstairs quickly and out onto the porch, thinking it must be a caretaker who'd seen the light on. The car lights went off, and the driver got out, and I saw from his posture it was my father.

He stood beside the truck in the moonlight, looking past the house toward the meadow and the sky. "Come out here, Louise," he said.

His voice was soft, but it carried in the air.

It was cold and I didn't have a coat on, but I walked down the steps into the yard. "I thought you were in Florida," I said.

"I don't go till Sunday," he said.

He walked around the side of the house, and I followed.

When I turned the corner, he was almost to the back fence where in summer the garden was—a dark figure backlit by snow. I was more afraid of him than I'd have been of any stranger.

I approached slowly, not knowing his mood and unsure of my own.

"I called Glen," he said without turning around. "He said you'd been there on your way to Hanover."

"Glen didn't know I was coming here."

"But I did."

"How could you have?"

He shifted slightly, his face catching the light and shadow of the moon. "Glen said you'd talked about finding Camille," he said, "and then you left that message on my machine."

"I didn't have much to go on," I said. "I called fourteen Parishes in Maine. One number didn't answer."

My father didn't say anything.

"I was going to look in your desk, in your computer … If you knew I was coming, why weren't you here?"

He was silent for a moment against the tone of my voice. Then he said, "I wanted to see what you'd do."

"I might have found out what I wanted to know."

"That was the risk," he said.

I shivered in the cold air, and he took off his coat and put it around my shoulders.

Across the meadow, mist rose from the hot springs into the colder air, and above the mist the moon tilted among Taurus and Orion and the Pleaides. My father pointed across the meadow where the elk were running out from the willows along the creek—cows and calves first, then three bulls, antlers raised and gleaming.

"Something spooked them," my father said.

I looked for what might have scared them but didn't see anything.

"Do you know what a moonflower is?" I asked.

"Yes. I've seen them."

"So have I," I said.

The elk passed through the mist, jumped the meadow fence, and crossed the road into the aspens on the other side.

My father turned from the empty meadow. "I'm cold," he said. "Let's go inside."

"You can have your jacket back."

I took off his jacket, but he walked away toward the house. I ran after him and caught his arm. "Why won't you tell me?"

He pulled away and kept walking, and I threw his jacket at him. It struck his back and fell to the ground. I chased him again and tackled him around the waist. His legs buckled, and he went down hard, with me on top of him. He struggled in the snow to right himself, tried to get purchase with his knees, but I had my arms around his chest and held on tightly. I rolled over, and my body weight pulled him with me.

He was bigger and stronger and finally wrenched free. "What do you want to know?" he asked.

I fell back into the snow, and he knelt beside me, his breath visible in the moonlight.

"Where is Camille?" I asked. I waited while he caught his breath. "How did you meet her?"

He leaned back on his heels and looked at the stars. "I met her in Aix-en-Provence," he said. "She was at the language school there. I'd just quit the anthropology program and went to France to take photographs. I wanted the sound of the language in my work." He paused, putting his bare hands under his armpits. "It was an idealistic notion, but I was young. Camille spoke beautiful French. When she finished her course, we lived for a few months in LaRochelle. I liked the boats, the fishermen and their wives, the beach. With Camille I felt freer than being alone."

"But you didn't stay there."

"I liked being the invisible foreigner, but she longed for home, and she convinced me I could take photographs anywhere, so we moved back to Maine, where she was from. We rented a small house two blocks from the water in Brunswick, and I became a caretaker of summer houses—gardener, repairman, winter watchman, which gave me time enough to take pictures. Camille got a job in a daycare for at-risk children. We got married that November, after she got pregnant."

"You wanted to?"

"By then I was making money. I had freelance newspaper assignments, I'd shot a few weddings and portraits, and I was showing my work at a gallery in Portland."

"Were you happy?"

"What does that mean? I liked my life. I still do."

"But something happened."

"One Monday in February I heard there was a Great Gray Owl in Ipswich, Massachusetts—a life bird for me. I wanted to see it. I'd been meaning to take some photographs to Boston anyway." His voice trailed away.

"Did you see the owl?"

"I saw the owl and delivered work to galleries in Boston, and on my way back I swung by a few houses I was caretaking. I was gone most of the day." He stopped again and looked down at me.

Already I heard the grief in his voice. The snow was cold under me, but I didn't move.

"She was dead when I got home," he said. "She'd looped a rope over a rafter and hanged herself." He shook his head. "There was no note."

I sat up. "The baby, too?"

My father put his head against my shoulder and put his arms around me and held me. He cried and I held him, too.

That night I called Glen and left a message that I knew about Camille and that our father had loved her, and he could call me if or when he wanted to know more. I phoned my mother, too, to let her know I was all right, though I didn't tell her where I was. We talked about her creep Walter.

The next two days I spent with my father in the loft. He showed me how to mix chemicals, how to judge the speed of an image, how to accentuate aspects of a print by shading it from the light. During those hours we didn't talk about anything deep or meaningful. We shared no special moment. But something had already happened to us in the snow. He had cut himself loose from his past, or I had freed myself from mine—whatever it was I didn't want it to end. I didn't ask about Camille, or why he divorced my mother or Lynn, or why he took photographs of children. I was patient. I still had the questions, but I didn't want the answers yet.

The last morning before he left for Florida, I did a load of clothes and helped him pack. We got his cameras and film ready, his lenses, his camping gear. He had to put together a folio of prints of ptarmigan for a magazine and I helped him assemble the pictures—brown summer birds, splotchy molting birds, pristine white winter birds. He had a photograph of a coyote striding three feet from a ptarmigan and not seeing it.

"The coyote was coming along the hill," he said. "I found the ptarmigan after the coyote passed."

"After you took the picture?"

"The bird was there," he said. "I didn't see it, either."

"And that day you took the picture of that black woman…" I nodded toward the photograph on the wall. "Why did you make her move?"

"I didn't make her."

"I was there," I said. "I heard you ask."

"I didn't make her," he said. "She wanted to."

That night I called Shirley and told her I was staying in Colorado for a few more days after my father left. I wanted to live in his house and learn about the quiet. I wanted to write Alex before I came back to San Francisco and to tell him one way or the other what I was going to do.

"You're crazy," Shirley said.

"I haven't made up my mind," I said. "I'm not crazy yet."

Then I called Dorrie and Irene. They each got on an extension phone.

"I'm with Daddy in Colorado," I said.

"What are you doing *there*?" Irene asked.

"Daddy's been teaching me how to take photographs and develop them."

"Are you in school?" Irene asked.

"No, but it's a little like that," I said.

"You're getting experience," Dorrie said.

"Exactly."

"Guess who called," Irene said.

"Who?"

"Glen," Irene said.

"What did he say?"

"He's studying music something," Irene said.

"Appreciation," said Dorrie.

"He said he was sitting around thinking of us," Irene said, "so he called."

"Good for Glen," I said.

"Are you coming to see us when you get home?" Dorrie asked.

"Would that be all right?"

"You can show us what you've learned about photographs," Dorrie said.

"Maybe we'll find a darkroom," I said. "I'll show you about light and shadow and how we feel things."

"I know how I feel things," Irene said.

"I know you do, sweetheart."

"With my hands."

I smiled. "That's part of it," I said. "Touching is a part of it."

"You feel with your heart and head together," Dorrie said.

"Right," I said. "We'll talk about that."

"And light and shadow," Dorrie said.

"I'll see you soon," I said, "when I get there."

The next morning when I woke, I heard my father's footsteps in the loft. I imagined he was checking his photo gear a last time. I got up and stuffed his clothes from the dryer into his suitcase. Then I got coffee and went outside onto the back step. It was cold and clear, except for the mist from the hot springs. Frost rimed the shed roof and the broken corral fence. The sun was up, hitting the sage hills and the barren aspens and the dark spruce. I went out to the garden and through the gate toward the creek. The red willows blazed a feathery line up the valley.

Out farther from the yard, I crossed the tracks of the elk and deer in the snow and saw where coyotes and rabbits had passed—all that lived there. I didn't know what I would say to Alex or what I would do with my life, but I felt I knew *me*. I whirled full circle, taking in the mountains and the hills and the meadow, and then I turned back toward the house and saw my father standing by the garden fence, watching me, coffee steaming from his cup into the morning light.

Author Biography

Kent Nelson grew up in Colorado Springs, Colorado and was a scholarship student at Yale University. He got a law degree from Harvard Law School, passed the Colorado Bar, and began writing fiction full time. To get by, he has worked a variety of jobs including doorman at a bar, tennis pro, innkeeper, hired man on an alfalfa ranch, city judge, and college professor.

He has published four novels, six collections of short stories, and 156 stories in magazines. His novel *Land That Moves, Land That Stands Still* won the Colorado Book Award and Reading the West Book Award, and his story collection *The Spirit Bird*, won the $15,000 Drue Heinz Literature Prize. His stories have been anthologized in The Best American Short Stories, The Best of the West, Pushcart, O. Henry, and The Best American Mystery Stories. He has held two grants from the NEA.

In addition to writing, Kent is an avid birder and has identified 767 species in North America and has searched for birds in Costa Rica, Ecuador, Bhutan, New Zealand, and Australia.

At Yale, he played varsity ice hockey and tennis and later was ranked #6 in the U.S. in 45+ squash. He has run the L.A. Marathon, the Anchorage Midnight Sun Marathon and the Pikes Peak Marathon twice, 26.3 miles, 7814 feet up and down.

He lives in Ouray, Colorado.